Forbid me

USA TODAY BESTSELLING AUTHOR
M. ROBINSON

Natalie,

Jacob's Lobster.

xo

Forbid Me

Dedication

To my VIP group

I love you.
I write all my books for you.
Thank you for being YOU.
Oh my God ladies…words cannot describe how much I love and appreciate every last one of you. The friendships and relationships that I have made with you are one of the best things that have ever happened to me. I wish I could name each one of you but it would take forever, just please know that you hold a very special place in my heart. You VIPs make my day, every single day.

THANK YOU!!!

Forbid Me

Boss man: Words cannot describe how much I love you. Thank you for ALWAYS being my best friend. I couldn't do this without you.

Dad: Thank you for always showing me what hard work is and what it can accomplish. For always telling me that I can do anything I put my mind to.

Mom: Thank you for ALWAYS being there for me no matter what. You are my best friend.

Julissa Rios: I love you and I am proud of you. Thank you for being a pain in my ass and for being my sister. I know you are always there for me when I need you.

Ysabelle & Gianna: Love you my babies.

Rebecca Marie: THANK YOU for an AMAZING cover. I wouldn't know what to do without you and your fabulous creativity.
Heather Moss: Thank you for everything that you do!! I wouldn't know what to do without you! You're. The. Best. PA. Ever!! You're NEVER leaving me!! XO
Silla Webb: Thank you so much for your edits and formatting! I love it and you!
Kevin Lajeunessa: Thank you for being my Jacob muse for this book! You did him justice! Follow him on Facebook: https://www.facebook.com/modelkevinlajeunesse/?fref=ts

M. Robinson

Michelle Tan: Best beta ever! **Argie Sokoli:** I couldn't do this without you. You're my chosen person. **Jen Dirty Girl:** Thanks for all your input and your friendship. **Tammy McGowan:** Thank you for all your support, feedback, and boo boo's you find! **Michele Henderson McMullen:** LOVE LOVE LOVE you!! **Dee Montoya:** I value our friendship more than anything. Thanks for always being honest. **Roxie Madar:** Thank you for all your amazing feedback and for your friendship, which I value more than anything.
Rebeka Christine Perales: You always make me smile. **Mary Jo Toth:** Your boo-boos are always great! **Ella Gram:** You're such a sweet and amazing person! Thank you for your kindness. **Michelle Kubik Follis:** You always make me laugh!! **Kimmie Kim:** Your friendship means everything to me. **Tricia Bartley:** Your comments and voice always make me smile! **Natasha Gentile:** Thanks for being gentle on my children and for all your amazing feeback.
Danielle Renee: Thank you for wanting to join team M. **Kristi Lynn:** Thanks for all your honesty and for joining team M. **Pam Batchelor:** Thanks for all your suggestions and for also wanting to join team M. **Jenn Hazen:** Thank you for everything!

To all my author buddies:
T.M. Frazier: I fucking love you, you fucking Ginger.
Jettie Woodruff: You complete me.

The C.O.P.A Cabana Girls:
I love you!!

To all the bloggers:

A HUGE THANK YOU for all the love and support you have shown me. I have made some amazing friendships with you that I hold dear to my heart. I know that without you I would be nothing!! I cannot THANK YOU enough!! Special thanks to Schmexy for sharing my exclusive prologue reveal and Like A Boss Book Promotions for hosting my tours!

Last but not least.

Forbid Me

YOU.
My readers.
THANK YOU!!

Without you...
I would be nothing.

Lily

"Stop," Jacob warned as I tried to pull him closer to me by his shirt.

"Oh, come on, everyone's inside. No one will see us."

It was nightfall. The bright full moon loomed over the horizon like a beacon. We were standing outside on the beach that held so many memories. It gave me a sense of comfort like it had when I was a child. We spent endless nights outside together.

Just. Like. This.

He looked up toward the house behind me. "Kid, I can see them. If I can see them, then they can see us."

I shrugged. "I don't care," I honestly spoke.

"You don't mean that."

"See… there's the problem, Jacob. I've always meant it."

He took a deep breath, his masculine chest lifting before he crossed his chiseled, muscular arms over his chest. The gesture immediately reminding me how they felt wrapped around my body.

"I love you. It's that simple for me." I shrugged again.

"I love you, too. You know that. I've always loved you, but that doesn't change the fact that this is wrong. What we're doing, what we've been doing since you were fifteen behind everyone's backs is fucking wrong."

"Why? Why is it so wrong? I'm not a child anymore. I'm twenty-four years old. I know you're ancient and all, but fuck." I grinned, trying to lighten the mood.

He chuckled, "You little shit."

"We'll figure it out. He has a right to know. They all do."

Forbid Me

He nodded, knowing I was right. "I won't lose you ever again. You're mine, Lillian."

The possessiveness of his words radiated all around me. His voice making me feel warm all over.

I beamed, peeking up at him through my lashes. I secretly loved it when he called me by my full name. It made me feel older for some reason. I know it didn't make any sense, what woman wanted to be older? No one would understand until they knew our history and walked a mile in my shoes. It took us a long time to get to this point, but we made it here nonetheless. Nowhere near where we needed to be. God only knows if we would ever get to *that* point.

Have you ever wanted something so badly that it consumed your very being? Something that you could practically taste on your tongue? Something that was all you thought about, day in and day out?

The feeling is so intense that it becomes a part of you. You could feel it under your skin, in your heart, consuming your mind.

That was Jacob to me.

He was my core.

I couldn't remember a time when I didn't want him.

When I didn't think about him.

When I didn't love him.

He put his arms around me, engulfing me in nothing but his scent and strong hold. He towered over me, making me feel so tiny against him. I loved that, too.

I stood on the tips of my toes, nestling my face in the crook of his neck and murmured, "Stay with me tonight." Rubbing my nose back and forth on his skin.

"You know I can't," he groaned. I knew my touch had an effect on him.

"I know you're old and it's way past your bedtime. I mean you are thirty-one after all."

He bit my neck making me yelp.

"Watch it."

I giggled, "Stay. I'll let you do things to me."

"Right." I knew he was grinning, I felt it against my cheek. "Because that's a problem. I can't keep clothes on you. All you want is for me to do things to you."

"All the more reason for you to stay."

"Kid, you're staying here tonight, in his house."

"So…"

"So?"

"He won't know, I promise. It will be our little secret," I tempted, using the same phrase I had since the beginning. Since *our* beginning. He pulled away and I followed suit. Jacob looked deep into my eyes with a perceptive smile on his face, reading my mind.

He was everything to me.

My heart.

My soul.

I was his…

My body.

My mind.

It had been and always would be that way.

Except, there was one problem. The same problem we've had since the beginning, and we were about to face it sooner than we thought.

The ocean breeze blowing the thin white curtains did little to cool the heat between us. I swear that girl had one temperature. Hot. Not in a good way either. But damn, she was so fucking adorable when she slept. She was always on my side of the bed, as close to me as possible, half of her body draped over mine. She didn't weigh more than a hundred and five pounds wet, but she always managed to take up the entire bed, no matter what size it was. She claimed that lobsters were supposed to sleep like that.

I guess we were fucking lobsters.

I never understood half the shit that came out of her mouth, but I loved her despite it. She was much wiser than her years. No one was like Lily. Trust me I would know. I had fucked enough women in an attempt to get her out of my heart.

No one even came close.

No one.

"Hey, you leaving me?" she asked in a sleepy voice. She hated getting up early. The girl could sleep all morning if I let her.

Forbid Me

I kissed her closed eyes and tried to scoot away. "Hell, yeah. I should have left last night."

"Where would the fun be in that?" She grabbed the edge of my boxers and pulled me toward her.

"Give me a curl, it's cold."

I hesitantly laid my body on top of hers, caging her in with my arms framing her face. I could never say no to her, which had always been one of our problems.

One.

She grinned not opening her eyes. "Mmm... so much better," she sighed contently. "My friend is up." She kissed my neck and along my jawline.

"I have to go."

"No, you have to stay."

"Kid—" She rocked her pussy against my hard cock, breaking my train of thought and flipping me over.

"The sun's not even up yet. I've never seen Lucas get up before noon." She tugged at my boxers, pulling them down and freeing my dick.

I should have thought about how things were different now. Lucas. The house. Everything, but I didn't. I knew in the back of my mind that I would be regretting my decision to not leave, to stay here with her. That was the beauty of Lily, when I was with her nothing else mattered, everything faded to black but her.

Lily was my own personal inferno.

Consuming. Intense. Destructive.

She kissed her way down my chest. Never taking her eyes off mine, she slid my cock into her warm, welcoming mouth. My back arched off the bed and my hand went to the back of her neck, gripping and pushing her throat deeper down my shaft.

"Fuck," I groaned, watching her naked body sway as she made love to me with her mouth. I sat up to get a better view and touch her, but before I even reached for her the door opened and I locked eyes with Lucas.

My heart dropped.

His murderous stare went from me to Lily, who was still...

Fucking. Blowing. Me.

"I'M GOING TO FUCKING KILL YOU!" he screamed while he lunged toward me at the same time.

Lily shrieked, jumping off the bed, allowing me to back away just in time to try and cover her with my body. The sheer white sheet wasn't doing much to shield her naked body. I fucking told her I needed to leave last night. I knew something like this was bound to happen.

"You need to calm down, Lucas," I coaxed with my hands out in front of me, grabbing my boxers from the edge of the bed and throwing them on. Not that it helped our current situation. It couldn't get any worse.

"Lucas, stop it! I love him!" Lily shouted behind me.

Fuck! Yes, it could.

His eyes widened and his mouth dropped open, all the color draining from his face.

She didn't falter, not that I expected her to. She never knew how to keep her damn mouth shut. "Lucas, I've loved him since I was a kid. You of all people should understand. Get over it!"

I turned around and glared at her. "You aren't helping," I gritted out.

She shook her head. "I don't care. I love you and it's time he knows! It's none of his business anyway."

"Luc—" His fist connected with my jaw before I even got his name out. My head whooshed back, taking half of my body with it. I stumbled, shaking it off, meeting his intense gaze.

I never thought it would come to this…

Bullshit…

Yes, I did.

Which is why I tried like hell to stay away from my best friend's baby sister.

Chapter 1

Lily

then

    I wouldn't say I was a nosey child, more like a curious one. I loved to read and watch documentaries that would make my older brother Lucas fall asleep. We were six, almost seven years apart. I was ten years old and he was sixteen. My mom used to say that I was a happy surprise, but I'm not stupid, I knew I was an accident. Lucas was never mean to me. He wasn't like most of my friend's brothers. He never picked on me or called me names. He never made me feel like I wasn't wanted.

    We were always close.

    He loved and protected me, often letting me hang out with him and his best friends, who were also like brothers to me. Dylan McGraw was almost seventeen and had hazel eyes with long blonde hair that went past his ears. I loved to tease him, telling him he had a girl's hairstyle. His girlfriend Aubrey didn't seem to care, I guess that's all that mattered. Austin Taylor was the youngest of the bunch. He was fifteen and had red hair, bright green eyes, and freckles all over his body. He used to let me connect the dots on his arms with a pen. I made all sorts of designs, and later in life he actually got one tattooed on his body.

    Then there was Jacob Foster. The thought of him alone made my belly flutter. He was the oldest, already seventeen, but I didn't care… he was *my* lobster. I loved him. He had called me Kid since the day I was born or so I was told. I used to hate it because I never wanted him to see me as a kid, but there would come a time where I would long to hear him call me just that. He had vibrant green eyes that spoke for themselves. I think he got that from his mom. He didn't have any resemblance to his dad, not even a little bit. His two younger sisters were a mixture of both of them, but Jacob was like his own person, just carrying a few of his mom's features. I could always tell his mood through his eyes, they would change to all different shades of green depending on his feelings. His eyes were like a living mood ring. He was tall, way taller than me, but it didn't matter. I knew one day I would grow up and he wouldn't be the giant that towered over me anymore. He was also much broader than the other boys with defined facial features. I think he was born with a ball cap on his head, he never took it off. The only time he ever did was when I would steal it off his head and put it on mine. It made me feel safe, like no one could hurt me when his hat was on my head.

My friends were all in love with my brother, which naturally I thought was disgusting. His dark hair and bright blue eyes had girls falling all over him since the day he was born, but it didn't matter. He already had his lobster and her name was Half-Pint, well not really, that's just what everyone called her. Her actual name was Alexandra, Alex for short. She was fourteen with dark brown hair and dark brown eyes like me. Lucas told me all the time that I reminded him of her. I didn't think so. I loved her. They loved each other. You would be a fool not to notice.

The boys didn't.

So I learned early on in life that boys were stupid.

Alex put up with way too much crap, from Lucas, from the boys, and from our families. I marched to the strings of my own guitar. If you didn't like it, too bad. You know where you could go...

Well, I don't want to brag or anything but I could sing and play the guitar like nobody's business. My mom used to say that I came out singing. That I sang before I could even talk. It was my God-given talent. Music had always been an outlet for me, I could always express myself through lyrics. It was therapeutic for me to get lost in the symmetry of words and rhythm. I showed enough natural talent with a guitar that my parents put me in lessons by the time I was six. Now my guitar never left my side.

You could usually find me hanging out in my room playing and singing at any time of the day, especially during the summer.

"Hey, Kid."

Jacob...

13

Forbid Me

I beamed, looking up at him from my bed with my guitar in my lap.

"New tunes?"

I enthusiastically nodded. He always noticed when I played new songs, which is why I often tried to learn new ones.

"I like it."

I smiled, big and wide, sweeping my hair behind my ears so he could see my face light up for him. He walked over to my desk and pulled out my chair to sit. I knew what he wanted. Jacob loved the classics like Jimmy Hendrix, Led Zeppelin, Santana, Lynyrd Skynyrd, The Rolling Stones, and Aerosmith. I had no idea who those people were, but I looked them up on my computer. I even bought music sheets with my allowance so I could play for him, begging my instructor to teach me how to play Jacob's favorites. Some of them were complicated songs, but to his astonishment I picked them up quickly. It only motivated him to teach me faster.

He called me a prodigy.

This would help me tremendously in my future. I guess in a way Jacob shaped and molded me for the success I would have in the years to come, although I never thanked him for it. I played Black Magic Woman on my guitar, my fingers gliding over the strings as if they were an extension of my own body. Strumming the precise high and low pitched tones effortlessly, with the skill of an experienced guitarist way beyond my years, the intensity vibrating against my core. I lost myself in the music, exactly how I always did.

Becoming one with my guitar. Hitting the last verse, making the chord amplify into the slow progression of the ending of the song. I closed my eyes and swayed my head along with the rhythm, biting my lip when it was over and opening my eyes.

His eyes were dilated and his mouth wide open. "Damn... Lillian. You are so talented," he breathed out when I finished.

I smiled again, big and wide. *He called me Lillian!*

"Hey, dickwad, what are you doing in here?" Lucas interrupted, much to my disappointment.

"Getting front row seats to the show of a lifetime."

I love him.

"I know, she's been playing that song for the last week. She's getting good. Come on, the boys are in my room."

"Where's Half-pint?"

"Studying."

He nodded and Lucas left.

"Want to come?" Jacob asked.

"Nah. I'm going to practice some more."

"Okay, play loud so I can hear from over there."

I grinned. "Okay."

He stood and rustled up my hair with his fingers, making me giggle before he left. I continued playing for a while, once again getting lost in the music, but the laughter from my brother's room started to get the best of me. The curiosity to know what they were talking about had my feet moving of their own accord. Before I knew it, I stood outside Lucas's door.

"Jesus Christ, you have no idea how fucking amazing it tastes, Lucas. Why haven't you tried it with Stacey? You've already had sex with her," Jacob questioned, as I hid further behind the wall to eavesdrop.

"There are no words to explain it. You're just going to have to try it," Austin added.

I chewed on my thumbnail, waiting for them to say what they ate. *Maybe I could eat it, too?*

"Shut the fuck up. I'm done having this conversation," Lucas answered with agitation in his tone. It's because he wanted to eat it with Alex. Stacey was a cover up, like Ken with Barbie.

"Eat her pussy already!" Jacob yelled out and everyone laughed though I didn't think there was anything funny about it.

"Just fucking do it. You can thank me later. Trust me, the way she will reciprocate will be enough for you to want to eat it again."

I shook my head and left. Disgusted with their conversation.

"Kid!" Jacob yelled out a while later.

I jumped from my bed. "Yeah?" I shouted back.

"Come downstairs. I'm in the kitchen."

I took a deep breath and went downstairs, walking into the kitchen. "What?"

"What do you mean what?" He laughed. "Come try this. It's my favorite food."

I glared at the plate of food in front of him and shook my head no.

15

"You'll like it. Come eat."

I grabbed the fork, picking up a piece of meat.

"I brought this over especially for you, Kid," he informed me and I immediately dropped my fork on the plate, making a loud noise against the glass.

"What's your problem?" he immediately asked.

"Nothin'."

"Then why aren't you looking at me? Did I do something?"

"No."

"Lillian," he coaxed.

Dang it, again with the Lillian. I took another deep breath and raised my eyes.

Concern and confusion spread all over his handsome face. "What's up, Kid?"

I folded my arms over my chest and whispered, "Are you eating cat?"

He jerked his head back looking at me like I was crazy.

"I may have overheard some stuff today."

"What stuff?" he followed, taking a sip of his drink.

"You said." I bit my lip and his eyebrows lowered.

"You said… you love to eat pussy."

He instantly spit out his drink and started coughing and choking. I ran behind him to grab some paper towels.

"Are you okay?" I patted his back to help.

He cleared his throat and coughed a few more times. "Yes, I just wasn't expecting you to say that."

"Well, at least you understand where I'm coming from then. I don't want to eat cat, Jacob. I don't even think that's legal. You could get in a lot of trouble. I don't want you guys to get in trouble. I thought you loved cats?" I was freaking out and rambling, throwing out as many questions as I could as I watched him clean up the mess with nervous movements. He finished. His eyes averted every which way before looking at me again.

It was now or never. "What's sex?"

"For fucks sake," I roared, my hand rubbing the back of my neck. "Fuck, I mean shit, I mean damn, Jesus," I rambled, making her giggle.

I took off my hat, placing it on the counter. Lily smiled and immediately grabbed it, placing it on her head. I never understood why she did that, but a sense of calm almost instantaneously came over her.

I ran both my hands through my hair and pulled it back in a frustrated gesture, rubbing at my temples for good measure.

"I don't think I'm the right person you should be talking to about this."

She shrugged her shoulders. "Who am I suppose to ask then?"

"Your mom."

"She tried to talk to me about it, but it didn't really make sense. She mumbled mostly. I don't think she really knows," she reasoned and now it was my turn to laugh.

"What do you want to know?"

"Do you love her?"

"Who?"

"The girl."

I cocked my head to the side. "Exactly how much do you know?"

"My mom says you're supposed to love that person. That it doesn't mean anything unless you love them." A sad expression fell over her face. "So, do you love her?"

I shook my head. "Not quite. Although, your mom's right, fuc… I mean making love… should be between two people that love each other. It should mean something."

"Oh," she breathed out. "Is that what you do?"

"Let's not talk about me. I'm talking about what applies to you, which is all that matters."

She nodded. "Well, maybe. Maybe one day… when I'm older. I mean… never mind."

I smiled. "One day, Lillian, you're going to have guys waiting in line for you. Trust me on that one."

She bit her lip like she wanted to say something.

17

"And I'm going to kick each one of their fucking asses if they hurt you."

She beamed again. I loved that I was able to ease her emotional turmoil.

She was a kid.

A sweet kid.

I wanted to keep her innocent for as long as I could.

Chapter 2

JACOB

now

I was fucking exhausted.

I had been working sixty plus hours a week for the last three years at Jones & McAllister, one of the most prestigious law firms in San Francisco. Whoever said trying to make partner would lighten my case load was talking out of their ass. So much shit happened in the last few years. More than I cared to remember. I felt like I was twenty-nine going on fifty. My plane landed in Nashville and I barely had time to take in my surroundings before I had to pick up my rental and check in at the Marriott Hotel. Not that it fucking mattered, I wasn't planning on using it for long. This was just temporary if things went as I planned.

I had drowned myself in work all these years to help me forget. I tried fucking her out of my mind by having sex with a countless number of women that didn't mean a damn thing to me.

Not one.

All of my colleagues and friends were getting married or starting families, but I was at a standstill. Every time I pictured my future, it was always with Lily by my side. I was done running, it was time to claim what was rightfully mine, what has always been mine.

When Mark, a friend from law school who was married with a kid on the way, asked me to come help get his new firm off the ground for a few months, I jumped at the chance, it was like fate was giving me a swift kick in the ass, cementing my decision. I was lucky my boss fucking loved me. Otherwise, I'd never be able to take an extended leave of absence like that. I had made the firm millions and at the end of the day… money always talks.

"Hello," I answered my cell phone.

Forbid Me

"Where the fuck are you?"

I yawned. "I'm on my way."

"Well hurry the fuck up. I've been at Bootleggers waiting for your sorry ass for the last hour."

"I thought we were going to talk about your law firm?"

"God, man, can you not think about work for one fucking second? Tiffany is out of town. I miss my wife and I'm drowning my sorrows in beer. Plus there's this chick singing on stage. She's a goddamn knockout. Completely your style, tiny, just the way you like them."

"I don't need you picking out pussy for me. I'll be there in a few." I hung up, quickly gazing up at the full moon and immediately shaking away the memories that threatened to resurface.

I parked on the side of the road only paying the meter for an hour. I pulled out my ID, showing it to the bouncer who gave me a quick nod before stepping aside. There were people everywhere. There was no way in hell I could find Mark. I looked down at my phone to text him when I heard it.

The soft strumming of a guitar immediately assaulted my senses, but that wasn't what made the hair on the end of my arms stand at attention. I closed my eyes needing to check my emotions and the thoughts that attacked my mind at rapid speed.

One right after the other.

They were disastrous and unforgiving.

The strumming of the guitar was effortless and defined. I would recognize it anywhere. No one could play like she could.

No one.

That voice…

It was smooth like silk but raw enough to give you chills.

That song…

Would be a permanent reminder of what I lost.

That night…

Would forever haunt me. My days and nights.

God… I couldn't think of that night without my cock getting hard and the shame engulfing me almost simultaneously. Metallica's lyrics of Nothing Else Matters took me back to another time, another place, where I pretended that she was mine…

I was always hers.

Always.

Her face…

Her eyes…

Her body…

I remembered it all, and I hadn't even looked up to see her. I didn't have to. She was engrained in my mind. In my heart. In my soul.

She sang the chorus over again. The emotions bleeding off the strings of her guitar and her voice. The guitar solo followed making the crowd scream and cheer for her talent. Her energy was fucking contagious, it always had been. I felt it all around me even though I still hadn't opened my eyes to take her in. I knew she was biting her fucking lip, it didn't matter how many damn times I told her she was going to bite it off. I'd memorized the feel of her lips against my mouth, the way I'd take that same goddamn lip and bite on it myself.

Wanting a piece of her.

Needing a piece of her.

Her voice dropped to a soft tone, as did her guitar. The song ended and the crowd went even wilder and ravenous for her.

"Well, hello there fucking Nashville!"

They hollered higher and louder. She always knew how to work a crowd.

"Welcome to Bootleggers! Who's gettin' fucked up tonight?"

"Yeah!" they shouted.

"Who's gettin' fucking laid tonight?"

They shouted again, whistling and clapping that time. I shook my head with a smile I didn't bother trying to hide.

"That's what I'm talking about! Down and dirty in the fuckin' South!" she yelled in the same southern drawl she hated as a child.

"I'm going to take a little break—"

"Booooooo!"

She giggled and my cock twitched.

"I know, darlins', I'm too fucking pretty to look at. I'll be back, I promise! In the meantime buy me a fuckin' shot! My name's Kid."

I immediately looked up, right at her. I swear to God my chest seized and she took my goddamn breath away. Wearing short daisy dukes and a minuscule shirt that had "Whiskey Makes Me Frisky" written across her breasts. The damn thing looked like it was as old as me. Her entire stomach bare, her belly button now pierced and her long dark hair cascading down her back, almost touching her ass. The tiny frame that I fucking loved was still the same, but she looked grown up. Older. Her legs, her fucking legs. I remembered them wrapped around me and I had to shake my head to erase the images that had my cock hard and my heart heavy.

I grinned, I fucking grinned, when I saw the cowboy boots she wore. I gave them to her. I thought she threw them away.

I guess she didn't.

Which gave me hope she hadn't thrown me away either.

Fuck me. I'm going to hell.

Now that I saw her…

There was no going back.

She was *mine*.

Consequences. Be. Damned.

Lily

"Kid," some random guy murmured from behind me.

I turned on the bar stool, cocking my head to the side with a smile.

"How about I buy you that shot?" He pointed at my shirt. "Whiskey right?"

I nodded toward Sam the bartender, raising two fingers and random placed a twenty on the bar. He spun to face me again. I was used to men hitting on me. It wasn't a new thing. It came with the job. But. I never fucked where I worked, that was a recipe for disaster.

"So, what's a little thing like you doing in a big city like Nashville?"

"Entertainin'," I simply stated.

"Ah. Is this the only kind of entertainment you offer?"

I licked my lips and leaned forward. "What other kinda entertainment do you have in mind?"

"One that involves me and you. Alone. Less clothing. Less talking."

"Wow, that work for ya back home?"

"As a matter of fact, it does."

I watched him grab the shot, handing me mine. I placed it in front of me and he followed suit.

"Here's to men and horses and the women who ride them."

"Cheers to that." He laughed as I clinked my glass against his, and then we both downed our shots. Mine went down smooth, I was a whiskey drinkin' kinda girl, but his, on the other hand, did not. He coughed and his eyes watered a lot.

Pussy.

"So… tell me about your name?"

I raised an eyebrow, placing my empty glass on the bar.

"Kid. That can't be your real name, so where did it come from?"

I smirked. "It comes—"

"From me. It comes from me, motherfucker."

All the air in my lungs left me in the blink of an eye, as did my smile. The color drained from my face while my heart and stomach sank to the ground.

Jacob.

There he was, striding up beside random and standing in front of me, cocky and confident as ever. I wanted nothing more than to wipe that smug look right off his goddamn face. I hadn't heard anything about him or talked to him in three years, let alone seen him. Alex was the only one who knew about *us,* and she knew better than to mention his name to me.

I. Fucking. Hated. Him.

"Excuse me?" random gritted out, his glare intently placed on the side of Jacob's face, who's glare was focused only on mine.

"You heard me. Now why don't you do yourself a favor and walk the fuck away before you won't be able to walk at all," he warned with a calm and tranquil tone that made me want to kick him in the head.

Jacob was never afraid of anyone and he had the scars to prove it, and I'm not talking about physical ones. Our stares locked, exactly how our hearts used to be. At least how I thought they were.

Lies. Nothing but lies.

Forbid Me

"Don't make me repeat myself, asshole," he added with the same hard edge to his voice, patience was never his virtue.

I barely paid random any mind when he backed away and left. Instead I cocked my head to the side, leaning back into the bar stool, folding my arms over my chest not breaking eye contact.

"Charming as ever, I see."

He pursed his lips in that same mouthwatering way he did when I was a child. Wearing a gray button-down shirt, a black tie hanging loose around his neck and black slacks had me questioning my resolve. Tonight he had favored a fedora over his ball cap.

This was grown up Jacob.

Devastatingly handsome.

"Good to know I still have an effect on you, *Kid*."

I narrowed my eyes at him and spoke with conviction. "I'd love to sit here and process how your delusional mind works, Jacob, but I can't get my head that far up your ass."

And… he fucking smiled. A shit-eating grin smile. "Same girl. Sluttier outfits."

"I'll be sure to remember that the next time I buy crotchless panties. Easier access and all that."

He scowled, his eyes dark and daunting, turning a deeper shade of green. I knew he hated the visual I just gave him.

"I wish I could say it was great seeing you, but let's be honest, the pleasure was all yours." I stood. "If you'll excuse me I have to go back to work." I stepped aside to leave, but at the last second I turned to look at his back. Getting closer to where he could feel my warmth. I stepped on the tips of my boots and rubbed my nose back and forth on the nook of his neck like I knew he loved, faintly breathing on him. My scent assaulting all his senses, just like I wanted it to.

"Now you, Jacob," I rasped against his ear. "You can go to hell."

And with that I walked away, not sparing him a second glance.

Chapter 3

JACOB

then

We were home on Christmas break from Ohio State, Dylan, Lucas, and I all got accepted. It was our freshman year and it proved to be challenging and different. We were all nineteen and grew up in the small town of Oak Island, North Carolina. Moving to a big city like Columbus was a drastic change for us, but I think it was one we all needed. Although dealing with Lucas's and Dylan's sour fucking faces every day made me question my decision to move in with them on a daily basis.

We lived off campus in a three-bedroom apartment, finally being on our own away from home, I thought this would be the time of our lives. But Dylan was miserable and he made the rest of us miserable, too. He missed the shit out of Aubrey, his girlfriend of three years. She was still back home finishing her senior year of high school along with Austin, who got accepted to Ohio State a few weeks ago too. I couldn't tell if he was excited or not. I never understood what was up with him, other than the fact that he fucked anything that had a hole and two legs. Always trying to be a rebel in a way. Dylan spent most of his time trying to talk to Aubrey, who happened to be busy more often than not. I think we all saw it coming, except maybe him.

Now Lucas… fuck, all the shit that had been going on between him and Alex throughout the years. He thought that no one knew, they both did. They thought we were oblivious to it all.

We weren't.

Especially me.

It made me sick to my fucking stomach just thinking about them in that way, she was like our little sister, always had been and always would be. Fucking following us around since she could crawl. We all loved her. Lucas wasn't good enough for her and I had to remind him constantly, making me sound like a goddamn broken record. I was just as exhausted from repeating the same shit over and over as I imagined he was sick of hearing it. I did everything I could to keep them apart. He needed to get his fucking head out of his ass and start seeing her the way we all did.

The way he was supposed to.

We were all sitting in Lucas's living room, arguing about what to watch on TV. Dylan and Aubrey cuddling in the armchair while Alex lay on the floor with a blanket and pillow, Lucas not far from her. Austin sprawled out on the love seat and I sprawled out on the other sofa.

"Whatcha guys watchin'?" Lily asked, walking into the room with her guitar around her neck. She was thirteen but appeared much younger, sweet and innocent, like Alex.

I smiled. "About to watch Freddy vs. Jason."

"What's that?" she replied, moving my legs to sit down beside me.

"A scary movie, Lily, you can't watch this. You won't sleep. Mom and Dad will kick my ass when they get home," Lucas called out from the floor, looking back at her.

Her face flushed, it was quick, but I saw it. She peered down at her lap before I gave it any more thought.

"Yes I will," she softly whispered, strumming a few strings on her guitar.

"Lily, you hate scary sh—"

"I'm fine," she argued, looking at him with wide eyes.

Lucas sighed and shook his head. "Whatever. Jacob's crashing here tonight so you won't be able to sneak into my room."

"I won't." She looked over at me from the corner of her eye, and I moved my stare back to the TV.

I assumed she was embarrassed since we were all so much older than her. Lucas turned back and lay down, scooting a little closer to Alex. I shook my head in disappointment. Lily placed her guitar on the ground next to the couch. I pulled the blanket from the back of the sofa and handed it to her. She smiled, taking it from me and laying it over both our bodies. The movie started and it didn't take long for her to curl up into a little ball, biting her fingernails and hiding her face in the blanket.

She screamed and jumped a few times throughout the movie, completely mortified every time it happened. When the movie was over Lucas offered to take Half-Pint home, Austin left saying he was meeting up with a girl, and Dylan and Aubrey left shortly after, too. I stayed on the couch channel surfing with a nervous Lily sitting beside me.

"Why are you so jittery?" I asked, looking at her.

She bit her lip before whispering, "I have to go to the bathroom."

I chuckled, "So go to the bathroom."

She bit her lip again. "I'm scared," she said loud enough for me to hear.

"Lillian."

She immediately turned toward me at the sound of her name, like she needed to hear me say it.

"It's fake. It's not real. It's just a movie."

She nodded and looked back at the TV. A few minutes later she still hadn't gotten up. The house was dark, the only light coming off the television screen. I stood up.

"Where are you going?" she questioned, trying to hide the panic in her voice.

"To the kitchen. I'll be right back. Do you want anything?"

"No," she replied uneasily.

I walked over to the light switch and turned on all the lights in the living room. I also turned on every light on my way to the kitchen. I grabbed a bottle of water and made my way to the bathroom, even though I didn't have to go. I made sure to turn on every light that led to it as well as the bathroom itself. I made my way back to the couch, not saying one word to her, taking off my ball cap, and lying back down in the same position I was in for the last few hours.

Not thinking twice about what I had just done.

Lily

I tried to hide the surge of emotions that I felt for him at that moment. I knew he turned on every light for me. He didn't have to

27

admit it or say it. He did it because he loved me. I left before he could see it written all over my face, grabbing his ball cap from the coffee table and placing it on my head. On my way to the bathroom, I made sure to check all around me once I was out of his sight. I also left the bathroom door open just in case. I left all the lights on when I went back to the couch, and it didn't take long for Jacob to get up pretending once again that he was going to the kitchen in order to turn them all back off.

We sat in comfortable silence until Lucas came back home, followed by my parents shortly after him. Everyone was getting ready to turn in, and I dreaded the fact that I had to sleep by myself. I was mentally kicking myself for watching that stupid movie.

Why would I watch a movie where the scary dude could get you while you were sleeping?

Lucas was about to shut off the TV and I started to internally panic.

Maybe I could sleep outside his door and they wouldn't notice?

"Lucas," Jacob said out of nowhere, making us both look at him.

"Let's sleep out here tonight. It's fucking hot in your room." He shrugged. "I don't care."

I bolted off the couch before he changed his mind.

"I'll get the blankets."

I made each of us our own little beds. Lucas on the love seat, Jacob on the sofa, and me on the armchair since I was the smallest. Lucas passed out a little while later as my eyes started shutting with exhaustion. I heard the TV click off and shortly after Jacob said, "Night, Kid."

I smiled into my blanket half asleep, with his ball cap still on top of my head, knowing he slept in the living room…

For. Me.

Chapter 4

Lily

now

"Ain't karma a bitch?" I announced, catching Jacob off guard as he stared at the now empty parking space that I assumed his car was parked in. "I guess you didn't get the memo about downtown being tow happy, huh?" I mocked, pulling out my car keys from my purse.

He took a deep breath, his deep penetrating stare moving from me back to the empty space. He was pissed, which only provoked me to continue to mess with him. If he thought I was the naïve girl he left three years ago then he had another thing coming.

"Looking at the parking spot isn't going to make your car magically appear."

He looked at me again, but this time there was something behind the intensity of his eyes that I couldn't quite place. Like it pained him to look at me.

Why?

"Shitty things happen to shitty people," I stated, smiling. He still hadn't said anything and that wasn't like Jacob at all. Especially when it came to my smart-ass mouth. His silence started making me feel uneasy, I knew he felt it.

Jacob knew me as well as I knew him.

Hours…

Days…

Years…

Couldn't change that, hell decades couldn't change that.

"What are you doing here so late anyway? The bar closed an hour ago," I asked, mostly because I wanted to shift the focus away from the effect he still had on me.

"Waiting for you," he finally spoke with a sincere expression on his face that made my heart flutter.

I scoffed, "I'm not a kid, Jacob. I don't need you to babysit me anymore."

He immediately stepped forward, making me subconsciously step back. My response didn't surprise him. It was almost as if he expected it.

"It's late, Lillian."

Fuck him for using my full name.

"No shit, Sherlock."

"What kind of boss lets you walk to your car by yourself this late at night?"

"The kind who minds his own goddamn business. I don't need anyone to look out for me. I've been doing a great job on my own these last few years."

He grimaced, not bothering to cover it up. It confused me more than anything.

Why?

"You never needed anyone to look out for you, Kid, but it never stopped me before and sure as hell won't stop me now."

I scowled. "Don't—" I stepped back again. The heel of my boot got caught on the pavement. My foot twisted. Jacob grabbed me around my waist, pulling me into his strong frame. My hands gripped his muscular arms, gasping at the sudden closeness between us, inadvertently peering up at him through my lashes. His hooded dilated eyes were the first thing I noticed. Then it was his lips, so fucking close to mine. All it would take was for one of us to speak and they would touch. We were a feather apart.

His breathing ran rapidly like mine, both of us waiting for the other to make the first move. I hated that my body wanted one thing and my mind told me another, both at war with each other.

My heart.

Betraying me once again.

It. Wanted. Him.

And that… I hated that, too.

All it would take is for me to say one word. One fucking word and my lips would be on hers. It would be as simple as that, and just as I was about to throw caution to the wind and claim her mouth the way I claimed her heart all those years ago, the spell was broken. The sound of a garbage can rattling nearby broke the passion that hovered between us. The same passion that had been there since I made her *mine*.

She pushed off my chest. "Call a cab, go home, Jacob," was all she said, stepping around me to leave.

"My cell phone died."

She turned with her cell phone out in her hand.

"I don't remember where my hotel is," I lied, but she didn't have to know that.

She cocked her head to the side with a questioning stare.

"I barely know how to get back to the airport. I can call a cab, but what good is that going to do? I have no idea where my car was even towed. The hotel address is programmed into my GPS, and I didn't even pay attention to the hotel's name."

If this were a few years ago, she would have known that everything that just spewed from my mouth was complete and utter bullshit.

Now I was a lawyer.

Enough said.

She bit her bottom lip. It took everything inside me not to bite it for her.

"You want to be responsible for me sleeping out on the side of the street?" I added for good measure.

The ice-cold demeanor she tried to portray didn't fool me. Lily was as sweet as they come.

She sighed. "Fine. Come on."

She turned and I grinned, placing my hands into the pockets of my slacks, following her a few streets over to her truck. She still drove the same Chevy truck that she begged her parents to buy her on her sixteenth birthday. It was the same exact truck Lucas had. She didn't care that she could barely see over the steering wheel. She loved her brother and looked up to him. I would be lying if I said it didn't pain my heart knowing we were in the same exact situation that would never end for us.

31

Forbid Me

She was still my best friend's baby sister.

She turned on the radio loud enough to where we couldn't have a conversation. I knew what she was doing, and I allowed her reclusive behavior. I would let her get her thoughts together because whether she wanted it or not we were putting everything on the fucking table. I was done running. It didn't take long for us to pull into her driveway. The soft landscape lighting highlighted the column features to her bungalow style home, screaming Lily, and I hadn't even walked inside yet. I followed her inside, shutting the door behind me as she dropped her keys and purse on the entry table.

Her house was small as shit but perfect for her. An open floor plan led to the kitchen and the living room. There was a hallway to the left, which I assumed led to her bedroom and bathroom. Black and white pictures were scattered on different walls. I noticed I wasn't in a single frame, not even in a group picture.

Motherfucker.

I remembered that picture, I was next to Half-Pint in that one. Little shit cut me out. I was about to call her out on it, but I heard a meow, a gray fat cat purred by my feet.

I bent down and picked him up. "Hey there," I greeted, rubbing behind his ears. "What's your cat's name?"

"Jacob," she shouted from the kitchen.

"Yeah?" I looked up as she walked back into the living room, leaning against the wall with a bottle of water in her hand.

"Jacob. That's his name."

I cocked my head to the side, an amused expression quickly falling over my face. "You named your cat after me?"

She folded her arms across her chest in defiance, and I knew the next thing that fell from her lips would be complete and utter bullshit.

"Well he's an asshole and he uses me." She smiled big and wide. "Seemed fitting," she spewed.

I stood there stunned. I wasn't expecting that.

She nodded toward the cat. "Don't eat that one."

I laughed, but that was Lily. Cold one second and hot the next. It was nice to see that some things hadn't changed.

"So, you do remember?"

"I remember a lot of things and because of those things, you're lucky you're even in my house."

"Lillian—"

"Don't," she paused to let her simple yet pungent word sink in. "The guest bedroom is down the hall to your right, I only have one bathroom and it's across from your bedroom. I have somewhere to be early tomorrow morning. Make sure you're gone by the time I get back."

Her venomous tone snapped me back to reality. "So, we can't be."

"No."

I pursed my lips trying to figure out a way to smooth this over. "At least let me treat you to breakfast." All I needed was more time with her, to remind her what she meant to me. "Please," I added.

She didn't utter one word before she turned and left the room. Barely giving me a second glance. I took it as a good sign. I made sure to wait till she finished up in the bathroom before going in there.

I was in her house and all I could do was think about...
How to stay there.

Lily

I hated that I let him come home with me.

I hated that he was in my fucking house.

I hated that he was sleeping right next door to me.

Most of all I hated that I wanted nothing more than to take him up on his offer for breakfast. The fact that I wanted to strap myself to my bed because I could feel my body being physically drawn to him as if he were a magnet pulling me into his vortex didn't help. I desperately tried not to let my mind wander to a time when I loved him. I dated several men throughout the years and I never let it get further than a few dates. I wouldn't get attached to another man. It wasn't in the cards for me, and a little part of me hated him for that, too. I had always been in love with the idea of love, and the first time I experienced it he showed me the reality of the fantasy I had in my head.

I was lonely.

Forbid Me

My brother was married to Alex, they had been for over two years. I was ecstatic for them. Words couldn't describe how much I longed for a relationship like theirs. It took them a long time to get to the place they were now. Alex had always been like a sister to me and now it was official, too. I didn't ever want to rely on another man like I did with Jacob. I wouldn't allow it. Of course, I had sex, but I also didn't give it out freely. I was never that kind of girl, and I wasn't going to start being one because Jacob hurt me. Plus I had a drawer full of battery-operated boyfriends and most of the time they finished the job those randoms couldn't perform. I ached for Jacob in the same way I always had, but I still hated him, and I hoped that emotion would never go away. I just had to stay strong and stand my ground.

At the end of the day, he was still the same good ol' boy that had fucked me over.

Get it together, Kid, just remember he's an asshole. Mind over matter.

I tossed and turned the entire night, waking up before my alarm, which was set for seven am. I lied. I didn't have to be anywhere. I just didn't want to spend any more time with him than was necessary, so I took my guitar and went to my favorite park down the street from my house. I got lost in my music, letting my confusion express itself through my lyrics and strings. It was ten am by the time I got back to my house.

I laid my guitar on the couch and walked into the guest bedroom, the bed was made and it looked like no one had even been in the room. For a quick second, I allowed myself to be sad that he didn't say goodbye to me though I quickly brushed that emotion away and out of my heart. I listened to my iPod, it was the only way to protect myself from the thoughts and sentiments that were brewing. I debated on whether or not to wash the sheets, I could smell him everywhere, his scent was as suffocating as it was addicting. I closed the door and turned to go into my bathroom to shower, needing to wash away the lingering traitorous thoughts of Jacob.

I opened the door and shrieked, placing my hand over my heart while my other hand was firmly placed on the doorknob. There was Jacob, in all his glory, freshly showered reaching for a towel.

My eyes went to the only place any self-respecting woman would look.

His cock.

Jesus.

It looked better than I remembered.

A perfectly placed V lay proudly between his hips that made me want to lean forward and trace it with my tongue. I had fallen into his strong, firm body last night but feeling it didn't do him justice now that I could see the pronounced definition of his impressive pecks. His arms were bigger than my thighs, and he wasn't even flexing.

I. Stopped. Breathing.

When my lustful glance finally met his, I noticed the cockiest fucking grin plastered on his face, and it immediately washed away all the lust I was feeling for him at that moment. It didn't matter that he was fully aware that he had an effect on me.

Fuck him.

I yanked out my earplugs. "What are you doing here?" I asked, seething.

"Exactly what it looks like," he replied, starting to dry off with the towel not bothering to cover his dick.

"No shit. But why are you showering here? I told you to leave before I got back."

"I asked you to go to breakfast with me," he simply stated only pissing me off further.

"I didn't say yes."

He smiled, getting out of the shower still not bothering to cover himself. "But you didn't say no either."

"Jacob—"

"Lillian, just let me fucking feed you," he argued with a husky tone, stepping into his slacks from last night.

"Fine, if that's what it will take to get you out of my life then so be it." I rolled my eyes and walked away, deciding to take a shower later.

We drove to the diner in silence. I took him to one of my favorite spots, if I had to suffer through breakfast, then it would at least be in a place I loved. The waitress took our orders while I sipped on my sweet tea. He ordered half the damn menu and I knew why he did it, he was buying more time with me.

"How long have you been working as the entertainment at the bar?" he asked, gazing at me with the exact same yearning he had in his eyes last night.

"Three years," I simply stated not wanting to give him more information than he deserved.

His eyes widened and a surprised expression quickly fell over him. "Don't you want to do something more with your life? I mean how much longer can you really work at a bar?"

I cocked an eyebrow. It was my turn to hold the surprised expression and like everything that involved Jacob, the pissed off one quickly followed.

I smiled. "Well, this was fun," I sarcastically stated. "Nice catching up with you." I stood and looked down at his confused demeanor. "Call me never."

He gripped my wrist before the last word even left my mouth.

"I didn't mean it like that."

I sighed, trying like hell to ignore how the mere touch of his hand around my wrist made my body warm all over and my heart skipped a few beats. After all these years, he still had an effect on me.

I was still his.

"What do you want, Jacob? Why are you really here?"

He flinched, it was quick, but I saw it. He let go of my wrist as he latched onto my hand, pulling me back down to my seat.

He spoke with conviction, "You, Lillian...

I. Want. You."

JACOB

then

I hadn't slept for three fucking days.

I was exhausted, mentally, physically, and especially emotionally. Austin and Alex were in a car accident. Let me rephrase that, Austin drove while he was shitfaced, raced a friend through the woods, and crashed into a fucking tree. They were both in a coma, Austin much more severe than Half-Pint. I wanted to wring my hands around his fucking neck, but it wouldn't help the situation, nothing would change the result of his decision. It was enough that Lucas may not ever talk to him again. Dylan and I tried our best to act as if we weren't fucking livid or wanting to kill him. If we gave Lucas any more ammunition, he may pull the plug on his goddamn life support.

We all flew in as soon as we got the phone calls from our mothers. I had been surviving off coffee and five-hour energy drinks. I don't think my body could have taken anymore, desperately needing to get some sleep before it officially gave out on me. I could have probably slept for days and still not felt human, yet I knew I wouldn't be getting any peaceful sleep until they woke up.

I left Austin's room and walked into Alex's. "Hey," I whispered, coming toward Lucas, who sat in the same chair in the corner of her room that he had been in for the last three days. "You been in to see Austin lately?"

"Yesterday."

"Lucas…"

"Don't," he snapped.

"We're all upset with him, but shit happens. He would never put Alex's life in danger on purpose. He was stupid and irresponsible, he's paying for it now." I eyed Alex's bed, putting on the best poker face I could master with Lucas.

This was bad.

This was the beginning of a long road ahead for all of us.

This is where we each placed our cars on different paths that would lead us to our own demise.

It all started here.

"And so is she," he added, making me turn back around to face him.

I begrudgingly nodded and followed it up with a long deep sigh. He was right and that was something I couldn't deny. "You going home to sleep?" I asked.

"Are you?" he countered.

I nodded again in understanding, putting my hands in my jean pockets, leaning against the wall with one foot over the other. I tried to shut my eyes but it was fucking hopeless, I couldn't fall asleep.

Lucas and Alex's moms walked in with Lily by their side, they had been here the whole time just taking cafeteria breaks here and there. It hadn't been more than a few months since I last saw all of them. I smiled, remembering the last time I saw Lily, she was scared shitless. Every time I saw her she reminded me more of Alex, I thought their personalities were so similar. I would learn later in life that I couldn't have been more wrong about that.

"Hey, Kid," I greeted.

She wrapped her arms around my waist as I tugged her into my side. She was so fucking sad. She was a thirteen-year-old kid, and I knew it was scary for her to handle life-changing moments like these. Fuck, I was twenty and I barely held it together. For some reason I took off my ball cap and placed it on her head, she was always stealing it from me and it was the first time that I actually put it on her.

A sense of calm came over her almost immediately, making me feel better.

"Hi," she softly spoke to her brother.

He smiled at her when she looked at him.

"Are you okay, Lucas?" she questioned, with concern and worry evident all over her face.

"I've been better."

She bowed her head with empathy. Lily was intuitive and cared a lot for others, which was a blessing and a curse. The girl loved everyone.

"Lily is exhausted. Can you take her home?" their Mom asked, pulling all of us away from our thoughts.

"I can't leave Jana," she whispered low not wanting to disturb her. Jana was in her own little world, holding Half-Pint's hand.

I always knew Lucas and Alex loved each other, we all did, but I think I was aware of it more than Dylan or Austin though I'm not quite sure why. I tried everything to keep them apart, but at that moment I couldn't be a fucking asshole. Lucas was hurting. I couldn't imagine being in his shoes if I felt like I was dying... it must have been like he was already in the grave.

He was about to open his mouth to say something, but I beat him to the punch. "I'll take her home," I stated.

"You sure? Robert is on call and he won't leave the hospital until something happens with Austin or Alex. Do you mind staying over? Lily can't be—"

"Mom," Lily interrupted, looking embarrassed.

I smiled again. She always had that effect on me. "It's okay, Kid, it's more for my benefit, I don't like to sleep in a house by myself."

She grinned, I could tell she knew I lied but appreciated the sentiment nonetheless.

"Thank you," their mom mouthed to me.

I winked at her as Lily gave Lucas a tight hug. Their mom kissed the top of her head, and then Lily wrapped her arms around me again as we walked out of the room together.

"Are you hungry?" I asked, looking at the time, surprised that it was ten fifteen pm.

She shook her head no, maintaining her stare out the passenger side window.

"Kid, let me feed you."

She just shrugged, it was completely unlike her not to talk. Most of the time you couldn't get her to stay quiet.

I pulled into the Dairy Queen drive-thru and ordered two blizzards with the works, hot fudge, peanuts, crushed Oreos, and chocolate chips. I saw her smiling from the corner of my eye. She took her blizzard and didn't have to be told again to eat something. I ate mine while I drove, and she finished hers before I was even halfway done, eyeing mine too. I handed it to her.

The Ryders' all had a sweet tooth.

I told Lily goodnight as we walked up the stairs, going into Lucas's bedroom to grab a pair of basketball shorts and a t-shirt from his dresser.

There was a soft knock on his door.

"Come in."

Lily walked in dressed for bed, once again looking sad and upset. "Will you stay with me until I fall asleep? It's not the scary dudes this time. I'm over that. It's just the last few nights I have been having nightmares of Austin and Alex. My mom told me what happened, and I keep picturing it in my sleep."

"Oh, Kid…" I sympathized.

Her eyes watered, and I was over to her in two strides, wrapping my arms around her tiny, small frame. "They're going to be okay."

"Promise?"

"Promise," I lied, knowing it was probably a bad idea, but she was a kid and didn't need to be worrying about grown-up things.

I followed her into her bedroom and sat in her office chair. It didn't take long for her breathing to even out letting me know she was fast asleep, silently wishing it could be that easy for me. I went to the bathroom aiming straight for the medicine cabinet needing something to help me sleep. I found some Nyquil and took it with me into Lucas's room. I took more than the suggested two teaspoons just because I needed to get some goddamn rest. I didn't want to think about anything else, I didn't want to worry about anything else, and I sure as fuck didn't want to envision anything else.

I lay down in Lucas's bed and it didn't take long for a dead sleep to drag me under as well.

Lily

I gasped and sat straight up in my bed from the same freaking nightmare I had been having for the last few nights. My lamp was on, and I didn't give it any thought as I got out of my bed and made my way into Lucas's bedroom. He always let me crawl into bed with him when I was scared.

That's just the type of amazing brother he was to me.

I missed him. I missed my parents being here. I missed Half-Pint and Austin. I wanted things to go back to the way they were a few days ago. I prayed every night and every morning for them to be okay, for them to wake up. I walked into his bedroom and it was then that I remembered that Lucas wasn't home with me, Jacob was. I bit my lip trying to decide what to do. I didn't want to go back to my room and be by myself. Jacob was passed out sleeping on Lucas's side of the bed. Lying on his back with one arm behind his head and the other on his stomach, he had the comforter pulled to his chest. A bottle of Nyquil sat on the nightstand, I felt bad waking him up to ask him if he could stay with me again, he looked exhausted on our drive home.

I slid into the bed, extremely careful not to wake him, leaving plenty of space in between us like I did with Lucas. As soon as I lay beside him I felt better.

I closed my eyes and for the first time in three nights…

I slept with no nightmares.

I was the first one to wake the next morning, looking out the window there was barely any light outside. I was about to wipe the sleep away from my eyes when I realized I was holding Jacob's hand. He was in the same position as last night and I was too, yet our hands had gravitated to each other. I guess we were both exhausted. I didn't want him to think that I was a baby, unable to sleep by myself, this being the second time he had to stay with me. I carefully made my way out of the bed and left before he woke up.

Bringing my hand that had been holding his to my face.

Smiling.

Chapter 6

Lily

now

I had been working double shifts at the bar for the last few days, keeping my mind occupied and away from Jacob. I couldn't believe he had the audacity to tell me that he wanted me. Of course he did, that was never the problem to begin with. He used to remind me all the damn time how much he wanted me, except back then I actually gave a fuck.

My cell phone screen lit up with Alex's picture. "Hello, it's me," I answered my standard greeting for everyone.

"Hello, it's you!" she replied with hers. "So, when were you going to tell me that you hung out with Jacob?"

"How do you know that?" I snapped.

"That's your reply?"

"I didn't hang out with him. I don't even like him."

"Lily…"

"What? I'm serious. I didn't hang out with him, he just showed up at my bar a few nights ago. Then he weaseled his way into spending the night at my house."

"You slept—"

"No! His car got towed because he's a fucking idiot. He proceeded to con me into bringing him back to my place, claiming he didn't know his hotel information. He was probably lying. It's what he's good at. How do you know I saw him?"

"He told me," she simply stated.

I bit my lip out of curiosity as to what the hell he told her, but I wouldn't ask.

"He said he had run into you and that you guys hung out."

It didn't mean I would stop her from telling me either. "Does Lucas—"

"Of course not." She hesitated for a few seconds. "Lily, why don't you hear him out?"

"Are you for real?" I scoffed, taken aback. "After everything he did to me? You think I would take him back? I'm sorry, Half-Pint, but I'm not you," I viscously spewed at the wrong person, immediately regretting my choice of words. "I'm sorry, I didn't mean that. I love you. I love that you're married to my brother, you're lobsters. I love that you're my sister."

"I know. You always speak before you think, it's a Ryder trait."

I laughed. It was.

"You're your own person, Lily, you have been since you could talk. I know Lucas put me through hell and back, but I never thought that he didn't love me. Not once. Jacob loves—"

"Jacob loves himself. Oh, and the good ol' boys. Not me, Half-Pint. Never me. When it came down to it, he made his decision. I didn't do it for him," I honestly divulged, knowing in my heart that I was right.

"It's a hard situation to be in for anyone. I mean look at how the boys treated me, and I'm not blood. You've always been Lucas's baby sister, even to me. They saw me as a kid, and I'm only two, three years younger than them. You're seven, but that doesn't take away from the fact that he loved you. That he still loves you."

"He didn't—"

"He did, Lily," she paused to let her words linger, "He does."

"Then he had a really shitty way of showing it."

"Yes. I'm not excusing his behavior. It was wrong, but he did it because he loves you."

I shook my head. "I don't see it that way. I know he's your best friend—"

"So are you. I think you owe it to yourself to hear him out. That's all. It could go in one ear and out the other, but I have to say it to you. I want you to be happy."

"I am happy. I love my life."

"It's been a rough few years—"

"Alex, I don't want to talk about this anymore. He's out of my life and that's where he's staying. End of story."

She sighed. "Well, I got my period this morning."

"Oh shit, I'm sorry, Alex." They had been trying to get pregnant since they got married over two years ago.

"It's okay. It's a Ryder, it will come when it wants to."

She said that for me more than anything. "I gotta get back to work. Talk soon okay?"

"Love you."

"Love you, too, give Lucas a hug and kiss for me."

"Always."

I hung up, my screen saver immediately displaying a picture of a full moon, the same one that still haunted my dreams.

Jesus Christ.

You could get into her house so fucking easy. I barely maneuvered the lock and walked right in. Her neighbor didn't even stop me, and she was outside watching me the entire time.

What kind of neighborhood is this?

I placed my tools on the table and made my way to the kitchen. Breakfast didn't go according to plan, she practically ran out the door when I told her I wanted her. The little shit was being more stubborn than usual, and I never thought that was possible. I didn't expect her to welcome me with open arms, but it looked like I had my work cut out for me. If she thought she could get rid of me that easy then she was in for one hell of a rude awakening.

I wasn't going anywhere but back into her life where I belonged.

It was around midnight when I finished fixing things in Lily's house. Grabbing a cold beer from her fridge, I made myself at home since she wouldn't be here for hours. I heard the front door open, but that wasn't what surprised me. What shocked the shit out of me was that she walked in holding a gun in her hands.

A bright pink gun.

"What the fuck, Kid?" I called out.

She jumped, turning in the direction of my voice, her gun now pointing at me. "Oh my God! I could have fucking shot you, you idiot! What the hell are you doing here?" she yelled.

"Put the gun down," I gritted through clenched teeth.

"Not until you tell me what you're doing in my house uninvited!"

I was over to her in three strides, grabbing the gun out of her hands before she even saw it coming. "What the hell are you doing with this?" I asked, placing it on her coffee table and turning to face her once again.

"Why does one carry a gun, Jacob?" she sarcastically stated, pissed off that I was able to take it away from her without any effort.

"I thought you were a robber. My door was unlocked. Where the hell is your car?"

"So you fucking walk inside?" I yelled at her. "I could have been a fucking rapist, Lillian! What are the hundred and five pounds of you going to do?"

"Shoot him!" she screamed with her hands out in front of her. "Hence, the fucking gun!"

I was in her face in one second flat, livid that she walked inside her house when I could have been anyone, furious that she was raising her fucking voice to me and hard as a rock that she had the balls to actually point a gun at me.

"First, taking the safety off the gun would be helpful and second, watch your fucking mouth."

"Oh, go to Hell."

"I've been there." I gripped the back of her neck and pulled her toward my mouth as her pupils dilated and her breathing hitched, not giving her a chance to think about it.

Not.

One.

Fucking.

Second.

"For the last three goddamn years."

My lips were on hers before she had a chance to blink, forceful, demanding, and urgent. She met each and every push and pull I delivered. My hands clutched the sides of her face as my tongue devoured her perfect pouty lips, biting her bottom lip, exactly the way I fantasized since the first moment I saw her a few days ago. Her soft tongue, her scent of peppermint and whiskey, the taste of her all around me had me groaning involuntarily. The memory of her didn't compare to this.

45

Forbid Me

To her.

She forcefully gripped the front of my shirt, yanking me closer to her, molding us into one person and kissing me as if her life depended on it. She moaned into my mouth, making my cock twitch. Suddenly she shoved me away from her, I thought she was going to rip my clothes off but instead she…

Fucking slapped me across the face.

Lily

Goddamn it.

I pushed him as hard as I could, knowing I needed a strong force to move him away from me. The cocky look on his face had me reacting on pure impulse and adrenaline. I raised my hand as far back as possible and slapped him across the face as hard as I could. His head whooshed back. The palm of my hand burned instantly from the impact, I shook it off. Shaking my head in disgust, not sure if it was aimed towards him or myself.

He turned back around with his hand on his cheek. I could already see the red handprint on his handsome face. Pleased with my handy work, I snidely smiled.

"What the actual fuck?!" he roared.

"Get. Out!"

"Not a chance in hell."

"You're breaking and entering. You would think with being a lawyer and all you would know this. I should call the cops and have you arrested."

"Try it," he threatened.

"Just leave, Jacob, it's what you're good at. I don't want you here."

"Bullshit."

He was in my face again in a nanosecond, backing me up against the wall and caging me in with his arms. His face mere inches from mine, I didn't cower. I held my chin up higher, meeting his intense crazed look.

I didn't falter. "I don't want you," I gritted out, each word more forceful then the next.

He cocked his head to the side with a raised eyebrow. "Is that right?" He moved his face a little closer, barely a centimeter setting us apart. I was engulfed in nothing but the dominance that he displayed over me in that minute, and I swear he could smell my arousal from it.

"So..." He softly kissed me. "If I reached into your panties..." He kissed me again. "Would I not find..." As he continued his assault on my lips. "You..." Running his tongue along my lips. "Wet..." Kissing me again. "For me?" he huskily rasped.

My body felt like it was set on fire. There wasn't an inch of me that didn't ache for him, that didn't want him. I craved his touch now as much as I did back then and he knew it. I licked my lips needing the moisture to soothe the burn he left behind. His eyes followed the simple gesture of my tongue. His desire overwhelmed me, but his love...

His love...

Fucking. Consumed. Me.

"I. Hate. You," I lied, seeing a hint of sadness passing swiftly through his eyes.

"No you don't," he growled. "You don't hate me at all, baby. What you hate is that you still love me." He pushed off the wall and took a step back. "This isn't over. It's far from fucking over, Kid."

And with that he left.

Except this time,

I knew he'd be back.

Chapter 7

Lily

then

"Mom! I'm bored."

It was summer. I was fourteen, almost fifteen, about to go into high school. Thank God Austin and Alex were okay and they were on the fast road to recovery. Alex was moving to California to live with Aubrey, which also meant she would be closer to Cole. Cole entered her life a few years ago and all he did was cause problems for her and my brother. He pretended to be a nice person but deep down I knew he wasn't.

"Honey, what are you doing up?" She looked so tired. She'd been looking extra tired over the last few weeks. Lucas had come home out of the blue one night a few weeks ago. He said he missed us, especially me, but I didn't buy it. Something was up.

"I don't know. I'm not sleepy anymore."

"Well, the boys are still sleeping. They got home late last night."

"Are they all here?"

"Your brother, Dylan, and Jacob. Dylan's in the guest bedroom, Jacob is in the living room on the couch."

I nodded.

"I'm going to go lay down, honey, I'll see you in a little while." She kissed my head and left.

I made myself a peanut butter and jelly sandwich, making sure to make one for Jacob, knowing he'd be hungry when he woke up. He was always hungry. I ate mine first and then brought his out on a plate along with some milk. He loved milk, too. It was almost ten and he was still sleeping. He never slept in, so they must have been out late.

I shook my head, setting the glass and dish on the coffee table. He lay on his back with one arm behind his head and the other placed on his chest, a thick blanket rested on top of him. With a mischievous smile I decided I was going to wake him up, and by that I mean I was going to jump on him and tackle his body.

He jolted awake, making me laugh at the funny, surprised expression on his face. "Time to wake up!" I laughed, tickling him under his arms.

He groggily smiled, trying to move me away while still half asleep.

"Come on, I made you some food! You never say no to food!" He still didn't pay me any mind, so I decided to lie on top of him, hoping my weight would make him wake up.

I positioned my entire body on him, and it was only then that I heard him order, "Lillian, no."

My eyes widened at the exact same time that his closed, his face overcome with embarrassment just as my mouth dropped open and I froze.

OH MY GOD, what was that?
Does that happen to all of them? Every morning?
I had never been more grateful to be a girl.

I should have moved. I should have jumped off his body. I should have said I was sorry. I did none of those things. I just lay there frozen on top of him not knowing what was the right or wrong thing to do. He didn't say or do anything either, I think he was just as shocked as I was.

"Jacob!" Dylan shouted from the kitchen. "Wake the fuck up!"

We both jumped, causing me to fly from his body and land by the armrest of the sofa. I looked everywhere around the room, except at him.

"I'm up!" he shouted back, sitting upright with the blanket bunching around his groin. I shook my head, mentally chastising myself because I had just looked at his midsection.

What the hell was wrong with me?

I could feel my cheeks turning scarlet red. He leaned forward grabbing his ball cap and placing it on top of his bedhead. He usually wore it backward but instead he set it on straight and I immediately

49

wondered if he was trying to hide from me. He grabbed the milk off the coffee table, drinking half of it down in one gulp. "Thanks," he murmured, placing it back on the table.

I nodded because I couldn't find the words that I wanted to say. *"I'm sorry for touching your thing."*

I bit my lip, wishing like hell my guitar was with me, at least I could play music to avoid the awkwardness between us. The one time I decided to leave it in my room, I'm punished for it.

He turned and looked right at me with an expression I had never seen before.

"Kid—"

"I'm sorry for touching your thing," I blurted, and he immediately broke out in laughter.

I shook my head, feeling stupid. "You know… your junk, your wiener…" I kept going and his head flew back laughing much harder and louder.

"Your friend. I'm sorry for touching your friend."

Damn.

This kid.

One minute I'm contemplating what the hell I'm going to say to her to explain what she felt up against her stomach and the next she's throwing out terms like your thing and your friend. My damn stomach hurt from laughing so hard, my muscles cramped up.

"It's okay," I smiled, catching my bearings.

"I forgot about that. I guess I didn't think you would have one… I mean not that you wouldn't… you're a dude… of course, you have one… not that I'm thinking about it… your wiener… it's just… I didn't know that they did that… it's really early… you know… and you were sleeping… does it do that every morning? What if you like… crushed it or something…" she rambled, still not lifting her eyes to me. "I'm going to stop talking now."

"Lillian."

She peeked up at me through her lashes.

"Don't sweat it."

She bit her lip. "Okay."

"Thanks for my sandwich and milk. I was hungry."

She grinned, the humiliation leaving her face. "You're always hungry."

"I'm a growing boy." I winked, making her smile wider.

Dylan walked in giving us an intense stare I couldn't quite place, looking from me to her and back at me again, shaking his head.

What the hell was that?

"You ready?" he asked, sitting beside Lily, rustling up her hair.

"Where's Lucas?"

"He's passed the fuck out. He's not going anywhere." He turned to Lily with a knowing look. "Where's my sandwich and milk?"

She shrugged, looking embarrassed.

"She likes me more than you," I interrupted, trying to make her feel more comfortable.

He cocked his head to the side wanting to say something but held it back. I arched an eyebrow with a questioning stare, but he scoffed, standing up like I was a fool because I didn't know what was behind his cryptic looks.

"Thanks for breakfast, Kid." I stood, tugging on the ends of her hair as I headed to the bathroom to get ready for a day of surfing.

Alex's parents owned a restaurant right on the beach where we spent most of our adolescence. We still left our surfboards in the back office, even though we hardly used them since we moved to Ohio. When we were back home, we hit the waves every chance we got. It was like riding a bike, you never forget yet always wished you could do it more. We spent most of the day in the water, only coming back in when we were hungry. Alex had our lunch ready for us just like old times.

"Good waves today?" she asked, bringing us our food.

"You bet," Dylan replied. "When do you leave for Cali?"

"In a few weeks. Aubrey is setting up our apartment now. You know how she is. She loves that stuff. All I need is a bed," she laughed.

He lowered his eyes to his food not noticing Alex's sad smile for him. Aubrey broke up with Dylan a year ago out of the blue, and as much as he pretended that he didn't give a flying fuck, we all knew he did. Three years was a long time to be with someone, and she worshiped the ground he walked on. Trust me, that was a hard thing to do when it came to Dylan, he was… well to put it mildly…

He was an asshole.

Controlling, dominant, crude, blunt, and those were the pleasant qualities.

"I'm nervous, though. I've never been away from home, and now I'm moving across the country."

"For Cole?" Dylan asked out of nowhere, making us both look at him.

She immediately shook her head. "No. For me."

"Half-Pint," I announced, bringing their attention back to me. "You'll be fine. California is beautiful, it's good to branch out and try new things. You might learn something."

She nodded, casually smiling.

"Plus we will come out to visit as much as we can, you know that," I reassuringly added.

"You better." She took one more look at Dylan and left. Alex was perceptive making me wonder later if she had figured out what was up with Dylan. Did she expect what he was about to say to me because I sure as hell didn't.

"What the fuck is your problem? What's going on with you? You're extra abrasive today," I questioned Dylan as soon as she was out of our sight. "I'm worried about Half-Pint, too, but she's got to grow up. We can't keep her a kid forever. She's an adult now."

He shrugged, glaring. "If I were you, Jacob, I'd be worried more about myself than anyone else."

I leaned into the table, narrowing my eyes at him. "Care to elaborate?"

"You are so damn clueless. It's like Lucas and Alex all over again."

I raised my eyebrows in surprise. "What the fuck are you talking about?"

"Lily. You know *Kid*? Lucas's baby sister? His fourteen-year-old baby sister?" he mocked, accenting the last few words. "I know you like them tiny, Jacob, but don't you think seven years is quite an age gap?"

I laughed. I had to. "You've gotta be shittin' me? You can't be serious. She's a kid."

"No shit."

"I see her as—"

"You see her as somethin' alright, I'm just not quite sure what that is yet."

I shook my head with wide eyes. Completely shocked we were even having this conversation. "This is a joke, right? You're fuckin' with me?"

"You know this is completely different from Lucas and Alex. Yeah… Alex is like our little sister, following us around and trying to be one of the boys since she could walk. Lucas isn't good enough for her and we both know that, which is why we have said our piece to them several times. But Lily, Lily *is* Lucas's baby sister. She's his blood. I guaran-fucking-tee you he will bury you in a grave alive if you so much as lay a goddamn finger on his sister."

I sat there, blown away, trying to take in everything he just said to me, but my mind couldn't process it, I was dumbfounded.

"I feel like you're already executing me, Dylan, and I didn't even get a goddamn trial. Whatever you're thinking, you need to stop. It's not like that. It's so far from that. It's absolutely asinine that I'm being accused of something that couldn't be more wrong."

"Listen, I'm not saying you're doing anything wrong but letting her—"

"Letting her?" I interrupted, caught even more off guard.

"Oh, come on, Jacob. You're not that fucking blind. The girl is in love with you. She's been in love with you for as long as I can remember."

"One, she's fourteen. She doesn't even know what love is. Shit, I'm twenty-one, and I don't even know what the hell it means."

He sighed. "You know what I mean."

"Obviously I don't."

"All I'm saying is she likes you, she has a crush on you, call it whatever you want, but it's been like that since… forever. It's blatantly obvious. Lucas has his head too far up Alex's ass to notice it. You don't think Half-Pint does? Oh, trust me, she's fully aware. But she's a girl, and to her it probably seems romantic and shit.

Jacob, you can't seriously sit there and fucking tell me you haven't noticed it?"

"I… I mean… I…" I mumbled.

"Wow," he replied in disbelief.

"It's not like that, at least not for me. I love her like I love Alex. I don't… I don't know what else to say to you. I don't know what else you expect me to say."

He stood, hovering above me. "She's not going to be fourteen forever, Jacob. Keep your dick in your pants. I don't want to hear I didn't warn you. Do you understand me?"

I nodded since I couldn't find the words to describe what I was thinking. Considering I had no fucking clue as to what led to this conversation in the first place. My relationship with Lily had been the same since she was born. I watched her get her diapers changed, we taught her how to ride her bike without training wheels. God, I had been a part of her life as much as Lucas had.

We all were. Our families had been best friends since before we were born.

I tried to eat my food, but my appetite was gone. I couldn't stop thinking about what he implied, and I spent the rest of the night and the next few days racking my brain for an answer.

It wouldn't be until a few years later I realized that I shouldn't have taken Dylan's warning so lightly.

Chapter 8
Lily
now

I stepped out of the shower, wrapping the towel around my body and securing it as I walked to my front door.

"Maverick!" I screamed, opening the door. "Jesus Christ! What are you doing here? You're like a stray cat that won't go away."

Jacob's hooded glare went from my face, down my body and back up again, leaving a trail of longing in its wake. The burning in his eyes immediately made my skin ache all over.

And then he fucked it up by talking.

"That's how you answer the door?"

"Of course not. I wouldn't have opened the door at all if I knew it was you standing behind it."

"Who the fuck is Maverick, Lillian?"

I snickered. "The only man in my life. The only man I need. He's all I've ever wanted."

"Kid…" he warned with a certain edge to his tone. "I'm done playing games with you. Who. The. Fuck. Is. Maverick?"

I grinned and shrugged. "Why don't you call him and find out?"

He looked out in the yard, his fists clenching at his sides and pushed past me, storming into my living room. "Maverick! Get your ass out here, you fucking pussy!" he called out.

"Interesting choice of words," I said, giving him a devious smile.

As if on cue, Maverick heard his name and came running toward him, rubbing his body against his legs purring.

Traitor.

Forbid Me

He peered down at the ground for a few seconds, smirking and shaking his head. "You, little shit, your cat's name is Maverick. You lied to me," he stated, looking at me.

"I learned from the best," I replied, slamming the door closed. "Can't you figure out you're not wanted?"

Maverick meowed and ran under my legs toward his food bowl.

User. Typical Man.

"Once again you're in my house uninvited! This is like bad deja vu. I'm going to call Dylan so he can arrest your sorry ass!"

He leaned against the wall, one leg over the other with his muscular arms placed over his solid chest. Once again devouring me with his eyes.

Bastard.

He looked sexy as sin and that's exactly what he was…

My own personal hell.

"You need to go," I ordered, my resolve breaking more as I took him in, every sexy inch.

He grinned, a mischievous gaze quickly replacing the heated one as if he could read my thoughts. I swallowed the saliva that had suddenly pooled in my mouth. My skin feeling flush all over and he wasn't even touching me. He pushed off the wall and for a second I thought he was coming toward me, but instead he made his way into my kitchen. Opened the fridge and grabbed a cold beer.

Unbelievable.

He twisted the cap off and placed it on my counter, not even bothering to throw it away. He took a few sips from the bottle and then made this deep exaggerated groan from deep within his chest. Normally this scenario would have turned me on. He looked good in my kitchen. My house was small, but Jacob made it appear much smaller. He looked huge in my tiny space.

"Since you made yourself at home, do you mind telling me the reason for this unpleasant surprise?"

The intensity that radiated off his demeanor had me weak in the knees and I found it hard to breathe. He slowly licked his lips with his predatory stare as he eyed me up and down, and I knew what ran through his mind. I should have moved, I should have left, but my feet were glued to the floor. I couldn't move them even if I wanted to. And the sad part was…

I didn't want to.

I did the only thing I could. I reminded myself of what he was, of who he was, and of what he did to me. "Hmm, I guess these days you're using me for my booze?"

"I never used you, Lillian," he simply stated, the words slipping past his lips effortlessly.

"So then what, Jacob? What did you do?"

"I loved you," he paused to let the meaning of his words sink in. "I love you."

I wanted to believe him. I swear to you I did, but I couldn't. I wouldn't go down that road again.

I wouldn't survive it.

"I hate you. I hate you so fucking much," I argued, my eyes watering, but I blinked them away.

"No you don't," he confidently coaxed, stepping toward me but this time I didn't step away. "You've loved me your entire life. I'm in your skin. I'm in your blood. I'm in your heart." Before I knew it, he stood in front of me, pulling my hair away from my face, grazing his knuckles against my cheek, and wiping away my tears. It was only then that I realized I was crying.

"I'm a part of you, baby, and I'm not going anywhere."

I closed my eyes and allowed myself to lean into his embrace.

Into his comfort.

Into his touch.

Into his words.

"I promise you," he whispered.

His words felt like a bucket of ice cold water fell on my scorching hot skin and I immediately opened my eyes, stepping away from him. It wasn't enough. Nothing ever was. I needed to place an equator of distance between us.

"You're a liar. That's all you ever do. That's all you've ever done. Actions, Jacob, actions always speak louder than words."

"I fucked up. Don't you think I know that? Do I look happy to you, baby?"

"Stop calling me that. I'm not your baby! I'm not your anything!" I yelled at him, wiping away the rest of my tears.

"That's where you're wrong. You're my everything."

"Get. Out," I gritted through clenched teeth.

"Stop fucking saying that. I'm here, Lillian. I'm right fucking here."

"Yes, you are, for how long, though? You're always here when it's convenient for you. So what? You will be here for a few weeks? For a few months? Until I'm attached to you again? Until I'm in love with you again? And then what? Hmm? Where do you even live? Because I know it's not here. So tell me… how long until you leave me again? We've done this dance before, Jacob. I have it memorized. I know you know it, you taught it to me," I viscously spewed.

He jerked back, hurt evident all over his handsome face. It killed me seeing him hurt even if I was the one purposely inflicting it. I hated hurting him. I wasn't that kind of person and I loathed him a little bit more because he was turning me into one.

"Now leave."

And to my surprise…

He did.

I left.

It took everything inside me to leave, but I did. I did it for her. Exactly the same way I had three years ago. I thought I was getting through to her, I could see it in her eyes. I was finally breaking through the thick wall she built because of me, but I wasn't getting anywhere with her tonight. I promised her an endless amount of things and the second it came out of my mouth I knew I fucked it up.

I sat in my car for I don't know how long, staring aimlessly at her closed blinds.

Waiting.

My phone rang taking me away from my thoughts. "Yeah?" I answered without checking who it was.

"Hey," Alex greeted. "Bad night?"

"You could say that."

"Lily?"

"You could say that, too." I threw my head back onto the headrest. "Am I fighting a losing battle, Half-Pint? Does she really hate me?"

"Hate is a really strong word. Lily couldn't hate anyone. You hurt her, Jacob. Bad."

"Like Lucas hurt you?"

"Comparable."

"I'm fucked."

She laughed. "But hey… I'm married to him now. Everything is possible, Jacob."

"How bad, Alex?" I asked, needing to know.

"It doesn't matter. It's in the past."

"How bad?"

She sighed. "Which time?"

"Jesus…" I rubbed my forehead.

"Lily is resilient. She's strong. She's like her brother. It's a Ryder trait."

"I did it for her. You have to believe me. I did it for her. I was such a mess back then Alex. If I had stayed, I would have destroyed us," I muttered.

"I'm sorry, Jacob, but she doesn't see it like that. I understand because I was in a similar situation like you were. She's not going to understand that, though. You betrayed her when all she wanted was you, ever since I can remember. You know that she would have given up everything for you. Plus you haven't been completely honest with her. She might be more understanding if she knows everything."

I banged my head against the headrest, but all I wanted to do was hurt someone.

Mostly me.

"What do I do, Half-Pint? She doesn't believe me. It doesn't matter what I say, she thinks I'm lying. I swear to God I'm not lying. I love her. I love her like I've never loved anyone before. She's all I want. She's all I've ever wanted."

She sniffed. "You're preaching to the wrong choir, Jacob. Words are just words, you have to prove it to her."

"How?"

"Actions, Jacob, actions always speak louder than words."

59

Forbid Me

At that exact moment, I saw her delicate fingers peek through the blinds. I smiled when I saw her eyes show through. Our eyes locked in the distance, setting my soul on fire.

"Done," I stated.

She.

Was.

Mine.

then

Cancer.
Found a lump in my breast…
Had it biopsied…
Stage three…
Breast cancer…
The words. The sentences. The significance.

They all jumbled together. It didn't matter what way I tried to say it or understand it, the end result was still the same.

She might die.

Exactly like my grandmother who died when I was barely seven. I hardly remembered her, what I did remember was the sadness all around me.

The crying.
The prayers.
The desperation.
The goodbyes.
Why is this happening?

I sat on the beach, my guitar in my hands and for the first time it didn't give me any comfort. The refuge I sought was nowhere in sight. I couldn't even get my fingers to move. When they finally did, it just sounded like noise. There was no life in my lyrics like there could be no life in my mother. A full moon was out tonight, darkness surrounding me like the sadness that reflected off my soul.

"Everyone is looking for you," Jacob whispered, sitting close to me as he placed his ball cap on my head, except this time I didn't feel his love.

I didn't feel anything.

Forbid Me

"My mom… my mom has…" I mumbled not being able to say it out loud.

It all made sense now, the random night Lucas came home. Her looking so tired all the time. My dad barely speaking. The boys staying close to Lucas. All the clues were right in front of me, but I was oblivious.

"How long have you known?" I found myself asking.

"Long enough."

"She's known for four months, my whole family has besides me."

"Lily, they didn't want to upset you."

"Because they think I'm a kid."

"No, because she's your mom."

"I will remember her, right? I'm fifteen. I've had plenty of years with her, plenty of memories with her. They won't go away? Even if she does, right?"

"Oh, baby," he sympathized.

He didn't hold me. He didn't dare touch me. He knew if he did I would fall apart. I would crumble right before his very eyes. Every inch of me would be gone.

"She's going to be okay, she's a fighter."

"Promise?"

"Kid, I don't want to make promises I can't keep to you, but I do promise this, I will be there every step of the way," he sincerely stated. "Good or bad, I'm here for you."

I nodded, blankly staring out into the water, watching the full moon reflect off it. "Do you believe in heaven?"

"Of course."

"Do you believe in hell?"

"Kid…"

"I never believed in hell. Why would anyone want to believe in something so evil? Something so bad?" Tears slid down my cheeks, I felt them dropping down the sides of my face. "Hell's on earth, Jacob. It's here with us."

He didn't say anything.

He didn't have to.

He knew I was right.

"You can't think like that. You have to stay strong. I know it's hard. I love your mom too, she's like a second mom to me. I don't know what to say to make it better for you. I wish I could take away your pain, Lily. I'm so sorry this is happening."

"You know I screamed at Lucas? We got into a huge fight. I yelled at him. We have never fought before. I made my brother feel bad that he didn't tell me. I told him I would never forgive him for this. He's hurting as much as I am and I added more to what he's already feeling. He has always been amazing to me, and I hurt him."

"He knows you didn't mean it. He knows you're upset. You hurt the ones you love, Kid."

I would learn soon enough how true that statement was.

"I remember everyone coming back to our house after my grandma's funeral. I remember all the food that everyone brought over. I remember my mom wouldn't let me eat anymore than a few sweets because she didn't want my stomach to get upset. I remember being really sad and going out onto our back porch and sitting on the swing. I didn't even hear you come out, I just remember a plate of every sweet known to man placed in front of me and looking up and finding you standing there. And for the first time that day, I smiled."

I could feel him staring at the side of my face.

"You remember that?"

He grabbed my hand, looking every bit as devastated as I felt.

"She's going to die, Jacob, I feel it. I know it in my heart that she's going to die," I wept.

"Lily—" his voice was torn.

"I know I'm not supposed to think like that, but I can't help it. I just know and I don't want to know…" I sobbed, barely being able to see him through my tears. "I don't want her to die… I don't want her to die… I don't want her to die… Jacob..."

He immediately pulled me into his arms, my face tucked into the nook of his neck. I broke down. I cried so hard my body was shaking. I couldn't control the tsunami of emotions and feelings that coursed through my body. He held me as tight as he could as if I was going to break and he was trying to hold me together.

At that moment, I needed him to embrace me.

"Make it go away…" I murmured loud enough for him to hear.

"What? What can I do?" he asked, pure panic and pain in his tone as he pulled away from me, looking deep into my eyes.

"Just make it all go away…"

His eyebrows lowered and he sighed in defeat as he slowly and cautiously grazed my cheek with his fingertips and then with the palm of his hand.

"I feel like I'm dying, Jacob, I feel like I'm fucking dying."

His face frowned and he leaned in and kissed away all my tears, each and every one of them. I tried to control my breathing, but it was no use. With his hands still on the sides of my face he whispered, "Shh…" over and over again against my skin.

I sucked in air that wasn't there for the taking and he never once stopped caressing my face with his hands and feathering kisses on my face. It was such an innocent gesture, but when I slowly turned my face to say something, anything, his lips were inches away from mine.

"Shh…" he murmured once again, feeling his breath against my lips.

Before I knew it our mouths were pressed up against each other. His lips were moist from my tears or maybe it was his but the only thing I knew to be true, was at that moment, in that hour, in that second…

I needed him.

I needed all of him.

We stayed just like that for what felt like an eternity although in reality it was only a few measly seconds? Or maybe it was minutes?

Who the hell cares?

A sudden urge to feel more, to want more…

Had me opening my mouth.

I'm going to hell.

I don't know how we got from one point to the other. One second she was strong as a fucking brick wall and the next she was bawling in my arms, telling me to make it go away. I wanted to comfort her. I needed to make her feel anything other than the despair that was consuming her. She was breaking my goddamn heart and it was my turn to find it hard to breathe. I never imagined there could be a pain like that. For whatever reason, I've always felt emotionally connected to Lily. I've always felt protective of her, attached even.

When I pulled her into my arms, I wanted to take away her pain. I wanted to make her feel safe. Reassure her that everything was going to be okay, even though I didn't know if it was. I didn't care if I had to lie to her to calm the despair that she was feeling, but when I opened my mouth to say the things that I was thinking.

I couldn't.

I couldn't lie to her. I never wanted to lie to her. Not about something I had no control over. So I did the only thing I could, I held her, I kissed away her tears, I made her feel like she was loved, desperately wanting to be there for her. In whatever way I could.

When I felt her breathing against my lips, I never imagined that they would find their way to mine. Like a goddamn magnetic pull that neither one of us could control.

My body had turned into lead. I couldn't move a muscle.

Not my hands that were still on the sides of her face, not my eyes that were still closed, and especially not my lips that were still pressed against hers. I didn't think, which was interesting since my mind felt like it was racing with nothing but memories of her. The second I felt her mouth open, I let myself get carried away. I followed the movement of her lips, but the second I felt her tongue touch mine I pulled away. I had to.

It was instinctual.

It was wrong.

She was fifteen fucking years old.

Then why did it feel…

So. Fucking. Right.

This is so wrong. I'm going to hell. Fuck me.

She saw the panic and turmoil in my eyes and I immediately felt bad. This wasn't about me, it was about her and her mom.

"I'm sorry. I shouldn't have done that," she apologized not looking one bit remorseful.

"Lily… I… we…" I muttered not being able to find the words to tell her that this couldn't happen, that it shouldn't have happened, that it was a mistake.

"I won't say a word. It will be our little secret."

And hearing her say those six words just confirmed how fucking wrong this really was. I instantly stood up, feeling ashamed and dirty. She peered up at me through her lashes with worry, concern, and sadness all wrapped up in one.

"Jacob, please don't run from me. I'm sorry, please don't go."

I stepped away from her, needing to place more distance between us.

"Lily, I'm sorry. I'm so fucking sorry." I shook my head as the guilt consumed me in ways I didn't think could be possible.

More tears slid down the sides of her beautiful face, and I couldn't take it anymore.

I turned around…

And left.

Chapter 10

Lily

now

"Lillian Ryder?" A young guy called out in the bar.

All the staff members turned to look at me and he followed their stares, walking towards me. "These are for you."

"Umm… I think you're wrong."

"Lillian Ryder, right?"

I nodded, confused.

"Then these are definitely for you." He placed a glass vase full of *my* favorite white hydrangeas on the bar. Another type of flower mixed in between them. "Please sign here."

"Who did you bone to get these, Wonder Pussy?" Tracey, the bartender, asked as the delivery boy walked away.

I racked my brain for a few seconds. "I haven't had sex with anyone in months. I honestly don't know who sent these."

She shrugged. "Meh, who the fuck sends plants anyway? Where are the roses?"

"I hate roses."

"You do?"

I nodded again. "Yeah."

"Why?"

"They die too fast. Plants can last forever." My eyes widened and my mouth dropped. There was only *one* person who would know that.

He wouldn't. Would he?

I grabbed the envelope and pulled out the card.

No more secrets. I love you.
Your Lobster

Forbid Me

I bit my lip as I took a deep breath, trying to pretend like the card didn't mean anything to me, like it didn't affect me.

"Forget-Me-Nots."

"Huh?" I looked up at her from the flowers even more baffled.

"The other flowers, they're Forget-Me-Nots."

"How on earth do you know that?"

"I'm full of useless information, it's my thing."

My cell phone pinged with a text message and I couldn't be more grateful for the small distraction. I swiped the screen not bothering to check who the sender was.

There hasn't been one day in the last three years when you haven't been my first and last thought.

I grinned.

Lily: Sounds like a personal problem.

I could picture him smiling and shaking his head.

Jacob: You little shit.

Lily: I see you discovered florists in the last three years. They're beautiful.

Jacob: Is that a thank you?

Lily: Maybe.

Jacob: That's just the beginning, babe.

I looked around the bar, contemplating what to say next.

Jacob: That lip is going to fall off, Kid. Then what am I going to kiss?

Lily: My ass.

I laughed. I couldn't help it.

Jacob: I have other plans for your ass, baby.

Lily: Dirty, old man.

Jacob: Watch it.

I rolled my eyes.

Lily: I hope this isn't you trying to stake your claim on me in my place of employment, Jacob?

Jacob: There is no staking claim when it already belongs to me, Kid.

Lily: I belong to no one.

Jacob: You. Belong. To. Me.

I could pretty much hear his dominance and conviction over the text message and it did nothing for my sense of resolve. It half turned me on and half pissed me off, I just didn't know which one would win out yet.

Lily: *Bye, Jacob.*

I placed my phone in my back pocket and went back to work. The next day I woke up from an intense dream with Jacob, he was kissing me all over my body, caressing, and touching me the only way he could. The one man that had ever made me feel as if I were made just for him. Always knowing my body better than I did. We didn't have sex, but it didn't matter, the hunger for him when I woke up the next morning was enough to have me immediately reaching over into my nightstand. My hand felt nothing but the bottom of the drawer.

"What the hell?" I sat up, turning over to look inside. It was completely empty with a single white note placed right in the middle.

I knew that handwriting.

If you want to see these toys again, you will have to go on a date with me. I can't guarantee they will still be in working condition.

Especially the bright pink one that looks like a rabbit.
Your Lobster

"Are you fucking kidding me?" I yelled to myself, reaching for my cell phone. He answered after one ring like he had been waiting for my call.

"Wet morning, baby?" he answered in an arrogant tone.

"Stop calling me that," I snapped.

"You know I could help you with your problem... all you have to do is say, 'Please.'"

"Fuck off."

He chuckled, "I'd rather fuck you."

"Jacob," I warned.

"I love it when you say my name," he rasped in a husky tone, not helping my current situation.

"Give. Them. Back!" I ordered through gritted teeth, losing my patience.

"Give what back?"

"You know what."

"Actually, I don't know, considering there was a whole arsenal in there. The only ones that made it are the ones I can use on you."

The possessiveness in his voice set my body on fire.

"Or," he paused. "You can use my toy. If I remember correctly you guys used to be really good friends, maybe it's time you were reacquainted," he added.

"We already went through this, Jacob. I'm the one always watching you walk away."

"The only reason I would ever leave you again, baby, would be to take you to another room and fuck you senseless."

My eyes widened and my throat became dry.

"I want you in my mouth, Lillian. I could taste you in my dream. I woke up knowing what I wanted for breakfast," he hesitated, letting his words linger. "I want you in my bed, but I *need* you in my life."

"Jacob," I pretty much panted, my will to keep him at bay breaking with each passing moment.

"You. Crave. Me," he said in a slow tone that it was dripping with seduction.

"Try to deny it, baby. I dare you," he continued.

"You're not playing fair."

"I'm not playing at all."

"Jacob, I mean it. I'm putting my fucking foot down. Give me back my toys," I ordered, completely serious. I was on my last leg of patience with him.

He laughed, a husky and throaty sound escaping from his mouth. "Your foot doesn't even make noise when you stomp it."

I scowled at my phone even though he couldn't see me and hung up. It instantly rang again. I didn't have to wonder who it was.

"What?" I roared into the phone.

"Don't hang up on me again."

"What are you going to do? Put me over your knee and spank me?"

"You would love that wouldn't you? Lying over my knee with your sweet pussy inches away from my cock."

I couldn't find the words to respond, so I didn't say one damn thing. I tried not to make a sound, but my erratic breathing gave me away.

"I love you, Lillian."

It flowed out of his mouth so easily, like he had been saying it to me every day for the past three years. Like there was no history between us, no bad blood that made me regret each and every moment I let him touch me.

Every moment I let him lie to me.

"I can't—"

"Can't or won't?" he interrupted. "Can't or won't, Kid?" he demanded yet again.

"I… I don't know."

"Yes, you do."

"I wish it were that easy, Jacob. I wish I could close my eyes and pretend that we didn't have this history between us."

"Baby, our history is exactly that. It's in the past."

"No. It's not. It's every time you look at me. Every time you talk to me. Every time you touch me. It's right there in front of me, reminding me that I wasn't enough for you to stay with me."

He sighed deeply, the frustration evident.

"Nothing has changed. Lucas is still my brother. He's still your best friend. I'm still his baby sister. You're still seven years older than me, except I'm not a kid anymore."

"Lily..."

"I gotta go." I hung up and turned my phone on silent.

I went to work that evening hoping it would take my mind off anything that had to do with Jacob. The more I talked to him, the harder it was becoming to resist him. The irony was that he used to say that exact same thing about me. I had no idea how we had come full circle. He had an effect on me like no other man ever had or even came close to.

"Hey, Maverick," I greeted, walking into my house and turning on the light. "Oh my God."

There in the corner of my living room was a huge fish tank. I placed my keys on the entry table, making my way toward a beautiful and exquisite aquarium. There were Clarion Angelfishes, Regal Tangs, Koi's, Moorish Idols, and those were just to name a

71

few. Hundreds of them swam around. Bright blue gravel coated the entire bottom, stone and coral bubblers everywhere, tropical plants scattered around, a massive rock castle displayed from one end of the tank to the other, with a pirate ship in one corner.

It was breathtaking.

But what really melted my heart were the two lobsters placed in the middle, their claws interlocked. I shook my head grabbing my phone from my back pocket. This must have cost him a small fortune.

Lily: I can't believe you did this. How did you pull it off?
Jacob: I have my ways.
Lily: I can't believe you still remember.
Jacob: I remember everything, Lily.

I didn't want to talk about that. We were having a nice moment and I wanted to keep it that way.

Lily: Should I be expecting a pony tomorrow? I always wanted one of those.
Jacob: Why would you want a pony when you have a stallion? You can ride me anytime you want.

I laughed.

Lily: It's beautiful. Thank you.
Jacob: You're beautiful.

I smiled.

Lily: Smooth. Good night.

The next day I found scattered notes around my house, my truck and at work. They were all love quotes from books and poems. The following morning I walked into my living room to find every movie we had seen together growing up on my coffee table, including Freddy vs. Jason. It was beyond me how the hell he was getting into my house without me noticing. He was definitely pulling out all the stops, and I would be lying if I said it wasn't working. Then Thursday came around and I found a brand new guitar sitting pretty on my couch with music sheets of all Jacob's favorites.

"Are you fucking insane?" I yelled at Jacob when he answered his cell phone.

"A simple thank you would suffice."

"Are you trying to buy my affection?"

"Depends. Is it working?"

"Oh my God, a Fender Pro Balboa, Jacob? Are you for real? This guitar is almost four thousand dollars!"

"Baby, you're worth it."

My eyes widened. "Why?"

"Why not?"

"No. Don't do that! Stop answering my questions with questions."

"Just so we're clear, are you yelling at me for buying you gifts?"

I shook my head even though he couldn't see me. "No. Don't twist things. You don't have to spend money on me. Especially this much money."

"Kid, I make a really good living. Who else am I supposed to spoil if not you?"

"I don't want you to."

"I don't remember asking you for permission."

"Ugh, you're so freaking frustrating."

"Just say when and where, and I'll fix that for you."

"I can't accept the guitar, Jacob," I stated, ignoring his suggestion that I knew he could follow through on.

"Lillian, just let me fucking spoil you."

I hung up. It was pointless to try to argue with him and I was beyond over it. I left my house immediately, my fingers twitching to play with the strings of the brand new guitar. Thursday nights were normally girl's night at Bootleggers, but tonight we were having a charity event called Guys and Dolls. Essentially we had quite a few people who volunteered to be auctioned off for a date with the highest bidder winning. We had been promoting it for a few weeks now and the turnout was above our expectations. It was the first time we were doing something like this and I welcomed the distraction. I played my last set before my break and walked out back, bumming a cigarette off my coworker. I only smoked when I was stressed or overwhelmed, it helped calm me down and right now I needed one badly. I was losing my composure among other things.

I took one puff before it was roughly ripped out of my hand and I came face to face with a pissed off...

Jacob.

Forbid Me

I watched her set down her guitar. Her new Fender nowhere to be seen. She was so fucking stubborn. I swear she was worse than her goddamn brother. I followed her out back to finish our conversation from earlier, it was far from over, but when I saw her light up a cigarette, my patience for this whole situation fucking snapped. I snatched the cigarette from her mouth much rougher than I intended to, but it infuriated me that she would be so careless with her health. I didn't know she had picked up this habit and I think that pissed me off more than anything.

"Do I need to remind you about the history of cancer you have in your family, Lillian?"

"No, you don't because I am not your responsibility! I am not a child!" she yelled, catching me off guard.

"Then stop fucking acting like one and watch your goddamn tone when you speak to me."

She stepped toward me not backing down, not that I expected her to.

"Why are you here? What do I have to do to make myself clear, Jacob? Nothing is going to happen between us. Nada. Do you understand? I don't want you. I don't love you. That ship has sailed and it's not coming back. It's sailed so far it's like the Titanic at the bottom of the fucking ocean!"

I cocked an eyebrow and folded my arms over my chest, her glare traveling from my face to my body. "You never were a good liar, Lily. It's time you stop acting like I don't know you."

She furiously shook her head. "You don't. You never did."

I chose my words carefully, lacing my tone with cockiness directed right at her. I took a step toward her, expecting her to step back.

She didn't.

"Is that right?" I replied arrogantly, centimeters from her lips. "I don't know you? Really? What part don't I know? Maybe I don't know the way you move your hair to cover the side of your face when you're nervous. Or maybe I don't know how you bite your bottom lip when you're deep into your strings. Or do you mean that I don't know the way you freak out if it's too dark in a room and you won't walk in? Or maybe I don't know that you bite your fingernails when you think no one is looking. Oh wait, here's a good one. I don't know that you're trembling in your skin right now. I don't know that your heart is beating a million miles a minute, your hands are clammy, and you can't swallow. How there are hundreds of thoughts going through your mind, but the top one being how bad you want me to kiss you. How bad you want me to fuck you. How bad you want me to claim every fucking inch of your perfect body," I paused to let my words sink in, and her flushed complexion gave away that everything I was saying was true.

"You're right. I don't know you. I don't see your gorgeous smile in my sleep. I don't hear that ridiculous giggle you have when I'm away from you. I don't see those dark brown eyes every time I close mine." I leaned in a little closer so she could feel my breath against her lips. "I don't stroke my cock to the memory of your sweet pussy pulsating down my shaft and the taste of your come dripping down my chin."

Her breathing hitched and her eyes dilated, all it would take was for me to kiss her, bite that goddamn bottom lip that had me hard just staring at it.

I didn't.

I wanted her…

Needed her…

To come to me.

"I'm pretty sure I know you. I know exactly who you are. You're the girl who still sleeps with the koala bear I won for her at the county fair eight years ago. The same girl who sleeps topless but keeps her panties on because she's afraid that something will crawl up her lady bits. Right?"

She licked her lips, trying to conceal the smile from my choice of words since she had only said that to me one time.

"Anymore doubts I can clear up for you today, baby?"

I swept her hair away from her face and the mere touch of her cheek against my fingers had me restraining myself from the impulse to back her up into the wall and remind her of who she really belonged to.

75

Forbid Me

"I'm not that person anymore," she whispered so low, her face betraying her own words.

"I love you. Can you let me back in here?" I touched her heart with my knuckle. "I belong there."

Her resolve was breaking, it was written all over her beautiful face. So it shocked the shit out of me when she said…

"No."

JACOB

then

It was Lily's sixteenth birthday.

I hadn't really seen or spoken to her since that night on the beach a few months ago. Every time I thought about it my cock got hard, only adding to the guilt that seemed to consume me. I went on an endless amount of so-called dates in an attempt to fuck her out of my mind. Nothing helped. It was still her face I saw when I was balls deep in other women.

Women being the keyword.

Lily was a kid.

A goddamn teenager.

We were all going through shit, especially Lucas and Alex, but most of all Austin. It seemed like a never-ending battle with him, one that any of us wouldn't be able to win. Most of all him. As for Lucas… well, he literally ate where he shit. He was now going to be a father to a little boy named Mason. Dylan, Austin, and I were spending spring break with Half-Pint in the next few weeks. None of us talked about it with either of them, we didn't have to with the hurt visible on both their faces.

Dylan was becoming more of an asshole if that was even possible. He treated women like fucking doormats and the worst part about it was that they loved it. I couldn't keep up with him anymore. I knew his asshole demeanor had to do with Aubrey. I sure as hell didn't know what caused her to break up with him, but it was enough to have both of them change in ways that I never saw coming.

I kept to myself and minded my own damn business. It felt safer that way. I couldn't stop myself from texting Lily that morning with happy birthday. The little shit didn't even respond. Lily knew me as well as I knew her, and she knew I fucking hated the silent treatment. It was much worse than ignoring me or blowing me off.

I wasn't planning on coming into town.

I stayed away from Oak Island because it allowed me to stay the fuck away from her. Her lack of response had me getting off the exit for North Carolina. A little after ten pm I reached for my phone when I neared the exit for Oak Island. I tried her again.

Jacob: Where are you?

It wasn't until I pulled into my parent's driveway that my phone pinged with a response.

Lily: What's it to you?

I chuckled. I couldn't help it.

Jacob: I'm back in town, Kid.

Lily: Good for you.

I laughed, louder that time.

Jacob: Where are you?

Lily: Out.

Jacob: Where. Lillian?

Lily: The Cove.

Jacob: How the fuck did you get in there?

Lily: It's called the power of boobs, Jacob.

I sneered, trying to block out the image of her fucking breasts offered on display. I put my Jeep in reverse and threw my phone in the passenger seat, not bothering to read her next text. It took every ounce of self-control to not punch the goddamn bouncer in the face for letting her into a twenty-one and older club. The place was packed when I walked in, I couldn't move a foot in front of me without ramming into some drunken ass.

I hated clubs.

The smell, the people, the sweat, all of it disgusted me. The desperation you could feel when you walked in, slutty fucking girls everywhere, and horny driven men following close behind them. Everything about it I despised, and knowing that Lily was among them made my blood boil and my temper ignite. Neither of which were needed when it came to her. I was a ticking fucking time bomb about to explode the longer it took to find her. As I made my way through the crowd, there was no sign of her whatsoever. I felt like a man that was walking into his execution, it didn't matter what way I chose to go, I was already going to be burned at the stake. There was no right or wrong answer.

Not. One.

It was when I saw her that I knew...

I was going to fucking Hell.

I took off from across the dance floor, hauling ass and shoving people out of the way. I took down anyone who was in my path of destruction, needing to get to her as fast as I could. She was dancing on some guy's lap, swaying her tiny body in ways that not only infuriated me but also turned me the fuck on. His hands moved from her waist up her body, feeling every inch of her skin.

She looked up when I was a few feet away.

It was as if she felt me.

I swear I saw her smirk and grind him harder. My fist was pulled back as I took my last step and it connected with the motherfuckers jaw before he even saw it coming. His face snapped back, taking half his body with him. I had to pull Lily away by her waist because the fucker was taking her down with him.

Pussy.

"Get up!" I roared, kicking him in the stomach, making him fall over again.

"Oh my God! Stop!" Lily yelled, trying to pull me back. "I don't even know him! We were just dancing!"

I ignored her. I knew I was being irrational, she was in an adult club for fucks sake and she wasn't acting like *my* Lily. Any hint of common sense seemed to fly out the fucking window when it came to her.

"She's a kid! She's sixteen! You like little girls, you piece of shit?" I kicked him again and he groaned, clutching at his waist and turning over.

"That's why you're upset?" Lily shouted, the hurt evident in her tone, and I immediately turned to look at her.

"You are such a dick!" She shoved me and stormed off.

Goddamn it.

I turned back around and saw the bouncers heading in our direction. I kicked the son of a bitch one last time and left, hauling ass in the same direction as Lily. I caught up with her outside, having left the club through the back door, exiting into the parking lot packed with cars, and the full moon looming over the horizon. I gripped her arm and roughly turned her toward me, it was then that I noticed she was dressed like a slut and her face was covered in makeup. Her appearance fueled the fire inside of me to the point of pain.

"What the fuck are you wearing?" I sneered, gripping her arm a little too tightly.

"What does it matter? I'm just a kid. What's wrong, Jacob? Is my little girl body revolting to you?"

"Enough," I gritted out, my jaw clenching from her tone.

Her slutty appearance, the thick black eyeliner on her dark, enticing eyes, it was messing with my head. She wore a glossy shine on her pouty lips, making them look more inviting. A short, tight, black dress that left very little to the imagination. Her tits and ass were pretty much hanging out, and I had to remind myself that she was only six-fucking-teen.

"Fuck you!"

"Watch. Your. Mouth. I have very little patience left, little girl," I warned, hanging on by a thread.

"I am not a little girl."

"Then stop acting like one."

"The guy inside didn't think I was a little girl or maybe that was just his hard cock," she scoffed too close to my face.

"I won't tell you again, Lillian, watch your fucking mouth."

"Forbid me."

The silkiness of her voice was like nothing I had ever heard from her mouth before. I growled and immediately let go of her arm, shaking away the inappropriate thought.

"What are you doing here?" I asked.

She folded her arms across her chest in defiance. All it did was remind me of how old she really was.

My mind was fucking with me.

"I should be the one asking you that question. It's my birthday, I'm here celebrating with some friends."

"Where are your friends?"

She shrugged. "They left with some guys."

I shook my head, disappointed. "Is that what you want for yourself, Kid, a one night stand? A guy who's going to fuck you, use you, and then dispose of you?"

She looked right at me and spoke with conviction. "How do you know I'm not using them?"

Lily

He jerked back like I had hit him, and I instantly regretted my words. "I mean… I just… it's been…" I muttered not being able to find the right words to express the hurt he had made me feel and everything I was going through. I couldn't talk to anyone about it.

"It's been hard for me. I don't have anyone."

"You have me," he interrupted, both of us caught off guard by his statement.

"I'm just your best friend's baby sister, and you're never around anymore."

"I wouldn't be here now if that were true," he simply stated, confusing me even more.

"Of course you would. I'm just a kid remember? You're looking out for me for Lucas."

"Did I kiss you for Lucas too?"

I gasped as my eyes widened. We hadn't spoken since that night on the beach, I got a random happy birthday text message from him this morning and now he comes here and attacks a guy I'm dancing with.

"Why are you here?" I found myself asking before I lost the courage.

"For you. I'm here for you. I know you're going through a lot of shit right now with your family. I wanted to make sure you were okay." His tone was torn but sincere. It shredded away the wall I had started to form when it came to him.

"That guy…" I looked down at the ground. "I wasn't going to go home with him. I mean… I don't… I haven't…"

I saw his shadow moving towards me. I desperately tried to control my breathing when he grabbed my chin and made me look up at him. I had never seen that look on his face, a mixture of pain, pleasure and complete and utter affection. It was terrifying in the best possible way.

Forbid Me

"That night on the beach. That was my first kiss. You're my—"

I. Kissed. Her.

I fucking devoured her.

The force of my kiss pushed her into the side of an SUV, I heard a loud thud as her back hit the door. I didn't falter, I couldn't stop myself. The sick part was I didn't want to. Hundreds of thoughts and questions crossed my mind, but it didn't matter because my heart already knew the answers. I pecked her lips at first, teasing her with the tip of my tongue, all along the outline of her pink pouty mouth. I softly, lightly kissed her, my tongue seeking out hers.

Needing to taste her.

Needing to feel her.

There was something agonizing and desperate in the way my mouth moved against hers. Her hands instantly reached up to try to touch me, but I intercepted them. Gripping both of her wrists in my hands, placing them above her head near the roof of the SUV. I couldn't let her touch me. I wouldn't be able to control my dick, that fucker had a mind of its own. I was already going to Hell for even thinking about taking her to Heaven. Her skin burned against my fingers. Searing and scarring me in ways I may never be able to recover from.

My fingers ran down her arms stopping when I reached her face. I wanted to caress her body, cup her breasts and make her moan from my touch.

Make. Her. Mine.

Instead I brushed her cheeks and down the back of her neck, pulling her closer to me, but not close enough. I wanted to mold us into one fucking person. I was the man who just kicked some guy's ass because he was craving her in the same way I desired at that moment. The same desire I felt for months.

What the fuck is wrong with me?

The inexperience of her tongue pushing into my mouth had me groaning at the taste of her and her body curving into mine with her pussy perfectly placed against my hard cock. I once again resisted the urge to rub up against her. She was so pure, and fuck me I wanted to taint her, mark her with my touch, let her ease my throbbing cock and make her remember me and only me. I gripped the sides of her face, kissing her with the passion and force of a starving man who had finally found food. She followed each and every lead.

"How am I supposed to stop, baby? How am I supposed to stop wanting you when I know you're only mine?" I groaned in between claiming her mouth over again. I couldn't stop. I was a crazed man, possessed with the need to brand her.

"Jacob..." she panted as I bit her bottom lip.

My cock throbbed and my heart pounded in my chest. I needed to stop this recklessness, but every time I tried to pull away, I was lured right back in. Just the slightest feel of her drove me over the edge and to the brink of insanity, and all we were doing was kissing. I kissed her one last time, letting my lips linger for a few more seconds. I rested my forehead on hers, my hands still clutched the sides of her face. Closing my eyes and breathing heavily. We were in our own little world.

Where everything felt right.

We both tried to find our breathing, and when I finally opened my eyes all I saw was...

My future.

Chapter 12

JACOB

now

I didn't do it to piss her off.

Well, maybe a little…

If she wanted to play hardball, then I would give her one hell of a game. I ordered a whiskey neat at the bar and sat back to enjoy the show.

Hoping like hell I wasn't going to regret this, too.

Lily

I sat in the backroom trying to get my shit together by taking deep breaths, wanting to regulate my rapidly beating heart from our confrontation.

"You can do this, Lily. He will be gone soon, he's not going to stick around. Just keep repeating that to yourself. He. Will. Be. Gone."

I took one last deep breath and made my way back to the stage, grabbing the first clipboard from Tracey. She winked at me and my eyebrows lowered not understanding the meaning behind her expression, but I grabbed the microphone nonetheless.

"Is everyone ready to spend some money?" I yelled. "We're going to start with the bachelorettes and then the bachelors, and let me tell you… phew!" I fanned myself. "These participants are fucking hot! Let's chat for a minute about the rules. Everyone is over twenty-one, and you can outbid as long as it's within the timeframe. No one can outbid once the participant has been purchased. Let's make this a great night, dig deep into those pockets people. All proceeds go to a fundraiser for breast cancer, a cause dear to my heart. Save the ta-ta's, save the women, and have a fucking blast. The highest bidder wins the bachelor or bachelorette for a date." I winked.

"What happens after that depends solely on the bidder and their prize. Remember folks, no means no!"

They laughed.

"We will start with our very own Bootleggers bartender, Tracey."

Each participant took about ten to fifteen minutes for their bids after their introduction, the donations were rolling in and patrons and participants were hyped up. It was the last bachelor of the night and it was near three am, all the women were riled up and this guy would definitely be bringing in a hefty donation. I grabbed the last clipboard and when I saw the name I looked up, right at him. I didn't realize he was still there until that moment when he was up on my stage.

To add insult to injury he grinned. A shit-eating grin that made my panties wet and heightened my pissed off mood. That's when he reached up to his ball cap, straightened it out so that the visor was toward the front. My mouth dropped open and my eyes widened instantaneously.

Son of a bitch.

I shook my head in disbelief that he was wearing that ball cap.

My. Ball. Cap.

He smiled big and wide, folding his arms across his broad chest, accenting his muscular build. I could easily see his form from where I stood.

What was he playing at?

The crowd screaming and chanting for more brought my attention back to them. I looked around the room mentally preparing myself if I could really do this. He tilted his head, gave me a slight nod and pursed his lips, challenging me in an arrogant and cocky demeanor, fueling my indecision. I didn't need the clipboard, so I threw it on the floor.

"This handsome gentleman is Jacob Foster, and he's a pain in the ass. You know the controlling, alpha type that usually gets what he wants. Except not this time," I added for good measure before looking back over at the crowd. "I'll start the bidding at fifty dollars? Do I hear fifty?"

"Fifty!" a girl in the front yelled with her hand in the air.

"Do I hear a hundred?"

"A hundred!" another girl called out.

It went on like this for God knows how long and all it did was made me hate him a little more at that moment.

"Do I hear eight hundred?" I found myself saying, trying to ignore the bottomless feeling forming in the pit of my stomach.

"Two thousand dollars," an older woman said, slapping down the money by my feet.

It was the highest bid of the night. Most of these people were college kids, maybe a little older, but this woman had to be in her forties. She was one of those women that you could tell was a knockout when she was younger, though she still looked amazing. I peered over at Jacob as he leaned back against the wall, placing his hand over his mouth and rubbing back and forth, examining me in a way I had never seen before. The scrutiny of his stare had my already overthinking mind going into overdrive and it shook me to my core.

"What exactly am I paying for?" the older woman seductively said, making me look down at her. She was looking right at Jacob, who was still only staring right at me.

"He is fucking gorgeous. Those eyes. I am going to have some fun with him. Three thousand dollars and that's my final offer."

I swear the whole bar got quiet. It didn't matter that we were in a crowded room. It felt like it was only the two of us. My heart was beating profoundly. I could feel it in my throat and at my temples. I swear he could feel it too. I took several deep breaths as I could feel his vigorous stare clear across the distance that separated us. We stood there, locking eyes, years and years of regret and mistakes piled up between us. It all came crashing down like a boulder had just exploded. I couldn't breathe as a suffocating feeling came over me.

"Did you hear me, little girl? Three thousand dollars, now give me my man to play with," she blurted in a tone I didn't appreciate. My eyes met her glare. If looks could kill, she'd be dead.

I bit my lip. Not wanting to look back at Jacob. I was terrified that I would see him being interested in another woman…

That wasn't me.

JACOB

I could hear everything the woman was saying to Lily, silently praying it would work. I hoped like hell my plan wasn't going to blow up in my fucking face. The thought of having to leave with someone that wasn't Lily was fucking revolting. I could physically feel her torment, the years of hurt that I caused her. It took everything inside me not to go to her and try to ease her pain anyway I could, but it wouldn't help. It would probably make things worse. She would have to make the first move. She had to give me something, even if it was just an inch that I could turn into a mile.

Lily's eyes widened as she peered down at her with daggers, shocked by her blunt outburst. There was also something in her face I couldn't place, something I had never seen before. For a second, I questioned whether I should stop this fucking bid and just take what's mine.

Her.

"My name's Kid, not little girl," Lily argued in a voice I instantly recognized and loved, making me smile.

"Thirty-one hundred dollars. The bidding is over. He's mine," Lily added almost knocking me the fuck over.

The woman backed away. Lily didn't look at me for the rest of the night. I would let her hide… for now. I waited for her outside when the bar closed. My car was parked in the same spot it was towed from. I stood, leaning against the passenger side door with my arms crossed over my chest and one leg placed over the other. I heard the door open and she walked out, looking gorgeous as fucking ever.

"Interesting little thing just happened, I went to pay my donation only to find out you already footed the bill."

I cocked my head to the side and grinned.

"I appreciate the gesture like you can't imagine, but now I think you took conceited to a whole different level, Jacob. You do realize you just spent thirty-one hundred dollars for a date with yourself right?" she said with the most adorable smirk.

"No. I paid four thousand dollars for you to have me, baby. Money well spent if you ask me. Not only does the charity get more funds, but you also get me. Alone."

She smiled and it lit up her entire face. "How much money do you have? I mean you've been here for a few weeks now. Do you even work?"

"Shit, that's all I do. Before I came here, I worked sixty-seventy hours a week. I have a lot of investments, my grandparents' trust, and I know how to spend my money wisely. I've been working on and off while I've been here, but I took a sabbatical for a while."

"Why?"

"Because of you."

"I'm not that gullible. You didn't even know I was here until the night you arrived, so try again, asshole."

I chuckled not ready to tell her the truth yet. "After I found you. I decided to take more time off." I pushed off my car. "I know what you're doing, baby, you're not going to get out of this."

"I wasn't planning on it."

"Is that right?" I whispered, stepping close to her. "By all means, what do you have planned?"

"Why? Are you pissed that I ruined your good time?"

"Like I give a fuck about that. Mrs. Robinson was a means to a goal. My good time is with you. It's always been you," I reminded, sweeping her hair away from her face. "I would have paid to not leave with her if she won."

Her face frowned. "Liar."

"Don't you understand me at all? I don't lie to you, Kid. I can't lie to you. Which is why I have spent the last three years away from you. It's why I left you in the first place. I'd rather stay away from you than lie to you again. It nearly killed me the first time."

She turned her face into my hand. "Jacob…"

"What, baby?"

"Please…"

"Please what?"

"Please don't hurt me again," she murmured loud enough for me to hear. Her words were like a sledgehammer to my heart. I knew I had crushed her, but to actually hear her say the words was like taking a bullet directly to my heart. I immediately pulled her into my arms and she let me, melting into my body the way I hoped for every night.

"I love you." I kissed the top of her head, hugging her tighter into my chest. "Give me a chance to prove it to you. That's all I want. I just need one more chance."

She hesitated a few seconds and I heard her take a deep breath, nodding into my neck and whispering,

"Okay."

Chapter 13

JACOB

then

Dylan, Austin and I were in California for spring break. We were staying with Alex and Aubrey at their place. Saying things were awkward between Dylan and Aubrey would be an understatement. We were at a fraternity party for Alex's boyfriend, Cole. She still hadn't told us they were together, but I caught them kissing and holding hands a few times. They assumed no one was looking. It was strange to see Half-Pint so grown up. It was just fucking weird that she was with Cole in the first place, but he seemed to make her happy. That's all that mattered to me.

"You're such an asshole," I stated to Dylan, who grinned.

"Why, whatever do you mean?" he asked with a smartass tone, pulling away from the random pussy.

"How many girls do you plan on fucking while we're here? You trying to make your way through the sorority house or just continue to piss off Aubrey?"

He laughed. "This has nothing to do with her."

"It has everything to do with her. She's staring at you right now, the hurt look on her face pains me, Dylan, and I have nothing to do with it."

He rolled his eyes. "She should have thought about that before she left me."

"Why don't you try talking to her? Maybe hear her out?"

"That would imply that I actually gave a fuck about her."

He pulled another girl toward him, and I watched Aubrey frown and then bow her head. I shook my head, needing to get away from them. I had my own problems and they came in the form of a tiny sixteen-year-old girl, who happened to text me at the exact same time I sat at the bar with a beer.

Lily: I miss you. :-)
I chuckled, my mood lightening.
Lily: You know you miss me. I'm a very miss-able kinda girl.
Jacob: Yes, sweet girl, you are.
Lily: What are you guys up to tonight?
Jacob: At Cole's fraternity party.
Lily: Why are you hanging out with the villain?
Jacob: I highly doubt your brother is Prince Charming.
Lily: No shit. He's an idiot.
Jacob: Watch your mouth.
Lily: They're lobsters. You can't come between that.
Jacob: What the fuck does that mean?
I could picture her smiling and biting her lip.
Lily: Lobsters mate for life.
Jacob: You sure about that?
Lily: Yes, proven fact. It's on the Internet too, so it must be true.
I grinned.
Jacob: Stop being so delicious.
Lily: When are you coming home?
Jacob: I don't know.
Lily: Can I come see you?
Jacob: Lily...
Lily: It will be our little secret. We can stay in a hotel. I promise not to hog the entire bed.
Jacob: What about your parents and Lucas?
Lily: What about them?
I sighed.
Jacob: Let me think about it.
Lily: Okay, make sure you think about me in the morning. For your friend. ;-)
I laughed so hard my head fell back.
Jacob: Good night.
Lily: Night.
I spent most of the night at the makeshift bar, people watching and thinking about Lily. I wanted to take her up on her offer and have her come see me. It would mean getting to spend

some alone time with her without having to look over my shoulder every other second.

I missed her.

I missed her like crazy.

I missed her more than I cared to admit or acknowledge.

A weekend in a hotel together would definitely test my willpower to resist her, but I wanted to just have her around me so badly. At that point, it seemed like a great idea to have her be with me in any way she could. There was no right or wrong response when it came to her, just endless questions that I couldn't answer or maybe it was that I just didn't want to. I watched Alex leave the house with Austin, but when she returned, she looked really upset.

"What's wrong?" I asked as I approached her with Dylan not far behind me.

"It's Austin. He's… he's… God. He's really messed up."

"Half-Pint—"

"No, Dylan, he told me."

"What did he say?" Dylan questioned her.

"He's on ecstasy."

"Shit," I breathed out. "Where is he?"

She shrugged. "I don't know. I'm really worried about him. He could—"

"It's fine," Dylan interrupted. "We'll go find him. Stay here till we get back."

She nodded with a sad smile. It didn't take us long to find Austin, he was a few streets down at an empty park.

"What the fuck, man?" Dylan roared as we walked up to him.

He was laying on a slide with his arms tucked under his head, looking up at the sky. I wondered what he thought about.

"Nice of you to join me, but if you came here to lecture me, I suggest you turn the fuck around. I'm not going to take any shit from either of you," he calmly stated, causing me to jerk back from the impact of his words.

"Jesus Christ, Austin," I rebutted. "What are you doing? This isn't you."

He scoffed, standing up right in front of us. "Who am I? Huh? You tell me, boys, because I have no fucking idea. I have spent the last twenty-one years of my life marching in line with all of you. I'm done. Do you hear me? Fucking done."

"What the hell are you talking about? You're not making any goddamn sense," Dylan countered, folding his arms over his chest. "Fuck, man, we know you went through some shit with the car accident but—"

"You don't know a goddamn thing. Your head's been so far up Aubrey's and every other girls' pussy, you can barely see straight."

Dylan immediately stepped toward him ready to kick his fucking ass. I placed my arm across his chest. "Relax," I ordered in a rough tone, looking back at Austin. "This the way you want to play it? We're your friends not your enemies asshole. You need to remember that while you're on this path of self-destruction that you so intently feel like continuing. What's next? Cocaine? Huh? What's it going to take for you to get your fucking shit together, Austin? Rehab? Fucking overdosing? Do you have a fucking death wish, bro? Please tell us so we know what to expect from your path of God knows what."

He snidely smiled with a look on his face I had never seen before.

"That's... fucking... rich... coming from you, Oh, Mighty Jacob." He shook his head with a devious stare directed only at me. I could see Dylan from the corner of my eye. He just seemed as baffled as I was.

"You want to judge me and point fingers? People who live in glass houses shouldn't throw stones..." Austin mocked in a tone I didn't appreciate.

"Stop speaking in code and just fucking spit it out already," I demanded.

"You want to talk about how I am living my life? Tell me that I'm fucking up? Well, shit, Jacob, why don't you look in the goddamn mirror?"

I jerked back like he had punched me in the fucking face.

"I saw you. I saw it all. I was there that night," Austin vaguely implied.

"What night?" I impatiently asked.

"The Cove."

My eyes widened and my stomach dropped, all the color from my face draining.

Forbid Me

"What's the matter, Jacob? Cat got your tongue?" Austin taunted.

Dylan looked back and forth between us. "What the fuck is he talking about?"

"Should I tell him?" Austin nodded, and I couldn't find the words to speak. The night replaying over in my mind as he stood in front of me waiting.

"Oh, come on, Jacob, we're all friends here, right? Isn't that what you just said to me. What are secrets between friends?"

"You don't know what you're talking about," I finally gritted out, my jaw clenching to the point of pain.

"I don't? Well, then why don't I refresh your memory and let Dylan decide if I'm right or wrong. You see… Dylan," he ridiculed still only looking at me.

"Jacob here isn't who he thinks he is. Holding himself up on a goddamn pedestal when he should be buried in the ground for what he wants to do. I was in town a few weeks ago, hanging out at The Cove downtown. I saw someone that looked like Lucas's baby sister and to my surprise it was actually her."

Dylan shut his eyes like he knew what the next words out of his mouth were going to be.

"So, of course, I made my way toward her. She was dry humping some cocksucker on the dance floor. I would have never thought the girl I saw as a little sister my whole life could move like that. It made me sick to watch it, what did it do to you, Jacob?"

I swallowed the saliva that had pooled in my mouth, my fists clenching at my sides.

"Then out of nowhere I see this guy haul ass through the crowd. I'm getting ready to throw down if some other motherfucker even lays a finger on her. Except, I'm nearly knocked on my ass when I see Jacob appear like her knight in shining armor. Isn't that right? After you proceeded to kick the guy's ass, I'm about to walk over and pat you on the fucking back for a job well done, but Lily shoves you and takes off like a bat out of hell. Jacob here not far behind her."

I tried to remain calm, but each word that came out of his mouth made me more aware of how fucked up the situation between she and I was.

"So I followed you, both of you. Would you like to tell Dylan what I saw? Or should I do the honor?"

I shut my eyes, the shame immediately filling my body.

"I watched you pretty much attack her in a parking lot on the side of a goddamn SUV. Tell me, bro, do little girls get you hard?"

"Enough," Dylan interjected, taking the words right out of my mouth. I didn't know if it was for my benefit or his, but I assumed it was both.

"Yeah... try watching it. Maybe Jacob can give you a private show like he gave me?"

"Austin," I warned on my last thread.

"Or do you only get hard when you think no one is watching?"

My body tensed and I could feel the vein on my neck pulsating with the rhythm of my heart.

"It's all good, Jacob, as long as there's grass on the field I say play ball."

I cold cocked him straight in the jaw. His face swayed back from the impact of my fist, but his body didn't move as if he expected it. Bracing himself for it, I never thought it would come to this. Especially with Austin being the one on the receiving end.

"You can say whatever the fuck you want about me, but you talk about Lily like that again and I will lay you the fuck out, Austin. I don't give a fuck who you are." I shook out my hand, the pain traveling up my arm.

Austin leaned over and spit out blood on the grass. "Truth hurts don't it, motherfucker?"

I stepped toward him and Dylan held me back stepping in between us. "Get out of here, Austin," he ordered.

Austin looked up surprised. "The Good Ol' Boys, huh? Yeah... you don't have to tell me twice."

He backed away still facing us, like he was trying to remember our faces or something, then turned and left. I could feel Dylan's glare burning a hole in the side of my face.

"Don't," I gritted out.

He backed away too. "There's nothing left to say." With that, he left taking his disappointment with him.

Forbid Me

I stood there for I don't know how long, my mind one big clusterfuck. Waiting. For what?

Who. The. Hell. Knows…

When my phone pinged with a text message, I reluctantly reached into my pocket and swiped over the screen.

Lily: You're my lobster.

I shook my head and replied,

I know.

Chapter 14

Lily

now

The smell of something delicious assaulted my senses before I even opened my front door. I stepped inside and the aroma was all around me. I smiled, walking toward my kitchen to find Jacob pouring me a glass of wine. He handed it to me with a cocky look on his face.

"How the hell do you keep getting into my house?"

He laughed. "You planning on kicking my ass out?"

"It all depends on your cooking skills."

"You little shit."

He wrapped his arm around my waist, pulling me into his strong arms.

"If you're a good girl I will let you have dessert," he huskily whispered into my ear, placing soft kisses down my neck.

"What do I get if I'm a bad girl?" I teased, leaning my head to the side to give him easier access.

"What are you inkling for? Mmm, you smell good enough to eat. Is that what you want me to do? Spread your legs like you know I love and taste your sweet pussy?"

Jacob had always been a dirty talker, even back then. It hadn't changed, that excited me in ways I didn't even know were possible. My body immediately felt warm all over. I found it hard to steady my breathing, let alone my voice.

"What do you think about that? How about we skip dinner and go right for dessert?" he rasped, moving his way down to my cleavage.

"I thought I had to be a good girl?" I finally spoke.

97

Forbid Me

"Is that even in your nature?" he taunted, doing something incredible with his tongue on his way inside my bra, never letting go of his strong hold around my waist.

"Fuck… baby… I missed you. Do you have any idea how much I love you?"

His actions set me on fire, but his words revived my very being, my heart and soul. I desperately wanted to say it back to him, but my mind was still protecting itself from him. My heart was yearning to say those three little words that I still felt so profoundly in my core. I just about lost it right then and there when he suddenly raised his face to look deeply into my eyes. He kissed my forehead and then the tip of my nose, exactly how he used to when I was a kid.

"I know, Lillian."

I bit my lip and my eyebrows lowered as I took in his simple yet powerful statement.

"Now I really want to kiss those take me lips, but I think my steak is burning."

I laughed. "Is that what I smell? I don't remember seeing a steak?"

"It's on the grill out back."

"I don't have a grill."

He smiled, pulling away from me. "You do now."

I shook my head as I walked toward the oven. "What's in here?" I pulled the oven door and he pushed it back closed.

"A surprise." He spanked my ass before walking toward the screen door. "Go shower."

I rolled my eyes but willingly listened for the first time in a long time. It didn't take long for me to get ready. I was never much for makeup even when I worked at the bar. I always thought less was more. I applied eyeliner and mascara, remembering that Jacob loved how it brought out my dark brown eyes, some blush, and lipgloss. I grinned while putting on my panties. I got dressed in a thin strap backless summer dress that was short and went down to a V in the front.

I took one last look at myself in the mirror, pleased with my appearance. Making my way back into the kitchen, my eyes widened and jaw dropped when I slid the screen door open and looked at my newly furnished and decorated backyard. There was a beautiful iron turquoise patio set, my favorite color. Soft lighting illuminated all around us, a grill that looked extremely expensive sat in the corner with so many dials I thought I would never be able to work it without his help. Which instantly made me think that he did that on purpose. There were tiki type decorations on the walls of the patio, making it look romantic yet masculine at the same time.

I stood there stunned as Jacob sat at the table, leaning back with his ankle over his knee, his fingers running over his mouth looking smug as ever, but sexy as sin. A mischievous grin displayed proudly on his handsome face, he hadn't shaved in a few days and his facial scruff was doing all sorts of things to my lady bits. I squirmed at the thought of it against my pussy and his eyes went straight to the source of my discomfort. The table was set with all sorts of plates that were covered and a bottle of wine chilled in the center.

"When did you do all this?" I asked, bringing his eyes back to my amazed face.

"Today," he simply stated not stopping the motion of his fingers from rubbing over his mouth.

"I… I don't… I don't even know what to say," I breathed out, stunned beyond belief.

He grinned. "A simple thank you would suffice." His eyes roamed all over my body. I blushed because I could tell he really loved my dress.

"No bra, huh? That's how you're playing it tonight?"

I shrugged, fully aware that I was wearing a cream colored dress. He cleared his throat and gestured for me to take a seat, pulling out my chair next to him.

"So… you know how to break and enter, fix stuff, cook, and decorate. You're like my very own Martha Stewart."

He laughed so loud his head fell back. "I'm a bachelor, if I don't know how to cook, I'll starve. I have two younger sisters and a mom, who have taught me a thing or two about decorating."

I nodded. "How are Jessie and Amanda?"

"They're good, both in college like you should be," he said with a sly smile.

"How's your mom? Alex says she's doing better," I answered, ignoring his comment about college.

He slightly nodded, leaning back in his chair again and moving his eyes to the table. I knew that was his subtle way of saying he didn't want to talk about it. A few years ago, around the time I left and moved to Nashville, his parents divorced suddenly. It was a huge surprise to all of us since they always seemed like they were the perfect couple. At least I never saw anything that said otherwise. His dad, Lee, moved out and left his mom, Ginger, everything. They owned a grocery store not far from my house, where they sold all sorts of tourist stuff and food. They also preserved a farm on his grandparent's old plantation in South Port that they only opened on Sundays, and I guess they sold it and split the profits.

His mom didn't take the divorce well. From what I heard it was bad. Alex said Lee moved away and hasn't been around for a while. I don't know if that's changed, but I'm assuming it hasn't given Jacob's shift in demeanor. I stood, catching him off guard, moving to sit on his lap.

"So… whatcha got for me?" I questioned, trying to lighten his sudden change in mood.

He smiled and kissed the tip of my nose, knowing exactly what I was doing.

"That's a loaded question if I've ever heard one," his tone happy and content once again.

I slapped his chest and tried to get off his lap, but he dragged me back on top of him, however, this time I straddled his lap with our faces a few inches apart.

"I thought we were going to eat?" I seductively feigned.

"I know what I want to eat."

I cocked my head to the side, peeking at him through my lashes.

"But I'll feed you first," he added, placing a few pieces of hair behind my ears. "Go, before I change my mind and feed myself first."

I reluctantly got off his lap, wanting to take him up on his offer, but a nervous feeling suddenly came over me so I reached for the wine, pouring each of us a glass. We hadn't been together for a very long time, and I was nervous that it wouldn't be everything he's built it up to be.

JACOB

I knew she was nervous, and as much as she tried to pretend and play it off by serving both of us some salad. Her deep breaths, that she didn't think I could hear, gave her away. I let her believe that I didn't realize what was going on because I didn't want to ruin our date by talking about her insecurities that would quickly fade away as soon as I placed my hands on her.

I would remind her of everything and make it all go away.

We finished eating our salads and then we started on our steaks   and loaded baked potatoes. She made the most delicious sound when she took her first bite of the steak and it made my cock twitch. I don't think she knew the effect she had on me.

"And the man can cook," she mumbled in between bites.

"I aim to please, baby."

"Did you just quote Christian Grey? What's next? A red room?"

"Christian Grey has nothing on me. By the time I am done with you, my name will be the only thing on your mind," I confidently replied, making her smirk.

We ate in comfortable silence, and I noticed that Lily was downing the wine like she had something to prove. While I impatiently waited for dessert, and I'm not talking about her being the course. I went inside and grabbed my last surprise that was in the fridge. When I walked back outside, she was taking the last few bites left of my baked potato since she had eaten all of hers. I placed the tray on the table, wondering if she would even notice what I set in front of her. She stared at it for a few seconds with an expression on her face that I couldn't read or pinpoint, and when she finally looked up at me, her eyes were glossy.

I knew.

"How?" she said so faintly I could barely hear her.

"Half-Pint."

Her face frowned and she lowered her eyebrows.

"She got the recipe from your mom."

She bit her lip and looked down at the peanut butter, chocolate Rice Krispies Treats covered in caramel. It was her favorite dessert and we could never find them anywhere.

"I don't know if it will taste as great as your mom's, but I had to try."

Tears streamed down her gorgeous face.

Shit.

"Kid, I didn't mean to make—"

"No," she wept. "Thank you, Jacob, this… God… I can't believe you did this."

"I love you," I simply stated.

She peered up at me with her makeup running and her lip quivering, making it one of the most beautiful things I had ever seen.

"I know. I've always known."

It wasn't what I was hoping to hear, but it was good enough for now. She cried while she ate them, and it was probably one of the most adorable things I had ever watched her do. She said they tasted exactly how they were supposed to and that only made her cry more. I tried not to laugh at her, but the smile on my face was enough for her to realize that I was pleased.

We went through almost two bottles of wine, so when she started cheesing and grinning like a fool, I knew she was drunk as shit. She kept leaning forward on the table, making the view down the front of her dress almost unbearable.

Almost.

It didn't stop me from taking in her creamy white skin that I knew felt like silk, the way her hair kept falling around her face, and the rosy flush of her skin. She cocked her head to the side with a mischievous glare.

"Whatcha lookin' at, Mr. Foster?"

"What's mine."

She stood up, giggling, grabbed my hand and wobbled her way inside as I followed close behind her.

"Whoa, where did that come from?" she chuckled, tripping over her own damn feet, but I quickly caught her before she fell. She led us into her bedroom. I knew where this was going when she sat me on the edge of her bed. I crossed my arms over my chest, amused with the show she was trying to give me.

"You're my famous," she laughed again, wanting to say favorite, I think, but I laughed too. It was contagious.

"I'm kind of surprised by how much wine you can take down."

She nodded all proud of herself, wearing the sloppiest, but most adorable fucking look on her face.

"I think we should do things to each other."

"Is that right?"

"Mmm hmm… I'll go first and then you can go or vice versa… or we can do it at the same time. Unless you want to fuck and then… that'd be cool."

"Do you have any idea what you just said, baby?"

She nodded again with that adorable face. "Yep… I have something to show you."

"I'm sure it's something I would really love to see."

She grabbed the hem of her already too short dress and hiked it up little by little till it reached the top of her thighs. She peeked up at me through her lashes.

"You ready?"

"I'm pretty sure I've seen it before, Kid."

"Nah-uh," she slurred, pulling up her dress to expose her panties that had a picture of a cat's face printed on them.

I busted out laughing.

I laughed so damn hard my stomach muscles cramped.

"Lily, is that a pussy on your panties?"

"Yep, do you wanna pet it? It wants to be petted," she taunted, making me stand up.

"Un-fucking-real, I am in a pussy infested house and all I get is blue balls." I walked to her and threw her over my shoulder. I slapped her ass as she giggles, carrying her back over to the bed to straddle my lap. She wrapped her arms around my neck and I gripped onto her plump round ass.

"Baby, you're drunk."

"Yessum." She kissed all over my face.

"I'm not fucking you. Not tonight."

She pulled away and tried to narrow her hazy eyes at me. "You don't want me?" She pouted.

Forbid Me

"I want you more than I have ever wanted anything in my life."

She sloppily smiled.

"But not like this, baby. You are drunk tonight, and I want you to remember everything I plan to do to your perfect body. Do you understand me?"

She nodded. "Mmm hmm."

I kissed along her collarbone.

"Does that mean you're leaving me?" she asked, her tone soft and low.

With doubt in me.

In us...

It's what I did to *her*.

It's what I did to *us*.

"Fuck no," I answered with a rough edge.

"Does that mean we can do a curl?" Her word for cuddle.

"Always," I breathed out, trying to stop myself from going further down her neck.

"Mmm-kay."

She reached for her dress and tried to take it off, but I reluctantly pulled it back down.

"Keep this on, Kid, I only have so much willpower left."

I spanked her ass again, this time making her yelp and then picked her up, lying her on the bed, pulling back the covers around her. I took off my clothes, only leaving on my boxer briefs. Lily took off her dress, throwing it on the ground. She grabbed the shirt I was just wearing and put it on, exactly how she did countless times before. I loved seeing it on her, knowing it used to be her thing. I turned off the light before lying right next to her, pulling her as close to my body as possible, she came effortlessly. She sighed contently and passed the fuck out within seconds. I don't know how long I laid there awake just holding her, taking in the feel of her tiny frame against my chest. Loving the feel of her in my arms again, never wanting it to end. I watched her sleep until my eyes gave way.

That night was the first time in a long time that I didn't dream about her. I didn't have to. She was in my arms.

And...

I vowed to never let her go again.

Chapter 15

Lily

then

I knocked on the hotel door.

To say I was nervous the entire flight to Ohio would have been an understatement. I told my parents that I was going to check out a few colleges with some friends. Normally they would have put up an argument, but I think they were relieved that I would be out of the house for a few days. Away from all the chaos with my mom's cancer and Lucas being a father now. It took me a few weeks to convince Jacob to let me come visit him. He had been acting a little strange after he got back to Ohio from spring break at Alex's. He told me he was just tired and overwhelmed from his last semester in college and preparing to take the LSAT for law school.

"Surprise!" I enthusiastically shouted.

"Hey, Kid," he answered the door with a huge smile on his face and I jumped into his arms. He picked me up off the ground and I wrapped my legs around his waist.

"How did you get here? I was just about to come pick you up. I thought your flight was landing in thirty minutes."

"I missed you, I wanted to surprise you," I said into the nook of his neck. "I'm so happy to see you."

"Me too, sweet girl, me too." He kissed the top of my head and then placed me back on the ground. "How was your flight?"

"Uneventful," I replied as he took my bag and guitar from the doorway to set it on the king size bed.

"One bed?" I arched an eyebrow, giving him a smug smile.

He chuckled. "Did you want me to get two?" he implied with the same cocky smile.

I jumped onto the left side of the bed, laying my face on the pillow. "I sleep on this side."

Forbid Me

"What if I wanted that side?"

I grinned. "Then I can sleep on you."

"I've shared a bed with you before, Kid. I'm pretty sure you'll sleep on me regardless."

I laughed. I had slept with him, Lucas, and the other boys several times. Our families were all friends since before we were even born. I grew up with all of them, taking vacations together every summer and endless amounts of sleepovers. It was never sexual, but I knew this time with Jacob it would be different.

Much different.

He placed his hands in his pockets with a look on his face that I couldn't place.

"Now what?" I questioned, turning over to lean on the headboard. "What sorts of fun stuff do you have planned for us?"

"First, I thought I would show you around Columbus."

"And then what?"

"I would feed you. Maybe if you're a good girl I'll even take you to a movie," he smirked.

"Like on a date? Or did we skip that whole step and moved right onto being boyfriend and girlfriend?" I asked as my heart beat out of my chest, needing to know the answer.

It's the only thing I thought about on the flight here, well not the only thing. I was sixteen and most of my friends weren't even virgins anymore, they had all experienced *something*. I had been kissed, twice, both times by Jacob, I don't know how any of this stuff worked, but I knew in my heart that I wanted it to be Jacob.

I always had.

He wouldn't have let me come visit if he didn't want me, right? Especially since we were sharing a bed…

"How about we take one step at a time? Huh? You're here, I'm here. Let's go with it."

I bit my lip, not exactly the words I wanted to hear, but not entirely awful either. I guess I could take that.

"Okay."

He reached out his hand for me and I quickly took it. We left the hotel and went to our first destination, The Jack Hanna Zoo and Aquarium. He held my hand the entire time, guiding me through the zoo and all the animals with our private behind the scenes tour.

Jacob knew I loved animals, it didn't matter what kind it was, if it was furry, I loved it.

"Awe! Look at the babies. I want to take one home," I said, looking inside the lion cub cages.

"Do you want to hold one?"

I immediately looked at him with a bemused expression on my face.

"I take that as a yes," he chuckled, nodding behind me. A man appeared out of nowhere opening the gates for us to follow. We had to stay toward the back until he brought one of the cubs over to us.

"This is Yoshi, he's six months old," the trainer informed us, setting him down on the ground. I crouched down to pet him and he wouldn't stop licking my hand.

"Yoshi loves the ladies," he added, making me laugh.

Jacob took some pictures of us. I was sad to leave Yoshi, but we needed to move on. The next room we walked into had a huge circular aquarium placed dead center.

"Wow," I sighed, letting go of Jacob's hand and walking around in complete amazement of all the colors represented by all the different fish and sea life. "I can't believe there are that many fish! You don't see this in the ocean at Oak Island."

"That you don't. Just a bunch of fucking sharks."

"Oh, I love this one!"

He looked at the chart. "That's a Clarion Angelfish."

"I love this one, too!"

"That's a Koi."

"What about that one?"

"A Regal Tang."

I pointed to hundreds and he named off each and every one.

"You know what's missing?" I asked, glancing at him.

"Hmm?"

"Lobsters."

He laughed at me.

"I'm serious. Look at this thing." I pointed at it. "There's a castle, a pirate ship, bright blue gravel, all the tropical plants, and all these beautiful fish. Where are the lobsters?"

107

He shrugged in a typical guy way, finding my banter amusing.

"One day I'm going to have a fish tank just like this, but mine is going to have lobsters, so it will kick this fish tank's ass."

"Sounds like a plan."

"A great plan."

He took me to Jeni's Ice Cream, which I guess was a pretty big deal in Columbus. When we walked in I understood why. My family was known to have a sweet tooth. It was actually a running joke that we could probably live off sweets if needed. This place had every flavor of ice cream under the sun available.

Jacob asked the lady behind the counter if there was an option where I could choose all the flavors I wanted. She said they didn't, but he used his powers of persuasion. By that I mean he smiled and said, "Please."

"Only for you. Don't tell anyone, though," she flirted.

"It's our little secret," I chimed in, grinning at Jacob.

"You have a really awesome big brother. I wish mine was like him."

I stopped grinning and Jacob pursed his lips. The atmosphere between us immediately changed. I feared what was going on in his head. I didn't think I looked that young. I bit my lip, his insecurity about us radiating off of him, and I hated that there was a sudden shift in our easygoing relationship.

I smirked, cocking my head to the side. "Awe, old man, she thinks you're my big brother, ain't that cute." I looked around the parlor and leaned on the counter. "Just so we're clear… he's actually my sugar daddy." I winked.

Jacob busted out laughing. I literally thought he was going to piss himself from my smart-ass response. The lady turned bright red. I ignored both their reactions and started to pick out all the flavors I wanted to eat.

Adding a few more just because she was a twat.

That was definitely one of the things I loved the most about Lily, she could take any situation and turn it into a positive one that usually left you laughing your ass off. The closer we got to heading back to the hotel the more anxious I became. I didn't know if she had certain expectations because of our sleeping arrangements. All I wanted was to hold her while we slept, that's the only reason I got a king size bed, but if there was one thing I knew about Lily, whatever she wanted or set her mind to, she fucking got.

I had lived in Ohio for four years and this was the first time I was doing any of the tourist shit, but it made her happy and that's all that mattered. I took her to a few more places that I knew she would love and then to my favorite spot for dinner. When I handed her my phone to pick out a movie, she said she wanted to rent one in our room instead. Stating that it was one of the best parts of staying in a hotel in the first place. I went with her request because fuck...

What other choice did I have?

We walked into the room and she said she needed to shower. It didn't take long for her to appear in the smallest towel invented by man.

All that ran through my head was that I was fucked.

"I feel so much better," she stated, laughing and sitting on the edge of the bed. Completely aware of the reaction she evoked in me by sitting in nothing but a towel with wet hair cascading down her face and her skin flushed, still slightly wet. She nodded in a seductive yet shy way that I had never seen before.

Fuck me.

I had to get the fuck out of there before my cock started to have a mind of its own.

I turned on the shower. Hoping like hell the cold water would drown out the thoughts that were occurring in my head... both goddamn heads. Visions of Lily bent over the bed and me slamming into her, Lily on the dresser and me on my knees, devouring her pussy, Lily riding my cock while I watched her tits bounce as I gripped her thighs so fucking hard, wanting to mark her. It was one right after the other, relentless and tempting, the sin of it all making it more addicting and maddening like the forbidden fruit she was. I was under the shower in three seconds flat, wanting to wash away the images of Lily, of us.

My. Best. Friend's. Baby. Sister.

Forbid Me

Looking so damn innocent. Knowing that she had never been touched before was way too much for my rigid cock that wanted nothing more than to sink into her sweet, tight virgin pussy.

Taking what I so desperately wanted to be mine.

I leaned my arm against the wall, my face resting against it with cold water running down my head and my entire body. I closed my eyes and my hand found my throbbing hard cock within seconds. I needed some release, but I couldn't go there with Lily yet, so I did the only thing I could.

I stroked myself picturing nothing but images of…

The way I would make her moan.

The way I would make her pant.

The way I would make her beg me to let her come.

I hit my head against the tile. "What the fuck am I doing?" I pleaded in agony.

I pictured her back arching and her nipples puckering when I licked and sucked them into my mouth. The sounds that would escape her tiny, breathless lips the closer I allowed her to get to her release. The way I would make her come and scream out my goddamn name over and over again until I was burned into her skin and she would only ever remember me.

Mine.

I pumped harder and faster, my hips moving in the opposite direction of my hand, imagining it was her pussy pulsating and tightening around my shaft to the brink of agony.

"Christ…" I groaned out a little too loudly on the edge of coming but not quite there. "Lily," I growled, hearing someone faintly gasp.

Lily.

I turned my head to the side, opening my eyes to find her watching me by the door, both of us wearing the same hooded gaze. Her chest was rising and falling with each pump of my hand stroking my cock, and I would be lying if I said it didn't turn me the fuck on.

My dick was getting harder to the point of pain.

"Say it," I ordered in a husky tone.

"What?" she panted, taking in the sight of me jacking off in front of her.

"Say my goddamn name."

Her eyes widened and her breathing hitched. "Jacob."

M. Robinson

I came so fucking hard that I saw stars as my entire body shook with the most intense orgasm I had ever experienced. She licked her lips and then bit her bottom one and for the millionth time I found myself wanting to bite it for her. I stepped out of the shower, wrapping a towel around my waist not bothering to dry myself. Avoiding the mirror like it was the goddamn plague. The shame overtaking me in ways I never thought possible. I took a deep, long breath and whispered, "Lillian—"

And she took off running.

Chapter 16

JACOB

now

It had been a few weeks since Lily was back to sleeping in my arms. I hadn't left her bed.

"Right," I said into the phone, talking to Jimmy, my coworker.

"When are you planning on heading back?" he asked as I watched Lily get out of her oversized truck that was still too big for her.

"Don't know yet."

"You are coming back right?"

Silence.

"Damn, man, you go from working around the clock to taking a two month sabbatical. Who are you and what have you done to Jacob?"

"I'm still working."

"Assisting," he corrected.

"I'm still making the firm and I money."

"Which is probably the only reason he's being so lenient about your little break."

"Don't forget the part that I'm damn good at what I do," I reminded.

"Arguing?"

"Defending."

"Hey!" Lily greeted when she opened the door.

"Motherfucker. That explains it, pussy whipped, who is she?"

I chuckled, shaking my head, grabbing her by the waist and making her squeal when she tried to walk by me.

"I gotta go." I hung up, kissing the back of her neck. "Did you think you could walk by me without me touching you? Especially when you're wearing that."

"It's a dress."

"It's a shirt you wear as a damn dress."

"I have a tiny torso."

"You are tiny everywhere, especially that tight little pussy of yours. It can tempt a saint."

She scoffed. "How would you know? My friend and I have not been reacquainted yet. My arsenal of toys could have stretched it all out by now."

I bit her neck.

"Ouch. What was that for?"

"You know why."

"Yeah… yeah… yeah… you don't want me to think you just want one thing." She turned to face me, cocking her head to the side, placing her hands on my chest. "What if I only want one thing, Jacob?"

"Is that right?"

"Yes, sir."

I leaned forward like I was going to kiss her but at the last second I clicked my teeth together like I was going to bite her.

"I could get used to you calling me sir."

"I could get used to you eating me out," she snidely smiled. "Both seem like they are never going to happen."

"Are you horny, baby? Is that what this is about?"

"You took away my toys, Jacob, what the hell do you think? I'm dying here. I can't use my hand. It doesn't work. It doesn't go fast enough or something, I don't know, it's like broken. I need my toys back!"

I laughed, my head falling back and she took the momentum to shove away and out of my arms.

"I think I just need to go to the sex shop and get a new B.O.B."

I stopped laughing.

"Yeah, a girl's got to do what a girl's got to do. Besides they love me there, they probably miss me. I'm a VIP member, you know… a Very Important Pussy."

I stepped toward her. "Are you trying to provoke me?"

"It depends, is it working?"

"What is it, baby? You want me to eat you and fuck that sweet pussy of yours right now?"

She looked down at her watch. "I could fit you in."

I grinned. "That's not how I remember it."

She narrowed her eyes at me and started to walk backward down the hall and into her bedroom with me following close behind. Our eyes locked the entire time, both of us knowing where this was going. She sat on the edge of the bed while I leaned my shoulder against the doorframe, my arms folded across my chest with one leg crossed over the other. I took in her disappointment that I hadn't followed her to the bed. I let a few seconds linger between us, wanting to remember her and this moment.

Just. Like. This.

"Stand up," I ordered in a harsh tone.

She didn't think twice about it.

"Take off your dress."

She reached for the hem.

"Slower."

She gradually lifted her dress over her creamy thighs, and I rubbed my fingers over my mouth already tasting her on my tongue. She threw her dress on the floor and stood in front of me in nothing but her bra and panties.

"Turn for me."

She did.

"You're so goddamn beautiful," I murmured, loud enough for her to hear.

She reached for her bra.

"No."

She cocked her head to the side with a questioning expression.

"That's my job. *I* get to strip you completely naked. *I* get to make you wet. *I* get to taste you. *I* get to make you come. It's mine. Do you understand me?"

She nodded and swallowed hard. The bedroom was the only place Lily ever took orders, the thought alone made her wet.

"Lay on the bed and close your eyes."

She was about to say something and I arched an eyebrow. "Be my good sweet girl and don't make me repeat myself."

She crawled on the bed making sure to give me a view of her voluptuous ass swaying with each movement she made. She took a deep breath and closed her eyes. I pushed off the wall and ripped off one of the hydrangeas from the vase on her bedside table. I took off my ball cap, setting it on the edge of the bed and placed the hydrangea on the tip of her nose. I kept her house stocked with them now just because I loved seeing her smile every time she looked at them. I spent too many years not seeing that damn smile.

I slowly moved it down her body, barely touching her skin but enough to where it left goose bumps in its wake. Once I reached her pussy, I pressed down firmer, moving it back and forth against her clit.

She sucked in a breath of air.

I continued to play with her for a few seconds. Setting the hydrangea on the nightstand, I took off her bra and then her panties, bringing them up to my face to smell her wetness.

"They're not scratch and sniff," she joked, her eyes still closed.

I grinned. "You do want me to put you over my knee, don't you?" I lay down next to her, my head pitched on my hand.

I licked my index and middle finger, rubbing her nipples until they were pebbled stones and then sucking them into my mouth. She gasped at the feel of my tongue and teeth. My fingers made their way down to where they wanted to be the most.

Her pussy.

I brushed along her lips before spreading her open, her bright red nub already standing at attention. I rubbed from her opening to her clit not staying in one place too long. I wanted to taste her, but I needed to know first…

"Tell me, Kid, how many *boys* have you been with?"

Lily

I immediately opened my eyes, partially from the memory of him doing this to me before and partially because of what he was asking.

"Don't ask questions you don't want the answer to," I coaxed, hoping it would work.

"Is that right?" he asked in a devilish tone. His eyes held nothing but mischief as his finger went right to my clit. He breathed into the side of my neck, making shivers crawl up my skin and throughout my entire body.

"You're not being a good girl…" He slapped my pussy, catching me completely off guard but making me want more.

"That feel good, baby?" he rasped, as he continued his assault on my clit.

"Yes…"

"Answer the question or I'll stop," he taunted.

"You wouldn't."

"Try me."

I recognized that tone. "Four," I simply stated.

His eyes glazed over with a predatory expression that made me clench my thighs.

"Including me," he stated as a question.

"Yes."

He leaned forward, close to my mouth. "Did they make you come?" he snapped in a tone I didn't appreciate but still made me wet.

"Don't make me ask you again."

"No."

I could feel him smiling against my face. His hand went back to my clit, manipulating the bundle of nerves until my legs spread wider and wider for him. He moved his fingers faster on my nub, playing me like I was a goddamn guitar.

"I'll tell you why they didn't make you come," he growled, looking deep into my eyes before making love to me with his mouth. He bit my bottom lip. I was so close to release, rotating my hips against his hand. I wasn't lying. I dated three guys after him and not one of them brought me close to orgasm. I mean it felt good, but I couldn't get there without toys, hence the arsenal I *used* to have.

"Because I am the only one who knows where and how to touch you, how to lick you and how hard to fuck you," he said in between kissing me, his voice laced with nothing but possession. "You're mine." He licked my lips and growled again. We passionately kissed, our tongues doing a sinful dance of want and need, his fingers moving faster and more demanding.

I whimpered into his mouth when he stopped. He kissed me one last time and moved his lips exactly where I wanted him. Licking, sucking, and tasting me in ways that had my eyes rolling to the back of my head, making all sorts of noises that I'd never heard before.

"Say it," he demanded against my most private area.

I panted, trying to catch my breath. "Jacob... Jacob, Jacob, Jacob," I repeated, coming all over his face.

Hearing her say that she had been with other guys was like taking a bullet to my fucking heart, but in the end it didn't matter.

Nobody has ever made me feel this kind of pain.

Nobody.

I was her first and I would be her last.

Lily was made for me. I knew her body better than she did. I taught her what she loved, what she craved, what she needed. I knew her down to her core. I made her come so hard, her juices were dripping down my beard. Her legs were squeezing my face so goddamn hard that I had to lock my arms around her thighs to hold her down. She finally came to when I was lying above her tiny body, framing her in with my arms around her face, overpowering her, consuming her, claiming her the only way I knew how. Her breathing was heavy and deep, her skin was bright pink, and she was slightly sweating. The smell of her arousal was all around me and she shined brightly with the afterglow of her orgasm. I would never tire of watching her come undone.

She was fucking breathtaking.

"Open your eyes. Look at me."

She did with a hooded gaze that made her dark brown eyes appear almost black.

"I want nothing between us, I need to feel all of you, Kid, every fucking inch. I've always used a condom except with you. Only you. I'm clean, I've been tested. Please tell me you're on the pill?"

She smiled.

I grabbed her leg and angled it upward, bending her knee so that her foot rested on my ass and hesitantly pushed in.

"Oh, God."

"Jesus, you're so fucking tight, so fucking wet, so fucking mine."

I thrust in, little by little, until I was fully inside her, stopping to relish in the joy and rapture that you get from the comfort of coming home.

The sensations of Lily and only Lily.

My mind was reeling with so many emotions I couldn't keep up.

The feel of her.

The taste of her.

The smell of her.

Just her. Always her.

I groaned when I was fully inside of her, resting my forehead on hers, our eyes locked, both of us in a trance like state. Her pussy fitting me like a goddamn glove, I could have come right then and there. We kissed and she moved her hips, I took her silent plea and began to thrust in and out of her. She moved her legs so that they were both wrapped around my lower back. Bringing me closer to her, and hugging around my neck. We kissed the entire time, not being able to get enough of each other. It seemed like hours went by and the whole world was left behind us.

Where there was no history and all that was left was us and our future.

"How do you do this to me? How have you always been able to do this to me?" she panted, her pussy pulsating down my shaft, tighter, making it hard to move.

"I love you," I simply stated.

"I'm going to come, Jacob, please…"

"Please what, baby?"

"Come with me." Her pussy clamped down and I thrust in and out a few more times because she felt so fucking good, until I couldn't hold back any longer and released my seed deep within her core.

Exactly where it belonged.

Chapter 17

Lily

then

I heard noises coming from the bathroom.

At first I walked toward the door because I thought maybe he was hurt or something. I was about to call out his name when I heard him cuss in a voice that seemed like he was dying. I opened the door and he immediately groaned my name without even realizing that I was standing right there.

Watching him.

I had never seen anything remotely close to the scene playing out before my eyes. I knew that guys masturbated, I wasn't that naïve, but I had never even seen a guy's dick before. And Jacob's... well, Jacob's... was fucking huge, his large hand barely covering it. His body was so tense, showing off every sleek muscle. His abs had contracted, emphasizing his six-pack and V right above his happy trail, which was doing all sorts of things to me. His back muscles flexed with every tug and pull. His body was a wonderland that I wanted to explore. I had the urge to lick the water droplets off him, standing in complete and utter awe of him. I wanted him more at that moment than I ever had before. He didn't stop when he saw me, and I watched with a fascinated regard as he stroked his dick while he was looking at me with the same captivating stare.

It was like a train wreck that you knew was going to end badly, but you couldn't look away even if you wanted to. There was no way in hell I wanted to. I was confused when he ordered me to say his name, but shit did it make my lady bits wet and pulsating in ways I'd never experienced before.

Watching him come as soon as I said his name wasn't helping my over stimulated situation down below. Causing my skin to burn, igniting the already fuming flames into my bloodstream.

Producing a tingly sensation that had me clenching my thighs from the unfamiliar sensations between my legs. The bubbly feeling in my stomach made me excited in ways I couldn't even begin to describe.

He never took his eyes away from mine. We were under a lustful spell that had us both rooted to the spot. He stepped out of the shower and I swear I thought he was coming to sweep me up in his arms and make me feel everything I just felt ten times over. So when he said my full name, it reminded me of why I loved it when he called me Lillian, and I took off like a bat out of hell. I ran toward the door and it was roughly slammed shut as soon as I opened it.

"What the fuck?" he roared. "Are you really going to leave like that?"

I turned to face him. "Yes... no... I don't know."

"The last thing I need right now is for you to act like a child."

My eyes widened, hurt.

"Shit," he drawled out.

I immediately turned to open the door, but he slammed it shut again behind me.

"I didn't mean it like that," he half-assed apologized.

I stepped away from the door, needing to put some space between us. I couldn't think when he was that close to me.

"Why are you running?"

I shrugged not knowing how to answer. When I saw his ball cap sitting on the nightstand, I instinctively grabbed it, placing it on my head. His face frowned, looking at me confused, and I tried like hell to not stare at his body that was still only in a towel.

"Answer me," he demanded.

I opened my mouth to say something, but nothing came out.

"Kid, it's me. Okay? It's. Me."

I peered down at the ground. He walked toward me, placing his fingers under my chin to get me to look at him.

"Why?"

"I got overwhelmed because I've never been in a situation like this before," I explained, trying to keep my voice from breaking. I cleared my throat. I didn't want him to see me cry. "I felt things I've never felt before, and I didn't know what to do next," I mumbled, desperately wanting to look at the ground again.

Forbid Me

"I have no experience when it comes to stuff like this. You're the only thing I know, what we've done are the only things I know. I'm sorry I'm not more experienced, but if you tell me what to do. I'll do—" he placed one finger on my lips, silencing me.

"Knowing that you're so pure is what's keeping me from throwing you over my shoulder and making you mine. It's your innocence that drives me fucking insane, Kid. I don't want to taint you, Lily."

"Oh…" I muttered, shocked.

He chuckled.

"Does that mean? I mean are we going to?"

"No."

I grimaced.

"Not because I don't want you. As much as we don't want to talk about it, Lily, you're sixteen, I'm twenty-three. Not only that but you're Lucas's baby sister. Do you have any idea what he would do to me if he found out you were here with me? What your parents would do?"

"I don't care. That doesn't matter to me. It's none of their business. It's my life. You're my life. I love you, Jacob. I've always loved you."

It was his turn to grimace. His reaction hurt me so much.

"Sweet girl, you don't know what that means."

"Yes, I do. I know the way you make me feel. I know that I'm happy when I'm with you. I know that I'm sad when I'm not. I know I think about you all the time. Most of all I know in my heart that you love me, too. As much as you don't want to admit it, you love me. I wouldn't be here if you didn't. You've always loved me. We're lobsters," I wallowed, not being able to stop the tears forming in my eyes.

"Lily, it's not like that—"

I stepped back as if he slapped me across the face. In a way he had. "You don't mean that."

"What we're doing is wrong."

"What?" She looked at me shocked like I smacked her in the face.

"That can't come as a surprise to you."

"Then why am I here?"

"Lillian, I should have never kissed you the first time, I shouldn't have kissed you the second time and God forbid me, I should have definitely not hauled you up for a weekend in a room alone with me. But your light, Kid, it draws me in like a moth to the flame. I can't stay away from you."

"See! You. Love. Me."

He sighed. "Let's just lay down, okay? Take a timeout. Watch a movie and just hang out. Alright?"

I bit my lip.

"I'll let you keep that hat." He grinned.

"This is your favorite hat. You always wear it."

He nodded, looking like he wanted to say more but held it back. "No scary movies?" he probed with the same sly smile.

"Deal."

He reached for my hand and I took it.

We watched two movies before Lily fell asleep in my arms. When I woke up, I was at the edge of the bed and she was pretty much sleeping on top of me. She was using me as a body pillow, her head on my chest, her arm around my stomach, and her leg draped over my thighs. I actually leaned forward to look at the whole other side of the bed, that didn't even look like it had been slept in. I cracked my neck, looking at the clock. It was nine am and Lily was still completely passed out on top of me.

"Kid." I shook her.

"Five more minutes."

I chuckled. "Come on it's your last day here. Let's go do something."

"In five minutes."

I sighed, laying back against the pillow and shut my eyes. When I woke up again it was eleven am, which was surprising because I never slept in. We were still in the same position, except Lily was lying even more on top of me, if that was even possible. She moved her knee up a little, immediately moving it back down when she felt the bulge in my gym shorts.

Forbid Me

The wide smile gave away that she was awake. "Your friend is up."

I laughed, big and throaty, making her smile bigger.

"That seems to be a running theme when you're around," I stated, placing my arm under my head to look at her.

She nudged her face into my chest. "We haven't made friends yet and he already loves me. Seems promising. I could officially meet him if you'd like?" She peered up at me through her lashes.

I shook my head no.

She shrugged. "It was worth a try."

"Well, we wasted all morning sleeping because of you."

"Meh, Ohio is overrated. I'd much rather hang out by the hotel pool today."

"I think I could arrange that."

Lily dressed in the bathroom while I changed into some board shorts and a gym shirt. When she came out, she had her hair in pigtails. My first thought was how much I wanted to grab those damn pigtails like handlebars and let her devour every inch of my fucking cock.

Goddamn it.

When she ran away from me last night, it was probably one of the worst moments of my entire life. I already felt like a piece of shit for what I allowed to happen. Having her literally running away from me just added fuel to the inferno around me.

Except Lily was the fire.

It wasn't a lie when I told her I couldn't stay away from her. She had this pull over me that I barely understood and it took everything inside me to not tell her that I loved her. Love wasn't something that was thrown around in my house. On the outside, my parents looked like they were the perfect couple. I guess in some ways they were, but not in the ways that mattered. They did their best to hide things from my sisters and me. I knew a lot of bad shit happened between them behind closed doors. I had found my mother crying more than once and it seemed to get worse since I left for college. I didn't know where I would be going to law school.

And I didn't have a fucking clue what I was doing with Lily in a hotel room.

I cared about her. I cared about her more than I probably should. I couldn't deny that. Where it would take me... us, was still yet to be determined. I didn't want to lead her on, and it killed me to think that I might be. That didn't stop me from having her here, holding her while she slept, and loving each and every second I was with her.

I was being a selfish fucking bastard.

"Hey!" she hollered, sitting next to me in the lounger. "What are you thinkin' about over here?"

"Hmm?"

"I leave you to go use the bathroom and I walk back and you look like you're questioning your manhood or something."

I laughed and so did she. "It's ok if you like men, baby, I will still always love you," she smirked.

"Cute, really cute, Kid. Don't tempt me, I'll show you just how much I fucking love pussy."

"Is that a promise or a threat?" she provoked, standing to grab something out of her bag.

I grabbed my cell phone, checking my messages.

Lucas: Hey, brother

Lucas: You around? Need to talk to you.

Lucas: Been trying to reach you all day.

Lucas: Where the fuck are you?

"Shit," I whispered to myself. He had texted four times in the last twenty hours. I had my phone on silent. I didn't want any interruptions.

Jacob: Sorry, man. Been crazy busy with finals.

I wasn't completely full of shit.

Lucas: You busy?

Jacob: What's up?

Lucas: It's Lily.

All the blood drained from my body. I couldn't even type without my fingers shaking. I was in deep shit. I wasn't ready for this conversation.

Jacob: What about her?

Lucas: You talk to her lately?

I didn't like where this was going.

Jacob: Why?

125

Forbid Me

Lucas: She's been acting weird. Secretive. You know that's not her, you can barely get her to shut the fuck up. You know she's in Ohio, right?

Jacob: She said something about that. Colleges, right?

Lucas: Exactly. You know as well as I do, Lily has no fucking interest in college. My parents are too occupied with my mom's illness to see past her bullshit. I think she's there for a guy.

My heart sank and I desperately tried to keep my cool. What the fuck could I say to that? "Yeah, bro, I'm that guy?"

Jacob: Maybe she changed her mind. She's young. She's got time.

Lucas: Lily? We are talking about my baby sister, right?

Jacob: All I'm saying is that maybe she wants to try something different. You know, get out of Oak Island and attend college. Do something different.

Lucas: Why be all guarded then? She's always told me everything. I just have a feeling it's a fucking guy, and the fact that she hasn't said anything to me about it makes me think he's a fucking douche. The last thing I need right now is for my baby sister to fall for some cocksucker who's just going to use her. She acts all tough, but I know this shit with my mom is eating away at her.

Jacob: Yeah.

Was all I could say, taking a deep breath.

Lucas: If you talk to her, see if you can get anything out of her, okay? I told Dylan the same thing.

Jacob: Of course.

Lucas: Thanks, brother. I gotta go get Mason. Catch ya later.

I looked at our text messages for I don't know how long, reading them over and over again. I finally just had to shake it off and threw my phone on the table, looking up to find Lily. When I did my eyes bulged out of my fucking head and I was out of my chair in two seconds flat to cover her before any other fuckers saw her.

"What the fuck are you wearing?" I roared, throwing a towel around her.

"It's called a bikini, Dad!"

"Lillian, do not fucking test me. Not right now."

"Why? What happened?"

"We're going back to the room so you can put some goddamn clothes on." I grabbed her hand, dragging her behind me.

"This is the only bikini I have."

"Then we're going to the fucking gift shop to buy you something that has more material than just some damn strings."

She halted, pulling her hand away from me. "No. There's no one even here. Have you looked around?"

I did. She was right. "Jesus Christ! All sense of fucking reason I have takes a flying leap when it comes to you."

She smiled.

"What am I going to do with you?" I rasped, brushing her cheek, needing to touch her.

She looked deep into my eyes with nothing but complete love and devotion for me and said,

"Anything you want."

Chapter 18

Lily

now

It had been two months that Jacob and I were together not counting the month that he wouldn't leave me alone. If you asked him, he would tell you three months, or even tell you since the day I was born.

He could be cheesy as shit like that.

Things were good. Things were great actually. He never left my house even though he had a hotel room or at least he says he did, I never saw it. Every time I asked him when he was going home, he would reply with, "I am home, baby, or you're my home, baby."

See? Cheesy shit.

I loved it.

I loved him.

I still hadn't said it to him, but I knew I didn't need to. He already knew it. He was trying to make partner at a law firm in San Francisco, but he didn't talk about it much. He was on the phone or his laptop a lot, so I knew he was still working. Jacob was always great at winning arguments, which I'm sure made him, an amazing lawyer. I don't know any bosses who would let you take off like he did. We didn't talk about what would happen after he left, how we would make it work. I guess we were enjoying playing house too much.

"Don't go," he murmured into the side of my neck from behind me. I giggled as he kissed along the nook.

"I have to go to work, Jacob."

"No, you don't."

"How am I going to pay my bills?"

"Me."

"How am I going to buy stuff?"

"Me."

"How am I going to—"

He peered up into the mirror, looking at me through our reflections. "I'll take care of everything. I'll take care of you."

I grinned. "Then what am I supposed to do?"

"Be with me," he simply stated.

"I am with you."

"Not when you're at work."

"Jacob…"

"I know this is important to you. I do. I know you love music and you're finally using the guitar I bought you and I see you started writing lyrics again, but in all honesty where are you planning on going with this?"

My eyebrows lowered. "What?"

He turned me to face him, caging me in with his arms. "Hear me out."

"I thought that's what I was doing."

"Lillian," he warned.

"I'm all ears."

"You've been working at the bar for three years. Almost four now."

I nodded.

"Where is it going?"

"I just want to play and sing."

"And I love that about you, sweet girl, but what about the future?"

"I'm just living a day at a time, Jacob."

"You have an amazing talent. I've always known that. Do you think maybe you're selling yourself short? Kid, you can't work at a bar for the rest of your life."

"I know."

"Listen, I know some people. Why don't you let—"

I jerked back. "You don't think I could do it on my own?"

"I didn't say that."

"You didn't have to."

"Lily, I'm just trying to help."

"By using your connections? For what exactly?"

"I don't know. Maybe get your music on the radio or at least book you a session in a studio to cut a demo. You're young. I mean right now it may seem okay, but it's not going to be that way forever."

I sighed. "I gotta go to work."

"This isn't over."

"I wouldn't dream of it."

He kissed the tip of my nose before moving away from me. I spent the entire drive to the bar thinking about what he said. As much as I hated to admit it, he was right. I didn't see a future until Jacob came back into the picture and that scared me more than anything. I was jumping right back in. Head first into being dependent on him, and I had yet to figure out if it was a good or bad thing.

It was getting late, only an hour left until the bar closed. I played my last set and went straight to the bar. I needed a drink.

"Hey, little girl," some random greeted with his two friends right alongside him.

"The name's Kid."

They were cute, if you liked the fraternity boy type.

"Kid," he corrected. "I'm Felix, this is Ryan and Eric."

"Howdy," I replied.

"Can we buy you a drink?"

"Whiskey."

"A girl after my own heart. A whiskey drinkin' girl."

"One and only."

They grinned. Each of them taking a shot and handing me one. I raised my glass and they followed suit.

"Here's to staying positive and testing negative."

They busted out laughing. I downed my shot and so did they.

"Lookie here, she didn't even cough," Eric stated.

"I'm not a pussy. Can't say the same for you."

"Feisty… now I like that," Felix chimed in.

I smiled, leaning back into my chair.

"How about another shot?" Ryan asked.

"By all means, boys."

They handed me another and I once again lifted it in the air. "Here's to girlfriends and wives, may they never meet."

"Phew," They breathed out, laughing.

"So are you a wife or a girlfriend?" Felix questioned.

"You first," I sarcastically replied.

They laughed again.

"Another shot?" Eric asked.

"I'm fine."

"That you are," Ryan said, looking me up and down.

"Wow, I haven't heard that one before."

"Tell me, Kid, do you give it as good as your mouth does?" Felix questioned.

"I should teach you fuckers a lesson for talking to her like that," Jacob chimed in, making all the color drain from my face, my heart immediately beating out of my chest and into my ears. It was as if he appeared out of thin air or something.

"You're lucky I respect her and this establishment enough to walk away without beating you fucking senseless. Go home and thank your lucky stars that you're not sleeping in the goddamn hospital tonight, assholes," he threatened, looking at each of them with a glare I had never seen before. It shook me to my core.

"Kid, get your stuff, we're leaving."

"You can't—" He grabbed Felix by the throat, pushing him back against the bar. My eyes widened and my breathing hitched.

He leaned into the side of his face. "What can't I do, motherfucker?" he gritted out, loud enough for me to hear.

"What was that? I can't hear you?" he mocked, Felix's face turning bright ass red.

"Jacob," I whispered, choosing my words carefully.

He turned and looked me up and down and then let go of his neck. Felix gasped for air as his friends went right to him, holding him up.

"You may want to consider getting new friends. One's that aren't such goddamn pussies," he snarled, gripping my arm, rushing us out of the bar. I tried hard to keep up, his stride being too much for me.

"You're going too fast," I pleaded as he forcefully pushed open the door, slamming it back against the wall.

"Can't we talk—"

"Not. Here."

"Jacob—"

He turned to face me. "I said I'm not doing this here. We will talk when we get home."

He opened my truck door and pretty much carried me into my seat, shutting the door before I could even say thank you and walked to his car. I was a nervous wreck the entire drive to my house, silently praying that he cooled off on the drive back by himself. His car was already in my driveway when I got home and the blinds were shut. It made my already nervous stomach more anxious. When I walked in, Jacob was sitting at the dining room table with a drink in his hands.

I rushed to him.

"So tell me, *Kid*…"

I stopped dead in my tracks a few feet away from him.

"Last time I checked you were *my* girlfriend, so is there a reason when that random asshole asked you if you were a girlfriend you didn't fucking bother to say yes?" he stated in an eerie tone not looking up from brushing the rim of his glass.

"Jacob—"

"By the way, you do give it as good as your mouth does, in case you're wondering," he sneered.

"You're not being fair."

"Is that right?"

"Yes. It's my place of employment. It's where I work. Why were you there?"

"Do I need a reason to come see you?"

I sighed, taking a deep breath. "They're stupid boys. It comes with the job, Jacob, since when do you act so insecure, mister high and mighty?"

He was over to me in three strides, making me gasp and backing me up into the wall.

"Watch it," he coaxed his eyes dark and daunting.

It was all in fun. Flirting was part of my job, it always had been, but from the look on Jacob's face there was nothing fun about it.

"Do I not give you enough attention, Lillian? Am I not inside you enough? Is that the goddamn problem?"

"I'm the entertainment—"

"In more ways than one?"

"Of course not, I've never…"

I narrowed my eyes at her, arching an eyebrow, trying to keep my temper at bay.

"I didn't know you were there."

"That was pretty damn clear."

"I was just flirting. It's not a big deal. You're making it out—"

"Don't even fucking try me, Lily."

"You're being unreasonable."

I snidely smiled. "Which part is unreasonable, Lily? The part that I drive to surprise *my* girlfriend at her job? Or the part that I find her flirting with three cocksuckers who are trying to get into her fucking pants? Or maybe it's the part that she downs the shots without even watching the glass to make sure they didn't drug it? Or how about the part where she denies being with me? Which fucking part of that is me being unreasonable?"

She bit her lip, contemplating what to say. "I didn't deny you. I just… I mean… we're taking things slow, Jacob. We're seeing each other. We haven't talked about anything else."

"Sticks and stones, Kid."

"No, don't be like that."

"Seeing each other?" I repeated in disbelief. "I fucking love you. I love you so much it hurts. I'm here because I can't leave you, forgoing everything for you."

"I didn't ask you to do that!"

"You didn't have to!" I roared.

"What do you want from me? I can't just forget about what you did to me! I can't just let it go like you expect me to! It's so fucking easy for you! I didn't leave you behind! I didn't fuck you over like you did me! I did nothing but love you! I'm trying, okay! I'm trying as hard as I can! I don't trust you with my heart. I'm terrified I'm going to wake up one day and you will have your bags packed at the door with one foot already outside."

I shuddered, feeling like the ceiling was caving in on me.

"Jacob…" she stepped toward me, causing me to step back.

"Don't," I said with a finger out in front of me. "Don't come near me right now."

She didn't listen, stepping toward me again. "Jacob…"

"No, Lily... just stop."

"I didn't mean—"

"You meant everything."

"Jacob…" she pleaded, but it was too late. The damage was done.

"What more do you want from me? I can't apologize any more than I have. I know I fucked up! But I lost you, too! Do you not realize that? Do you not think that it fucking killed me to walk away from you? To leave you! Do you think I'm that much of a heartless bastard! You let me back in between your legs and your goddamn bed, but that's it. Is this payback, Lily? Is this your way of punishing me for my mistakes?"

"You know that's not true."

"I know nothing. Not one damn thing. I thought… I thought you were *mine* because I've never fucking stopped being yours."

She grimaced.

"I need a break."

"What?" she replied, taken aback.

"You heard me." I walked to the door and opened it.

"You're leaving me again?" she whispered.

"No, I'm leaving before I say something I regret."

I slammed the door…

And left.

JACOB

then

I wanted to take her to a nice dinner for our last night together, but she was insistent that we stay in and order pizza. She showered first and when I walked back out into the room, she was wearing my t-shirt that looked more like a dress on her and my hat that I gave her.

I'd never seen her look so sexy.

She caught me staring at her. "Sorry, I didn't pack enough clothes. I guess I was excited."

"It looks better on you."

She looked down at herself and then back at me with confusion. "I look like I'm wearing a potato sack."

"Keep it."

She grinned, nodding. "I rented us a movie."

I sat down next to her, dragging her over to me by her waist and she squealed.

"What did you get, sweet girl?"

"9 ½ weeks."

"What's that?" I kissed the top of her head.

"I don't know, but the guy looked hot."

I laughed.

"Not hotter than you, of course."

I turned off the lights and spooned her, pressing play. Once the movie started I realized it was an older film, I hadn't seen Kim Basinger in anything in years, let alone Mickey Rourke. It didn't take long to realize that it was an erotic film, and part of me wondered if Lily did it on purpose. The fascinated regard on her face as she watched Kim masturbate was a memory I'll take to the grave. My arm slowly moved on its own accord, from her waist down to the side of her thigh. Her creamy, velvety skin brushing beneath my fingers, her eyes instantly went from the screen to my hand.

"Lillian," I huskily groaned and she swallowed hard. "Tell me, Kid…"

She bit her lip, making my cock twitch and I knew she felt it against her ass. My fingers moved at a slow torturous speed for where I really yearned to touch her. My shirt had ridden up her hips to expose her lace pink panties and lower abdomen. She watched my fingers move with the same enthralled gaze that she did with the scene in the movie.

"Have you ever touched yourself?"

She hesitantly shook her head no, and I lost my shit. Her lips parted and her tongue peered out slowly licking her lips. I reached out to stroke the side of her cheek. Her face leaned into my fingers. Shifting my hand to the back of her head, I gently brought her over to me. My lips found hers instantly. It started with just a peck until I opened my mouth to her and she sought out my tongue. This kiss was so much different from our last. That kiss was urgent and demanding, this one was soft, like we were both exploring each other's mouths for the first time. Our tongues twisted as we tasted each other. It felt so fucking amazing.

She felt amazing.

But like anything with Lily it turned into something else entirely. I urgently pulled the sides of her face, kissing her more aggressively than before. I knew that I needed to slow down, but damn I couldn't help myself. I wanted her so damn bad. All the buildup, months of anticipation, longing, and desire that I had kept safely bottled up were at the surface. It was more than I could have ever imagined. I was ready to lose my load.

Her delicate fingers moved down my chest in a slow agonizing motion. I held my breath. Her hands traced my pecs and moved down to the contours of my abs. I had been touched there, several times, more times than I fucking cared to count. This was different. This was so expressive and emotional, so goddamn loving.

This was Lily.

Nothing could have prepared me for this moment. Her panting and moaning beneath me would be forever entrenched in my mind. Our legs entwined, rubbing together and moving all around the bed. I kissed her jaw line, her neck, and deliberately made my way back up to her lips. I no longer had any control over my movements as I gripped her waist, turning us both over to have her lay on top of me. Her breathing escalated when she realized what I had done, but that didn't stop her from swaying her body against mine, dry humping the shit out of my fucking cock.

"Fuck... Lily," I growled into her mouth. "We need to stop," I half-ass requested.

"I don't want to stop."

"Jesus, last night you're running from me when you see my cock and now you're grinding your pussy against me like a goddamn pro. Which one is it, Lily? Because you can't have it both ways."

"I want you," she breathed out in between kissing me. "I want it to be you."

"Kid, you don't know what you're saying."

"Stop saying that," she urged in a desperate plea.

I continued to devour her mouth, soon my hands started to roam, attacking her body. She encouraged me by making all sorts of fucking sounds that didn't help keep my hands away from places they shouldn't be.

"Jacob..."

I would never forget the raspy way she said my name. It was full of emotion, mixed with pure lust. I cupped the side of her breast making her moan loudly, vibrating against my chest and down to my cock. That was all it took for me...

To buck her off.

Lily

"What the fuck?" I instinctively shouted as I watched him get off the bed.

He was in my face in two seconds flat. "Watch. Your. Mouth," he threatened, accentuating each word.

I shook my head with a heated expression. "Are you for real? I just felt your dick all over me, Jacob, and now you're worried about my swearing?"

He stepped back and away from me. "We can't do this," he stated like it pained him to say it.

Forbid Me

"Can't do what exactly? Can't hang out? Can't do sleepovers? Can't kiss? Can't dry fuck? Please, tell me what we can't do because you're giving me whiplash!" I yelled not being able to control my emotions.

"I'm not going to tell you again," he warned with the same hard edge in his tone, only further pissing me off.

I scowled, stood on the bed, and spoke with conviction never taking my glare off his. "FUCK, FUCK, FUCK, FUCK, FUCK! FUCK YOU!"

His composure was calm and collected and the only expression that changed on his face was his pursed lips, which immediately had me unsettled for what he was going to do.

"Say it one more time, Lillian, I will have no choice but to take you over my knee and spank that little fucking ass of yours."

My eyes widened. That was not what I expected… the thought alone made me want to keep going. Instead, I sat back down confused by my emotions.

"You wouldn't."

What the hell is wrong with me?

He didn't falter. "I'm the adult here. I shouldn't have let that happen. It's not your fault, it's mine."

"I don't know what you want from me? You're hot one minute, you're cold the next. I'm not twelve, Jacob. I'm sixteen. Most of my friends aren't even virgins anymore."

"I am sorry, Lily, you're right. I have been leading you on, but that's only because I don't know what to do. I know I should stay far away from you, but I can't find the strength to do that yet. I have to let you go, Kid."

I cocked my head to the side, frustrated. "Fine. I'll go and fu…" I hesitated from the glare in his eyes. "I'll go sleep with some guy and then maybe you'll touch me. I won't be pure and innocent anymore and you don't have to feel bad for stealing my virtue."

The glare in his eyes didn't disappear if anything they got darker.

"I'm twenty-three, Kid. That's seven years older than you. Do you know what we're doing is illegal? Do you have any idea how much shit I could get into for having a minor in my hotel room?"

"Who's going to tell? I'm not!"

"Is that what you want for yourself? You want me to fuck you and then what? Hmm? Tell me since you have all the answers."

I frowned. "I don't know. I thought... I thought we could be together. Why is that so hard to understand?"

He took a deep breath and looked at the ceiling for what seemed like forever, even though it was probably just seconds before peering down at me.

"Lily, I was there when you were born. I held you when you were a baby."

My eyebrows lowered as I took in his words. I didn't know that.

"Lucas wanted a baby sister so bad. Not a brother, he had three of those. He wanted you. Do you have any idea how much shit we gave him about that? He didn't care, Lucas loved you before you were even born, and the second I held you, I did too. We all did. It's so easy for you to say that... to want that. I can't. I'm supposed to see you like they do, but I never have." He rubbed his fingers over his lips like the words coming out of his mouth made him feel dirty.

"I don't know what that means and wish more than anything I could tell you what it did because it's eating me fucking alive. I've watched you take your first step, I've watched you say your first word, and I've been there for every significant moment in your entire life, Lillian. Every. Single. One. And now here I am trying to take something from you that doesn't fucking belong to me, and if Lucas or our parents found out they would bury me alive."

My eyes watered. It was the sweetest, saddest thing anyone has ever said to me, and the fact that it was coming out of Jacob's mouth made it that more intense. I knew what he was saying was right, but I tried to ignore it. In the end...

"I don't care," I stated. "Do you hear me? I. Don't. Care."

He sighed, his chest rising. "I'm sorry, Lily, but I do."

"So now what? I go home and pretend that I don't love you?"

He shut his eyes and bowed his head as soon as the words left my mouth and he wasn't allowed to hide from me.

Not after all this.

"You know what? You're right. I should grow up and explore new things. It's not fair to you. I'll make sure to go home and hang out with *boys* my own age."

He instantly opened his eyes, peering up at me through his lashes, his resolve breaking.

"You know… experience age appropriate things, because it's not wrong if it's two sixteen-year-olds being together and fucking, it's only wrong if it's you and I. Did I get it right? Do I understand the rules now? I'm just a *kid* so it might take me a little while."

"Lily..." he rasped. "Don't."

I stormed off the bed, grabbing my clothes and throwing them in my bag.

"Fuck…" he breathed out.

"Don't do what? What am I not supposed to do? I'm only sixteen years old and all. I'm immature. I can't have adult feelings and emotions. I'm your best friend's baby sister, that's all. I don't have to be told twice that I'm not wanted."

"You're acting like a goddamn child."

"Who cares! It's how you see me anyway! It's not going to change anything! I'm giving you what you want! If this is how you see me, then this is how I'll act!"

"That's not what I'm saying. You're twisting my words. I want you more than anything and that is so fucking wrong. You are not ready to have sex with me or anyone else for that matter. That much you proved last night, sweet girl. You and I should not have happened, Lily, I've been selfish this far, but I have to take a step back," he roughly grabbed my arm, turning me to face him.

I pushed him. I pushed him as hard as I could. His head jerking back from my reaction.

"Don't touch me! You never get to touch me again!"

"Kid…"

"Exactly."

We both faced off, neither one of us backing down.

"I'll be sure to tell Lucas and my parents you said hi since they're so damn important to you."

I scoffed. "What the fuck, Lily?"

I looked at him one more time, grabbed my bag…

And left.

Chapter 20
JACOB

now

I just needed a break.

Just one goddamn minute to myself.

I wanted to catch my bearings and compose my thoughts. I had to step away from the situation before it escalated to the point of no return. I couldn't control my temper when it came to Lily. I think that's why she loved to provoke me in the first place. Watching her with those fuckers made my blood boil just thinking about it. I don't know what else I could do to make this right. I was out of answers, out of options. I couldn't fucking think straight. I took a walk, trying to figure out what I could do for her to let me back in, mentally chastising myself that I had done this to us. There was no going back. I couldn't change the past knowing that ship had sailed.

All I could create was a future.

I walked around her neighborhood aimlessly, knowing it wasn't going to go over well when I walked back into her house. I took a deep breath before turning the knob on her front door. It wouldn't turn.

That little shit.

I grabbed my keys from my pocket and unlocked the door. She was nowhere to be found when I walked in, but I could hear her shuffling around her room as I walked back there.

"What the fuck are you doing?" I roared as I watched her place all my stuff in a bag on her bed.

She gasped and turned around with her hand over her heart. "How the hell do you keep getting into my house?"

I held out the key in front of me. Her eyes widened, immediately reaching for it. She wasn't fast enough. I placed that bitch back into my pocket.

Forbid Me

"You made a key? Give it to me!"

I folded my arms over my chest and leaned my shoulder into the door frame. "Come and get it."

"Un-fucking-believe-able."

"I've been called worse, baby."

She shook her head, going right back to throwing my shit into a bag.

"Do you honestly think that's going to work?" I asked with an arrogant tone. "I'm not going anywhere and neither are *you*."

She grabbed the vase from the nightstand, aiming it right at me. I cocked my head to the side daring her to do it. She bit her lip, placing the vase back on the nightstand.

"Good girl."

She narrowed her eyes at me. "How many times do I have to watch you walk away from me? Huh? How many damn times?"

"You know the definition of a break, right? I went for a damn walk, Lily."

"I don't care what you did. You turned your back on me, again! Again your back greeted me."

"You can think what you want, but I did no such thing. Things were escalating quickly so I left before it got out of hand."

"Who's acting like a child now?"

"By my definition… you are."

"Oh my God! I didn't do anything wrong tonight. You totally blew a dumb situation out of proportion."

"Is that what I did?" I mocked.

"Stop! Stop doing that!"

"Lillian, let me remind you to watch your damn tone when you speak to me. I'm standing right in front of you. Right fucking here!"

"Ugh! You're so frustrating… I don't want you here anymore. Now, I'm the one that needs a break."

"I'll sleep in the guest bedroom," I simply stated.

"This isn't your house! I'm not asking you. I'm telling you."

"I'm not leaving," I breathed out.

"Fine," she sneered, going straight to her closet. She tore a few things off the hangers and threw the contents into another bag. "I'll leave."

I shook my head, walking to the kitchen to grab a cold beer from the fridge. I gulped it down in three swigs before opening another. She stormed out into the living room, her bag over her shoulder.

"You know what…"

"What, baby?"

"You're a real piece of work, you dick."

She turned and slammed the door behind her. I sat at the dining room table, taking another swig of my beer.

Waiting.

Lily

He had a lot of nerve.

Making a key to *my* house.

Walking back in like he had done nothing wrong in the first place.

Telling me that he wasn't leaving and neither was I… well I showed him.

I'd be lying if I said I wasn't shocked as shit that he was letting me leave. I didn't want to leave my house, but what other choice did I have? I would go to Tracey's. I got in my truck, throwing my bag in the passenger seat. I took a long, deep breath, putting my key in the ignition.

I turned it.

"What the fuck?"

I turned it again.

Nothing…

I kept it turned with my foot on the brake.

Nothing…

"What. The. Fuck?" I shouted to myself, slamming my hands against the steering wheel. This was the last thing I needed. I hated knowing I had to walk in there and ask him for help. My truck never gave me any problems. I grabbed the keys and walked back to my front door.

"My truck—"

I stopped dead in my tracks.

Forbid Me

There was Jacob, leaned back in the chair, his muscular arms over his firm solid chest stretching out the sleeves of his shirt with his ankle crossed over his knee, wearing nothing but a cocky grin. Sitting pretty right next to him on the dining room table was...

My. Truck. Battery.

"You can't do this!"

"I believe I just did, Lily."

"So this is what you're going to do for the rest of our lives? Leave when *you* want but when I try to, you're going to take my truck apart?"

"Look what it's done for your perspective. You're picturing our future together. That's a step in the right direction."

I shook my head, un-amused.

"You want this to be over? All you have to do is say you're sorry. It's that simple. Apologize for being a little shit." He grinned.

"I will do no such thing. I didn't do anything wrong. You need to say you're sorry," I argued.

"I'm sorry."

My eyes widened, surprised that it was that easy.

"I'm sorry that I didn't beat the living shit out of those guys." He stood. "I'm sorry that I have more respect for you, not to take out my frustration on their fucking faces." He stepped toward me. "I'm sorry that you're so damn beautiful that men can't help themselves." Another step. "I'm sorry for breaking your perfect heart, time and time again." Another step. "I'm sorry that you can't get past our history and look forward to our future." Last step. "But most of all." He placed his mouth against my lips.

"I'm sorry that I'm going to have to teach you a lesson for being such a bad girl."

He leaned forward catching me by my waist, picking me up and throwing me over his muscular shoulder like a damn rag doll. My ass was right in his face. He had a strong hold around the back of my knees to keep me from thrashing around. He used his hand like a vise on my wrists to keep me from fighting him.

"What are you doing?" I shrieked, stunned by the turn of events.

I could feel him smiling against my leg and then he smacked my ass.

Hard.

"Ouch! What the fuck?"

He spanked me harder two more times as he walked. "That was for your mouth," he said, spanking me again. "That was for your flirting." He spanked me three times. I thrashed on his shoulder, trying to break free, but his hold was too strong.

"That was for being a stubborn little shit and not admitting when you're wrong. For denying me what is mine. Lastly, for being so fucking careless and putting your life in danger," he scolded, smacking me three more times so hard it echoed off the walls.

"Oh my God! Stop! I'm not going to be able to sit for days!" I begged, with my ass burning from the impact of his strong hand.

"That's the point." He spanked me again, not as hard but still making me jolt.

"I'm sorry! I'm sorry!" I shouted for mercy.

And the bastard fucking chuckled.

It took everything inside me not to tell him off, but I knew it wouldn't be in my best interest. He gently placed me on the dining room table next to the truck battery. I hissed upon contact, my ass not welcoming the hard surface.

"Relax," he encouraged as I gave him a death stare, biting my tongue from saying something I would regret.

"What, baby?" he coaxed. "I'll rub that sweet ass, make it better."

I wanted to say he would be lucky if he ever saw me naked again.

"If you act like a child, Lily, I'm going to treat you like one."

I narrowed my eyes at him and he smiled. He started to unbutton my blouse. "I'm going to tell you how it's going to go, sweet girl." He slid it off my shoulders. "You're going to be a good girl." He took it off and threw it on the table. "You're going to sit here," he paused. "Just like this." He unclasped my bra, throwing that on the table as well. "You're going to stop with the bullshit of the past." He unbuttoned my jean skirt.

"You're going to forgive me." He glided it down my legs, tossing it in the pile with the rest of my clothes. "You're going to stop flirting with *boys* who barely know how to stroke their own cocks before I go to fucking jail." He kissed the tip of my nose and got down on his knees, peering up at me with a look of lust, skimming my panties down my thighs.

"Lastly, Kid, you're going to tell me." He kissed my thigh.

"That you love me."

My. Heart. Dropped.

"I will reward you with burying my face into your sweet pussy and making you come down my beard."

"Jacob…"

"Say it, Lillian," I ordered. "We both know you want to. I can see it all over your pretty face, especially now. You're mine. Only mine. Always been mine, always will be mine. Say what I need to hear."

I was done with the bullshit and I was laying down the law. I won't pretend that I didn't love spanking her ass and that my cock wasn't throbbing, just waiting to sink balls deep into home. Her intense, conflicting stare never left mine. She'd been fighting an internal battle within herself. It didn't matter.

I would win.

Her love for me…

Would conquer.

I gripped her thighs and dragged her closer to the edge of the table, giving her an incentive, kneading her thighs, waiting for her to say the three words that would put us both out of our misery.

"I love you, Lillian Michelle Ryder. I love you more than anything in this world. I promise you that I will never leave your side and I will never lie to you again. I will never hurt you again. I'm here for the long run. No matter what."

She bit her lip with a look of pain.

"Please, Kid…" I breathed out. "Trust me."

She took a deep breath and said,

"I love you."

Chapter 21

JACOB

then

Austin took off. Dropped out of college, and no one had heard from him since.

Lucas was adapting to fatherhood with his son Mason, and the co-parenting situation was working great for them.

Dylan was looking into the police academy. He wanted to join Special Ops.

Alex was officially with Cole and for the most part, seemed really happy.

Me? Well, I was in fucking hell.

It had been three months since I last saw or spoke to Lily. Not from lack of trying. She wouldn't answer my calls or return any of my text messages.

Nothing.

It was like she fell off the face of the earth. The only reason I knew what was going on with her was because of Lucas. He kept me somewhat updated without even knowing that he was doing so. This was not what I wanted, but definitely what I needed…

I hated *that* more than anything.

I drowned myself in school and applications for law school. I even tried to go on countless dates that never led to anything, other than me counting down the minutes till I could go home. At least there I could wallow in my own personal misery that I had no one to blame but myself.

I was fucking miserable.

I missed her ridiculously contagious laugh. I missed her metaphors that I barely ever understood. I missed her made up words that only made sense in her head. I missed her infectious smile. I missed her dark brown eyes that held more expression than any other person I knew.

I. Missed. *Her*. All of her.

The list was endless.

I listened to every song that reminded me of her on my iPod. I had listened to them so damn much I was starting to memorize every word. You'd think I was a goddamn girl with a broken heart, not a fucking grown ass man.

Damn, I sounded like a pussy.

I grabbed the picture I hid in my drawer, looking at it as I lay on my bed. It was the one I took of her at the zoo when we were in Ohio. She was holding the lion cub in her arms, looking at him with so much happiness and love. It was my favorite part of our weekend together. She didn't stop talking about that aquarium for the rest of the day. I impulsively reached for my phone to text her, hoping like hell she would finally answer.

Jacob: You can't ignore me forever, Kid.

I threw my phone on the bed and went to take a shower. I didn't expect her to text me back, Lily was a stubborn little shit. I threw my towel on my desk, putting on a pair of gym shorts when my phone pinged with a text message. My eyebrows lowered as I grabbed it off the bed still not expecting it to be Lily.

Lily: Watch me.

I chuckled, I couldn't help it. I was thrilled she actually answered me. I wouldn't have cared if she replied telling me to go fuck myself. The point was that she finally responded.

Jacob: I miss you.

Lily: Good for you.

I sighed.

Jacob: Kid...

Lily: Jacob...

I shook my head.

Jacob: What are you doing?

Lily: I'm on a date.

My head jerked back. I had to read the text several times before I processed what the fuck she said.

Lily: With this guy I'm seeing and we're about to watch 91/2 Weeks. Peace out.

"Are you fucking kidding me?" I roared out loud to myself.

Jacob: Where are you?
I waited for what felt like forever with no response.
Jacob: Do not fuck with me. Where. Are. You?"
Still no answer.

I paced around my room, raking my hands through my hair, wanting to rip it out of my damn head. I looked at her picture one last time, changed my clothes, grabbed my phone and keys and took the next flight out. I was lucky enough to find an immediate flight and arrive three hours later. It was almost eleven pm when I paid the cab driver at the end of her driveway. As I walked up to the porch steps, I tried to come up with an excuse to tell her parents as to why I was there in the first place.

Her head jerked back and her eyes widened when she opened the front door.

"What are you doing here?"

I barged inside ready to lay the motherfucker out.

"Where is he?" I gritted out low enough to where her parents couldn't hear me.

She cocked her head to the side and looked at me like I was crazy. "Where's who?"

I leaned in toward her face. "Don't fuck with me, Lillian," I warned. "Where. Is. He?"

"If you're referring to my date… you just missed him. Or are you referring to my brother that you love so much?" she spewed. "Because he doesn't live here anymore as you probably know."

I took a deep breath, stepping away from her, finally being able to relax. "Where are your parents?"

"My mom has another round of chemo this weekend. They're staying at the hospital."

"Did your parents know that fucker was here?" I asked, trying to ignore all the images of them being alone together.

"Do my parents know you're here?" she sarcastically stated with a wide smile, shutting the door and walking away from me.

It was then that I realized what I had just done. It was like I had been moving on autopilot for the last few hours, losing all sense of reason. Exactly the way it always was when it came to her.

Shit.

I followed her into her bedroom, standing by the door as I watched her sit on the bed with the rumpled sheets all around her. She looked at me with a confused expression and then quickly realized where my intense glare focused.

She grinned.

"What exactly went down in here, Lily?"

"Oh, what ever do you mean, Jacob?" she mocked in a condescending tone. "I'm a kid remember? We just watched a movie. I was as good as I was when you and I watched the same movie." She winked and then smiled.

"Let's try this again. What the fuck happened here?"

She put her finger up to her lips and peered up at the ceiling. "Hmm… well. Steve is *my* age, he's *not* my brother's best friend, and he has *no* relationship with my parents… so it doesn't really matter what happened because it's not illegal and it's not wrong, right? Plus he's perfectly okay with being with me in public," she sassed, nodding. "Oh, and it's none of your damn business."

"What. Happened?" I gritted out, giving her one last chance to come clean. My fists clenched at my sides to the point of pain.

"Nothing that hasn't happened before."

And then…

I lost my shit.

Again.

Lily

He was over to me in three strides, laying me back on my bed, his huge, muscular frame looming over me.

"And what exactly has happened before, Lillian?" he asked in a tone I didn't recognize, scaring me and thrilling me in ways that I found it hard to breathe.

I didn't cower. "I experienced things. You know? The way you wanted me to," I spitefully answered. "I can show you all the new stuff I've learned, see if it's up to your standards." I reached up to touch him, but he intercepted my hands, locking my wrists together with one hand, pushing them above my head. I never saw it

M. Robinson

coming, it happened so fast. He wouldn't ever let me touch him, and I didn't understand why.

"Don't," he ordered on his last thread.

I didn't falter. "I can't tell you how amazing it is to finally know what everyone is talking about. I thought I would never be able to get rid of this ache. Unlike you... *he* actually gives me what I'm begging for."

He jerked back like I had slapped him across the face. "Did he fuck you?"

"You don't have to have sex to have an orgasm, Jacob. His fingers and mouth do just fine."

I saw it.

The. String. Snapped.

It was as clear as day. His eyes glazed over like a possessed man. His jaw clenched. His appearance hardened in a way that will forever be embedded in my mind. His strong grip suddenly tightened on my wrists, as his body tensed. Before I could process what was happening, he cocked his arm back and slammed his fist on the bed near my head, making me jolt.

"Is that right?" He lifted my dress, exposing my legs and stomach.

"Tell me, baby?" He brushed his fingers around my belly button. "Did he make your eyes roll to the back of your head?" They moved down to my panties. "Did your back arch off the bed?" He gently touched along the edges, swiping his fingers into the elastic and making it snap.

I shuddered.

"Did your thighs clench like they do with me?" Slowly pulling them down, inch by inch, leaving a trail of desire in its wake. The predatory stare in his eyes as he looked at my most sacred area was a memory I'll take to my grave.

"You're so fucking beautiful, Lillian, so goddamn beautiful," he groaned on the side of my neck as he placed soft kisses down to my cleavage, removing my strapless bra and dress in one swift movement. He tossed it aside, leaving me much more exposed than before. His mouth sucked on my nipple as his hand caressed my other breast. I writhed beneath him, trying to break loose from the grip he still had on my wrists, but I couldn't.

151

Forbid Me

He was so strong.

So consuming.

So empowering.

I felt him everywhere, every inch of my skin tingling from his touch, all overwhelming and all at once.

I was done for. No one would ever be able to make me feel like this.

Just Jacob.

Only *him*.

I could feel his erection on my wet core, and he purposely moved his hips, creating a delicious sensation that sent shivers all over my body.

He looked up at me with hooded eyes. "I want to taste you, baby, I want to taste you so fucking bad."

I moaned in response, sucking in my bottom lip and arching my back for him to do exactly what he was pleading.

"Do not move your arms. Do you understand me?" he ordered against my dry lips.

I nodded, not being able to find words to reply. He let go of my wrists and kissed his way down my body, leaning forward when he was where I wanted him the most. He inhaled my scent and I almost died of embarrassment, but it was quickly replaced by an ache he created when he licked all along my heat.

"Fuck…" he breathed out before taking my bundle of nerves into his mouth and sucking in a forceful yet tender back and forth motion.

I had never felt anything like it before. My breathing became heavy, feeling my chest rise and fall. My legs started to shake, and I couldn't keep my eyes open. I had no idea what to do with my hands. I felt like I was going to explode. When I felt his fingers at my opening, I almost died right then and there.

"You're so fucking tight. Jesus Christ, Lily, what are you doing to me?" he growled in ecstasy.

I couldn't take it anymore. The way his mouth devoured me and his fingers made love to me was too much for me to control. The room started to spin and my breathing faltered.

I exhaled.

I panted.

I clenched.

I felt like I was coming apart and being ripped open. I couldn't control my movements let alone my breathing. I made all sorts of noises that seemed foreign coming out of my mouth. The room caved in on me, as spasms consumed my body then constricted, squeezing Jacob's head so hard that I felt his facial hair in my bones. The sounds that were dripping from his mouth were enough to push me over the edge.

I gasped and screamed out, "Oh my God, Jacob!"

"You are mine. Do you hear me, Lillian? Mine!"

Watching…

Tasting…

Feeling…

Smelling…

Hearing…

Lily came apart, and knowing that I was the cause of it had pre-come dripping down my cock. I rested my forehead on her lower abdomen, both of us desperately trying to catch our bearings. It was just as intense for me as it was for her, the throbbing in my jeans only proving my point, and she didn't even touch me. I couldn't have her hands on me. I wouldn't be able to hold back.

"Shhh…" I whispered, trying to help Lily even out her breathing. I could hear and feel her heart pounding out of her chest. "Shhh… baby…" I repeated, mentally preparing myself for what was to come.

"Jacob," she coaxed, knowing I needed her encouragement to look at her. I took a deep breath and moved to lie by her side, wiping off her come from my lips and beard.

She was glowing.

I had never seen her look more beautiful than I did at that very moment and it hit me like a ton of fucking bricks.

I was blinded by her.

Consumed by her.

Wrecked by her.

She owned each and every part of me, right down to my soul.

Forbid Me

I. Loved. Her.

We stared at each other for I don't know how long, knowing that as soon as one of us opened our mouths to say something, anything, we would forever lose this moment. Everything would change again and not knowing if it would be good or bad was the hardest pill to swallow.

"Don't get mad, okay?" she said, breaking the silence between us with a shaky voice.

"Words every man loves to hear, Kid."

She nervously laughed. "I love you."

I wanted to say it so fucking bad, it was right there on the tip of my tongue, dying and pleading to come out.

I couldn't.

It would only make things worse, if it were even possible at that point.

"I lied to you."

"Excuse me?" I replied, confused.

She hesitated for a few seconds before saying, "I wanted it to be you, Jacob. I just wanted it to be you."

My eyes widened and my jaw dropped, feeling like a bucket of ice-cold water was poured down my body. I closed my eyes, I had to, but it didn't make it any less real.

"Please, Lily, please tell me it's not what I'm thinking," I begged, already knowing the answer.

"I'm sorry, Jacob. I love you!" she justified.

I immediately stood, my hand over my mouth, feeling like I was going to throw up. "Do you have any idea what you've just done? I would have never… Fuck me…" I breathed out. "I would have never…" I couldn't even say it. I couldn't even look at her. The shame engulfing me in ways that I couldn't even fucking see straight. "Lily, put some goddamn clothes on. I can't look at you like that right now."

She did as she was told, barely making any noise. I paced around the room, tugging at my hair, trying to keep my composure from breaking and saying something I would regret.

"How could you do this to me? After everything I've told you. After everything I've expressed. After everything I've shared. After all of it!" The bile raised in my throat. "Do you think this is a game? What the fuck, Lily?" I yelled at her, finally looking at her.

She still looked so damn stunning that it took my breath away, physically killing me. I was suffocating in her afterglow, the smell of her all around me. Taking me under and consuming me in ways that I didn't think I could ever recover from.

"I don't regret it," she simply stated, sitting on the edge of her bed.

I took in her disheveled hair, her rosy cheeks, her swollen bottom lip that I knew she had been biting, the way her dress hung off her shoulder, exposing her neck and collarbone. Her stomach was showing and her thighs were bare, my scent, my touch, my love was all over her.

That's when I realized...

I. Didn't. Either.

Not one fucking second of it.

And that...

Scared me more than anything.

"Why would you lie to me, Kid?"

She shrugged. "You wouldn't touch me. What choice did I have? I know it's not right, but I love you. I have no other excuse, it's my only reason."

I sighed, calming down. "So there's no Steve?"

"There's a Steve. I went on a few dates with him. He kissed me once, but it didn't feel right. I felt nothing, no spark, no butterflies... not like I do with you..." She bowed her head. "Something special happened between us, Jacob, and I really wish you could see that."

I bent down, sitting on the balls of my feet in front of her. Her eyes watered and it nearly broke my heart. I took off my hat and placed it on her head.

"You left this behind."

She instantly smiled and it warmed my heart. The damage was done. There was no going back...

"What am I going to do with you, Kid?" I shook my head, hugging her tiny frame.

"Will you stay with me?"

I chuckled. "Try and make me leave."

I scooted her up on the bed, took off my shirt, and jeans to sleep in my boxer briefs. She pulled off her dress, threw it on the floor and put on the shirt I was just wearing. I grinned, turned off the light, and lay next to her. Tugging her against my body, she fit perfectly. She slept wrapped up in my arms for the rest of the night, and we spent whatever was left of the weekend together and I flew back home Sunday night…

Except this time,

Lily was embedded in my heart.

Chapter 22

Lily

now

"Where are we going?" I asked as he took the exit for I65 N.

"I told you I'm kidnapping you," Jacob replied, reaching over and squeezing my thigh. I squealed, slapping his hand away. I hated when he did that.

"It's not kidnapping if I already know."

"Can't I just surprise you?"

I raised my eyebrow and cocked my head to the side.

"Yeah... good point."

I smiled.

"Your birthday is coming up."

"My birthday isn't for another six weeks."

He narrowed his eyes at me. "I'm aware of when your birthday is, Kid," he stated, reaching for my thigh again, but I intercepted his hand at the last second.

"Ohhh! Did you see that, big man? Gotta be quicker than that. I have cat-like reflexes."

He scowled and took his hat off my head.

"Hey! That's mine!"

He used that to his advantage and squeezed my thigh. "What was that?" he mocked, squeezing tighter. "I'm sorry I didn't catch that? Cat like what?"

I thrashed, squealing and laughing at the same time until he finally let go.

"Actually it's mine. You have your own." He set it backward on his head.

"Still looks better on me."

"You're such a little shit," he chuckled.

"I'm aware," I smirk at him. "Now... you were saying."

"You mean before I was rudely interrupted?"

"Yes, before that."

He shook his head, grinning. "Everyone is coming for your birthday."

"Oh? You know about that?" I asked, surprised.

"Of course I do. Lucas has been hounding me for the last six months to come."

She bit her lip.

"Say it," he ordered.

"Would you have come? I mean, if we still weren't talking."

"How did I know you were going to ask that," he stated as a question.

"You're a lawyer."

"Would you have wanted me to?"

"Oh no!" I shook my head. "You are not using your lawyer tactics on me, buddy, I asked you first."

He chuckled. "You're too smart for your own good, Kid," he hesitated for a few seconds. "The truth?"

"Always."

"I was planning on coming."

"You lie," I teased, making him look at me with a sincere expression.

"How many times do I have to tell you that I don't lie to you, Lily?"

"You might want to retract that statement, Mr. Lawyer."

"It had been a long time since we… well, you know. I was going to come, for you," he added, ignoring what I called him out on.

"In what sense of the word?"

"In any sense you would allow me. Until you blew me off and told me to eat shit, then I would have made myself a key to your house and spent weeks reminding you of why you're *mine*."

My face frowned. "Wait a second, did you know?"

"Did I know what, sweet girl?"

"Did you know where I lived? That first night at the bar, was that planned?"

"No, that night was pure luck. I knew where you lived and Lucas had mentioned you worked in a bar, I didn't know it was Bootleggers, though. I was planning on texting Alex the next morning to ask her, but fate intervened and you were right there in front of me."

"So, you came to Nashville for me?"

He smiled with a slight grin. "I came here to help my friend Mark from law school get his firm off the ground."

"That's not what I asked."

I chuckled. "You were the plan all along, baby. You were the motivation, the firm was my excuse."

I smirked. "Look where you're driving before you crash, big man."

He smiled with his face once again content. "Consider this a pre-celebration for your twenty-third birthday."

"Ah… does that mean I get two presents?" I joked.

"I was planning on giving you multiples, but if you only want two I guess I'll have to comply, it is your birthday after all," he replied with a smirk.

"Nope, your idea is better, multiples it is. Who am I to take away your happiness?" I retorted, laughing.

I turned up the radio, sat back in my seat and enjoyed the comfortable silence. Four hours later and we were getting off at exit 35.

"What the hell is in Alabama?" I questioned, looking at him like he was crazy.

"A little piece of paradise, sweet girl."

We pulled up to a place that looked like a condominium. A valet greeted us and took our bags. The place was exquisite, and I subconsciously looked down at my clothes as we walked up to the front desk, not that Jacob was dressed any better than I was. Just his standard attire of a surfer shirt, cargo shorts, and flip-flops.

"Checking in," he stated to the attendant behind the counter who was too busy *checking* him out.

I stood next to him and looked at her, angling my head to the side. "Like what you see?"

"Ma'am, I... I… I…" she mumbled.

"Eyes on the screen, sweetheart. This one is taken. All mine, and I don't share with anyone."

I could see Jacob grinning like a fool from the corner of my eye so I leaned in close to his ear. "See? I can lay my claim, too."

He busted out laughing. I gave the attendant a smart-ass smile.

"Here are your keys to the penthouse," she muttered, catching me off guard.

Penthouse?

"Thanks." He signed the paperwork and grabbed my hand.

I turned at the last second. "Bye," I said to her, making her turn bright ass red.

We went up to the top floor that led to one condo. He unlocked the door and opened it for me. I walked into one of the biggest foyers I had ever seen. I made my way inside, taking in every last detail from the trey ceilings to the marble floors. There were three bedrooms, two master suites, two living rooms, a game room, and a wraparound balcony that took up the entire side of the building. The view of the beach was breathtaking. I think I could see my house from there.

I walked back inside to Jacob making us drinks at the bar.

"Exactly how much money do you make?" I found myself needing to know.

"Enough for you not to work, stay at home, and be my sex slave," he simply stated.

"You're not like a drug lord on the side, right? I'm not going to get locked up unexpectedly. I'll tell you right now, I'm way too pretty for prison. I'll be someone's fiddle in no time."

He laughed so hard his head fell back.

"Why you laughin'? Have you taken a good look at yourself in the mirror lately? You'll be someone's bitch, too. Fresh meat for Manuel, he will have you shanking people in the big yard and doing care packages in no time. Yelling at you to make his mud and suck his—"

He raised his eyebrows with a challenging yet amused expression.

"Orange is the New Black," I simply stated.

"First off, I don't let anyone yell at me. Your pretty little ass can account for that one. Second, this is my boss' penthouse."

"Ohhhh."

"I asked the concierge to stock the fridge and bar." He looked me up and down, his demeanor quickly turning predatory. "I think it's time for your first gift. Why don't you go get naked and lay on the bed so I can lick your asshole."

JACOB

Her eyes widened, dilating. "Stop trying to do things to my butthole!"

"Then stop sitting on my finger when you're riding me."

She rolled her eyes. "I don't want to do that right now, anyways."

I took a sip of my drink. "And what makes you think you have a choice in the matter, Kid?"

"Because no means no." She grinned and took off running.

I caught her around the waist before she even made it out of the room, giggling as I threw her over my shoulder like a ragdoll.

"No! No! I didn't do anything this time! I don't want to play this game! I don't even like this game!" she panicked, thrashing around, but she was no match for me.

I chuckled, smacking her ass lightly. "Relax." I walked into the game room, sitting her on the pool table. "If I want in…" I leaned in close to her face. "I'm getting in." I kissed her lips softly. "Here's how it's going to go. I'm going to eat your sweet little pussy right here on the edge of this pool table. Then when I've made you come enough, when your juices are dripping down my beard…" I rasped in between kissing her.

"I'm going to take you into the kitchen and you're going to suck my cock. For our next stop, we'll go into the master suite, dining room, living room, foyer… and see how many positions and rooms I can fuck you in until you can't stand." I licked along the edge of her lips.

"What about the balcony?" she purred.

"I've never been an exhibitionist, baby. Nobody sees your naked body but me." I claimed her mouth before she could answer, and I spent the rest of the morning inside her.

After we took showers we went to grab lunch, but at the last minute we decided to take it to go. It was a beautiful day and we wanted to take advantage of it. We sat on the beach, eating our sandwiches, and taking a breather, I lived for moments like these when everything was just simple.

"I know you want to go in there, Jacob, I can see it written all over your face."

We were watching the wave's crash on the beach.

"I think you might actually be twitching."

I grabbed her hand and kissed it. "That's not the point of this weekend. It's about you."

"Umm… that's really sweet and all, but I kinda want to read this book, and let me tell ya… it'll only benefit you."

"Is that right now?"

"Go!" she said, laughing, shaking her head that I wanted back in already. "I can entertain myself for a few hours, the waves are calling your name."

"Be good and stay put. I want to know where you are while I'm in the water."

"That sounded very Fatal Attraction," she sassed.

"You do want me to put you over my knee again, don't you?"

"It was your shoulder. Get it right, and… no."

I kissed her. Spending the next few hours in the waves surfing, it felt so damn good to be doing it again. Except this time Lily was sitting on the beach waiting for me. I remembered wanting that so bad for so many years. That was the point of this weekend. I wanted to relive our childhood *together*, even if it was just for a few days.

It was near dusk by the time I got back to the beach and that was the only problem with the ocean, you could get lost in it. I took her to a nice dinner and we made love on the balcony when we got back. Only after I made sure no one could see her from the beach. I didn't give a fuck about me.

We slept in the next morning, thanks to her. I took her to the Arena The Next Level, it was a huge indoor amusement park with all kinds of arcade games, and they even had laser tag. She was as competitive as they come. When I beat her at every single game, she claimed I was cheating and didn't want to play with me anymore, so I took her on the Ferris Wheel and reminded her that she wanted to play with me just fine. We were both exhausted when we got back to the penthouse, so we decided to order in and relax in the hot tub.

Lily put way too many bubbles in not realizing it had jets until I decided to explore how many uses I could get out of the streams. We spent a good hour mopping up the floor when we were done.

If you ask me it was time well spent, watching Lily on her hands and knees soaking up the water with towels was an extra bonus.

It was the last day of our stay and it felt like we just got there. Since she loved animals, I knew taking her to the Dolphins Down Under would be a memory she would adore. It was a rare thing to see dolphins anywhere in the ocean in Oak Island. I booked us the private tour and the look on her face was priceless when she realized what we were doing. We got to snorkel, swim, and hang out with the dolphins, Lily actually cried when it was time for us to head back.

"Wow… this is beautiful, Jacob," she breathed out as we took our seats at the restaurant inside the marina, our view being the ocean. We were able to use the shower on the boat to get dressed.

"I can't believe you did all this. This has been one of the best weekends of my life. Thank you."

I smiled. "It's not over." I reached into my pocket and took out the wrapped box, placing it on the table.

"What is that?"

"How many times do I have to tell you? When someone hands you a gift all you have to do is say thank you."

She picked it up. "You wrapped it so nicely," she expressed, opening it and gasping when she saw the bracelet.

"I wanted to give it to you while we were alone or else I would have waited for your actual birthday."

She looked at all the charms, grabbing the lobster one first and biting her lip.

"That one's my favorite, too. There's a cowboy boot, a surfboard, a guitar, a cancer ribbon, a cat, and, of course, the lobster. I know it looks really bare still, but I figured we could add to it throughout the rest of our lives together."

She immediately got out of her chair before I got the last word out, almost knocking me out of mine.

"I love you. I love you so much," she whispered into my neck, squeezing me tight.

"I love you, too."

Forbid Me

"This was the best birthday ever," she stated, sitting up in my lap.

"We still have all night," I reminded her. "I'll have no mercy on you, sweet girl. I won't stop until I'm etched in your skin, beating with your heart, not knowing where you end and I begin. I need to lose myself in you."

She looked deep into my eyes and breathed out,

"Promise?"

then

"Happy birthday to you, happy birthday to you, happy birthday dear Mason, happy birthday to you!" everyone sang, as my nephew clapped his chubby little hands together with a great big smile on his face.

It was his 1st birthday party. My mom pulled out all the stops. It looked like Elmo threw up in here with Elmo balloons, streamers, tablecloths, cups and, of course, the cake. She was a step away from painting the damn room red. I thought we might need an intervention for her or maybe just a chill pill. Everyone was there having a great time, and that's all that mattered in the end. There wasn't much that made my mom smile or laugh these days. She pretended as well as I did. I guess we all did, but the evidence of what was happening to her was right there in front of our eyes, a daily reminder of something none of us could stop.

The boys were all there and it was great to have everyone together again. Austin was the only one missing, he was still gone, but at least he would send postcards every so often from different parts of the world. I knew it helped everyone's worry over where he was and what he was doing. It had been six months since Jacob and I had first messed around. They graduated from Ohio State three months ago and Dylan and he moved back. Dylan was renting a house in South Port. Jacob was still undecided on where he wanted to go to law school. He was renting an apartment near the beach in the meantime.

I would be lying if I said it didn't hurt me that we hadn't talked about where he was applying. I knew there were several out of state schools he was interested in and even more acceptance letters, but that was it. He didn't ask for my opinion and I didn't offer it. We were talking on the phone or texting every day before he moved back and it was still the same. Except now I got to see him all the time. We had messed around a few more times, but he still wouldn't let me touch him. To say it sucked to be sneaking around behind everyone's backs would have been an understatement.

I walked into my bedroom needing a break from everyone. If I watched Lucas and Alex make puppy eyes at each other from across the room one more time I was going to smash their heads together. Even after all these years they were still playing this stupid damn game of cat and mouse.

They belong together, plain and simple.

I sat on my bed with my guitar, playing and singing Everybody Hurts by R.E.M. I closed my eyes to the soft strum of the melody, getting lost in the lyrics of the song. Sometimes the only solace I could find was with my guitar, my emotions running wild with everything that was going on around me.

Lucas and Alex…

My mom…

Jacob.

I sang the last chorus of the song again, not wanting my comfort to end, strumming out the last harmony perfectly and letting it vibrate against my chest. I sat there for a few seconds, contemplating how the words reflected my life and how much I could relate to them. I took a deep breath, opening my eyes only to find Jacob looking at me with a gaze I didn't recognize. Almost like it pained him to look at me.

I smiled, trying to break the unexpected tension between us.

He was leaning against the wall, his arms folded over his chest, dark and daunting.

"How long have you been standing there?" I asked.

"Long enough."

I lowered my eyebrows as he continued with his inquisitive stare that I couldn't quite place.

"That lip is going to fall off, Kid."

"Can't be any worse than when you bite it."

He faintly smiled. "Why so sad?"

"It's just the song, Jacob."

"Liar."

I shrugged. I didn't know what else to say. Actually, I did. Except, I was afraid to share it with him. The last thing I needed was for him to think that I couldn't handle us.

"Lily, maybe we—"

"Don't you think it's a little late for that," I interrupted.

He leaned his head against the door, looking up at the ceiling for what felt like forever.

"I never wanted to hurt you. That's the last thing I've ever wanted to do. You know that, right?"

I nodded. "Of course."

He pushed off the wall and I stood, ready for whatever he had to throw at me. So I was shocked as shit when he pulled me into his arms to kiss me. His hands cupping my face with such love and tenderness that it made me weak in the knees.

"Fuck, Lily," he groaned into my mouth.

I kissed him harder with as much passion as I could muster. We kissed for I don't know how long, getting lost in each other just as I had with my guitar.

"Holy shit!" Alex cussed, walking in on us.

We immediately stepped away from each other, both of our hands in the air in dismay.

"Oh my God! Lucas is going to kill you. He's going to murder you and hide the body. I'm going to know about it, I'm going to be an accomplice!" she shouted.

"Shhh..." Jacob hushed, immediately going to her and pulling her inside, shutting the door behind him. "It's not what you think."

"Not what I think? Did I not just walk in on you kissing Lucas's baby sister? His *sixteen*-year-old sister! Oh my God, Jacob, you're twenty-three! You could go to jail. Please tell me that's all you guys are doing!"

"Shhh… calm down, someone will hear you," he silenced her again.

"That's what you're concerned about?!"

I stepped toward her with a sincere expression displayed all over my face. "Alex, I love him," I chimed in, grabbing her arm to look at me. "I've always loved him."

I needed her to understand that this was serious, it wasn't a school girl crush. Jacob was my core. He was my *everything*. She

167

had to understand that, her more than anyone had to know where I was coming from.

What I felt…

We were one in the same.

"Lillian, stop saying that. You don't know what you're saying. You don't even know what that means," Jacob ordered in a demanding tone.

I hated when he pulled that card on me. All it did was piss me off. He knew what I said was true, but for some reason it made him feel better to say it or something.

"You love me, too! You just can't say it out loud," I replied, ready for battle, not caring that Alex was sitting right there watching it all.

"Stop! I mean it," he urged in a desperate voice.

"Stop what? The truth? You wouldn't keep kissing me if you didn't love me. Who cares about our ages, it's just a fucking number," I reminded him for what felt like the millionth damn time.

"Watch your mouth," he ordered with a finger in my face.

I shoved away his finger. "Screw you! You're not my dad. I'm not a child."

"Then stop fucking acting like one."

"Oh my God," Alex interrupted, making us both look at her. She looked like she had just seen a ghost. "She's the girl, isn't she? The one from last spring break? Jesus, how long has this been going on?" she asked with wide eyes going back and forth between us.

I wanted to say since birth, but I didn't think it was the time or place to get that deep into how I felt.

"Nothing. Is. Going. On," Jacob gritted out.

"Stop. Saying. That." I clenched my fists, looking from him to her. "Why are you looking at us like that? You more than anyone should understand this."

She immediately stood. "Me?" she argued. "What do I have to do with any of this?"

"You!" I pointed at her. "You love my brother, my brother loves you. You have loved each other since you were kids! The only reason you're not together is because everyone else won't mind their own goddamn business and just let it be. You would think you're related or something. It's so fucking stupid!"

There. I finally said it. Someone finally fucking said it.

"Lillian, watch your mouth," Jacob scolded with a heated composure.

"Oh my God!"

Why isn't anyone listening to me?

"Fuck you! Are you going to stand there and pretend you're not one of the main reasons they aren't together? You have been butting into their business since the beginning. You all have. I'm over it. It's stupid. They love each other, exactly the way we do! Except you can't get over the fact that I'm Lucas's sister. Who cares? I don't and neither should you."

Alex shook her head, stepping back.

"You more than anyone can understand what it's like, Alex. Please don't stand there and be all judgmental, age is just a number. I've grown up with these boys as much as you have. It's not like he's old enough to be my father or anything, now that would be gross."

"Lily, it's against the law," she reminded.

If I heard that one more time...

"Fuck the law," I let out.

Jacob was over to me in two strides. "I will not tell you again. Watch your fucking mouth."

I put my hands up in the air, exhausted with all of this. There was only so much I could take, and I was reaching my breaking point.

"You know what? You two can stay in here and wallow in all this negative energy. I'm not going to stand by and allow it to affect me. I know you'll come find me, Jacob, because you LOVE me! So let's see who's right and who's wrong. I guarantee you that I won't be waiting long, stew on that for a little bit." I turned and left.

Knowing in my heart.

He would follow me.

Alex sat down again, resting her elbows on her legs and laying her head in her hands. Neither one of us said anything for the longest time. My head hammered with the silence.

How could I have been so careless?

169

Forbid Me

"I don't know how it happened, Alex, I swear to God I don't," I honestly spoke, needing her to hear me say it. Needing her to understand. "One second she's five years old running around in pigtails and then the next she's sixteen. I tried. I tried like hell to ignore it. To ignore her, but you know Lily, she does what she wants, exactly like her brother. After your accident, she started opening up to me, and I let her because she was a kid and she needed a friend. I liked being around her, she reminded me so much of you. I don't fucking know," I sighed.

"Have you?"

"Fuck. No. All we do is kiss and that sounds a lot worse than it is," I lied, it was a lot worse than that. I lied to one of my best friend's because I didn't want her to judge me. I already felt like a piece of shit. I didn't need someone else reminding me what I already knew to be true. "We've kissed a few times and it didn't start till her sixteenth birthday. I swear to God that girl is like a tornado and I can't help but be sucked in."

She raised her eyes to me, blown away from what I said. Or maybe it was just from the whole fucking situation.

"She's going to be seventeen soon. I know that doesn't make it any better, I know it doesn't make it right. Fuck, Half-Pint, she's not wrong. I think I'm in love with her, how fucked up is that?"

I was in love with her, but I couldn't bring myself to fully admit it out loud, especially to Alex. I needed someone else's perspective and Lily was right, Alex would understand more than anyone and I had done everything in my power to keep her and Lucas apart. I hated myself for that, especially at that moment when faced with her and the truth all around me, smacking me right in the goddamn face. She watched me pace around the room until I finally stopped and sat down in the desk chair, facing her, hunched forward with my arms on my legs.

"I have no idea what to say," she softly said.

"I'm sorry, Alex. All these years, all I've ever done is... I mean... with Lucas and you... I just. Fuck... this is my fucking karma."

She opened her mouth to say something, but nothing came out.

"I know you don't have to say it. I know," I admitted, knowing that she wanted to say that I was right.

"Does anyone know?"

"Of course not."

"What are you doing in her room? You know that could have been Lucas walking in here. Do you have any idea how bad he's going to beat you for this? Oh my God, Jacob, he's going to murder you."

I lowered my eyes and peered at the ground, rubbing my hair back and forth, wanting to tear it the fuck out. "I know. You have no idea how many nights I've lost sleep because of this. I need to get away from her. It's one of the reasons I'm applying to law school so far away. I need to put distance between us."

"Does she know?"

I shook my head.

"Oh man…"

"I've made my bed and now I have to lie in it. This is the only thing I can do to make things right." It nearly killed me to say it.

"She's going to hate you."

I sighed, knowing that she was right. Lily wouldn't forgive me for this. "It is what it is. I can't keep leading her on like this. I am sending mixed signals all the time, but I can't help it. I can't explain it either."

"You don't have to. I understand."

I looked deep into her eyes. "Half-Pint, it was never about you. It was Lucas. None of us thought he was right for you. You deserve, you deserve someone like Cole."

"It doesn't matter anymore. It's in the past."

"I'm sorry, I'm sorry if I ever influenced anything that caused you pain. I love you," I sincerely spoke.

She nodded. "I know. Everything happens for a reason."

"You're not going to tell—"

"I promise… but if this shit hits the fan, because it's eventually going to, I'm going to claim I didn't know anything. I'll pretend to be just as surprised as everyone else."

I laughed and stood. "I'm going to—"

"Go."

She watched me leave, realizing that Lily was right. It didn't take me long to go after her.

Forbid Me

Confirming that I did love her...

After all.

I found her on the beach by the pier. Sitting at the exact same spot when she found out her mom had cancer. I sat beside her. My hat was safely placed on her head and she looked like she'd been crying which was completely different from the girl that had left the room.

My carefree Lily was gone.

She stared off in front of her not looking away from the waves, almost as if she was in a trance.

"You're leaving," she stated.

"How did you—" I paused. "You heard."

"I thought..." she shook her head. "I thought you were going to tell her that you love me. I thought you were going to tell her that you wanted to be with me. I thought you were going to tell her everything I've so badly wanted to hear." She swallowed hard, her voice breaking, mimicking my heart.

"You didn't tell her any of those things. You *think* you love me? I could understand why you lied about us just kissing, but Christ, Jacob... your karma? Really?"

"Lily... it wasn't... I didn't... fuck..." I breathed out, frustrated. "What was I supposed to say?"

"How the hell should I know? You never tell me anything. I knew you were applying to out of state schools because I thought you wanted to get the best education, not because you wanted to get away from me," she swallowed her voice finally breaking, fresh tears falling down her beautiful face.

I wanted to hold her.

I wanted to comfort her.

I wanted to tell her that everything was going to be okay.

That I loved her.

I did none of those things. I sat there and watched the love of my life cry.

For me.

For everything I had done, for everything I couldn't bring myself to say, for everything that she had overheard... for all of it.

"I'm sorry, Kid. I'm so fucking sorry," I whispered, trying to keep my own voice from breaking.

"Just go, Jacob," she sniffed still not looking at me.

"What?"

"You heard me. Just fucking go," she whispered so low like she didn't really want to say it.

"What about you?"

"What about me? I'm going to sit here. Watch the sun go down. Go home to my parents and continue to watch my mom die a little more every day," she sobbed, wiping away her tears. "Alone. Because the guy I love doesn't want me…" she broke down, and I couldn't take it anymore. I tried to pull her into my arms, but she pushed me away.

"Don't!" she shouted. "Just go! It's what you want to do anyways."

"Lily, you know that's not true."

"What I thought I knew proved to be one big lie, so no, Jacob, I know nothing. Not one thing."

"What am I doing to you? Look at you. This is my fault. I can't keep doing this to you, Kid, it's fucking killing me!"

"It's always about you! What you feel, what you need, you, you, you! You don't listen to me, you don't hear me, and you blow me off because you think I'm a kid. I'm not a kid, Jacob. I may only be sixteen, but that doesn't matter. I'm watching my mom die. Every day. No one talks about it. No one says anything when she's throwing up all fucking day. No one says anything when she can't get out of bed because the chemo is literally eating her from the inside out. No one says anything when she can't eat, when she can't move, when she can barely fucking talk! So, tell me, is that something a kid would see?"

I bowed my head, ashamed and remorseful.

"I wish I didn't love you."

I immediately raised my eyes to her. The look on her face crushed my already breaking heart.

"I wish I could stop loving you just so you would know how it feels."

"That's not fair, Lily," I finally spoke.

"It doesn't make it any less true. Just go… I don't want you here anymore."

"I wish it were that easy."

173

Forbid Me

She stood, looking down at me. "It is. Just watch me do it." She took one last look at me and left.

I watched the girl that I loved more than anything walk away from me, except this time...

She took my heart with her.

Chapter 24
Lily
now

"Lily, why is there men's cologne in your bathroom?" Lucas asked, walking back into the living room.

Shit.

I thought I hid everything Jacob in my house. He was adamant that *all* his stuff was staying in my house. We had talked about it, and we weren't ready to tell anyone yet. We wanted to enjoy being together without having it be ruined by my brother, especially on my birthday weekend. I had picked him and Alex up from the airport. They were staying in my guest bedroom for the next two days. Mason was with his mom for the weekend to my disappointment, I miss my little dude.

"What?" I played dumb.

"The cologne, Lillian. Who's is it?"

I looked around the room, my heart pounding in my chest.

"Bo!" Alex yelled at him, slapping him in the chest. That had been her childhood nickname for him. "Leave her alone. She's twenty-three, she's allowed to have sex."

"The fuck she is," he roared.

The front door opened at that exact moment, and of course in walked Dylan and then Jacob, both not bothering to knock. All three of them built like mountains, making my house look tiny. I was saddened Austin couldn't make it. He was stuck in New York, saying something about his girlfriend Briggs. Although, nobody knew if they were actually together or not, they had the craziest relationship. He texted me a picture of his new tattoo on his arm and it warmed my heart as soon as it appeared on my phone. He had gotten a tattoo of one of my random drawings I used to draw with a marker on his freckles as a child. Austin was covered in tattoos now and my design seemed tiny in comparison to his others, but I loved the gesture.

Jacob picked up Alex from the floor, squeezing her tight in his arms. "Look at you, Half-Pint, all grown up."

She laughed as he set her back down. "You say that every time you see me. I'm digging the beard." She tugged on it.

Yeah… me too.

"Hey, bro," Jacob greeted Lucas. They hugged, smacking each other's backs.

Dylan came over to me and did the same thing to me that Jacob had done to Alex. "Hey, there, rock star. Can't wait to see you perform. I hear you're a big deal around these parts."

I smiled as he set me back down on the ground. "Yeah, I do what I can," I replied, grinning.

Jacob mischievously looked at me. "I don't get a hug, Kid?"

"I see you all the time," it slipped from my lips.

"You do?" Lucas questioned, grabbing Alex from behind around her waist. "You mean, old man Jacob here isn't working his life away anymore?"

I bit my lip.

"You know your baby sister, Lucas. She's hard to ignore."

"No shit. So who's the fucker she's seeing?"

Jacob cocked an eyebrow.

"You met him yet? Do we need to pay a little visit?" Lucas added.

"Yeah…" Jacob nodded. "I've seen him around a few times in passing. She always has this smile and glow about her when he's around. I haven't met him yet, though, but he makes her happy, Lucas, and at the end of the day isn't that all that matters?"

"Who the fuck are you? And what have you done with, Jacob?" Dylan argued, making me laugh.

"Why does everyone keep saying this to me lately? You're right. Let's find him and lay him the fuck out, Special Agent McGraw," Jacob mocked, only looking at me.

"Oh my God," Alex chimed in. "We just got here. Can we eat before you guys start plotting out ways to end up in jail? I'm starving." She linked her arm with mine. "Or you know what? You guys can stand here and continue playing G.I. Joes. Lily and I will go to lunch. I'm sure we can find someone who will hang out with us."

Lucas picked her up off the ground, throwing her over his shoulder. "Nice try." He smacked her ass and she yelped. "Let's go, Half-Pint's hungry and you know how she gets."

She giggled and winked at me as he carried her out the door, and I knew Jacob was dying to do the same to me.

These goddamn good ol' boys with their caveman tendencies.

I took them to my favorite diner to grab some lunch. I hadn't been there since Jacob and I went on our first morning together. I sat us at a booth, sitting down next to him, Alex and Lucas across from us, and Dylan at the side. Jacob squeezed my thigh as soon as I sat down because of the seat I had picked. I glared at him while everyone looked at their menus and he didn't pay me any mind, looking over his own menu.

"This damn table, I barely fit," Jacob said, trying to nudge it but it wouldn't budge. The table being so long that the boys all looked uncomfortable while Alex and I were just fine. I laughed at the thought.

"What time does Aubrey get in?" I asked Alex, Dylan pretending like he wasn't listening to every word.

"Umm... I think she said four this afternoon. Something with Jeremy's schedule, I don't know, it didn't make sense, but they had to change their flight," Alex replied, sipping her cherry coke.

"God, they've been together forever now. How are they doing?"

She shrugged. "I guess good. I don't see them very often."

"You live in the same town."

She shrugged again.

"You chasin' any pussy while you're here?" Dylan asked Jacob, wanting to change the subject. Except I was the only one who knew why.

"Not chasing," he simply stated.

Alex narrowed her eyes at me with a questioning expression, and I looked down at my menu. Jacob's hand quickly found my thigh again, rubbing it up and down, close to my panties. I tried to move his hand away, but he wouldn't budge, only squeezing my thigh to get me to stop.

I cleared my throat to avoid yelping.

"You okay?" Jacob asked, knowing damn well I wasn't.

"Mmm hmm…"

If he was trying to make his presence known, then he was doing a damn good job of it. Dylan and Lucas might be clueless enough not to notice it, but Alex… no way in hell she missed it.

"Wow, the man who's one step away from being a manwhore, suddenly has very few words for his latest putang? I call bullshit," Dylan laughed, never one to hold back. "Must be someone special."

"You could say that," Jacob retorted as he cupped my sex, and I gasped.

Alex's gaze shifted back and forth between us.

"Are you sure you're okay?" Jacob asked again, and I could feel him grinning.

I wiped my mouth. "Yep. Just kicked the table by accident."

"Are you next, bro? Does Alex need to start planning a wedding? You know she's going to jump on that shit," Lucas laughed, kissing the top of her head, but Alex didn't answer. She was too busy piecing together the puzzle that sat in front of her.

"Is she coming out?" Dylan questioned.

"How do you know she's not here right now?" Jacob beamed as I bowed my head again, trying to fight him off under the table.

"Maybe she's sitting at this table," Jacob stated, and I just knew everyone was looking at me.

What the hell is he doing?

I looked up with a smile. "You know he's fucking with you right?"

"My baby sister is too damn smart for the likes of you."

"Is that right?" Jacob chuckled, squeezing my leg one last time before finally letting go.

I could breathe. "In other news… I'm going to go to the bathroom."

I got out of there faster than a bat out of hell.

JACOB

I knew it was out of character for me to purposely provoke her, especially in front of Lucas, but at that moment I didn't care if he found out. I was over them fucking with me. Knowing I was going to have to spend the entire weekend out of Lily's bed just added to my agitation, and frustrated the fuck out of me. We finished lunch and then Lily took us to her bar, Lucas and Dylan wanted to check it out before tonight.

I sat with Alex at the bar while she showed the boys around. There were pictures of her all over the walls, and I could tell by the look on both their faces they were extremely proud of her.

"How long?" Alex asked, taking me away from my thoughts and making me look at her.

"How long, Jacob?"

"Since I've been here."

Her eyes widened. "That was almost five months ago!" She slapped my chest. "Neither one of you have said a word."

"You've had your own shit to worry about, Half-Pint. How's that going?"

"The same, but you're changing the subject."

"Hey… I guess I'm just dying to be an uncle."

"Does she know?"

I knew what she referred to and I shook my head no.

She sighed. "Jacob… you can't not tell her."

"I will. When the time is right, I will tell her."

"Have you spoken to him? Your dad?"

"Off and on," I simply stated. It was the truth.

"Your mom is doing great. I stop by and check on her at least twice a month."

"I know."

"This…" She looked over at Lily. "It's different this time, right? Because I swear, Jacob, if you hurt—"

"I want to marry her."

Her head jerked back, stunned.

"I would marry her right now if I didn't have to deal with your husband."

She sighed. "Yeah…"

I watched as Lucas pulled Lily to him, kissing her on the head and looking down at her with such love and adoration.

"He's going to fucking kill me."

She nodded. "Yeah… Lily has been through a lot these last few years. You know that. It's one of the reasons she moved here."

"I know what you're doing, Half-Pint, and yes it was *one* of the reasons, but we both know the truth. She left because of me. No one else."

"It's in the past."

"Sometimes. Other times it's blatantly right in front of me when she looks at me and tries to look past what I did."

"Jacob, it was a lot to take in. Anyone would have done what you did. I honestly think if you told her it would bring you closer. It would give both of you closure, and she wouldn't look at you that way anymore."

The guys came back before I could answer. I didn't take my eyes off Lily, silently praying that Alex was right.

Lily

I played my last set of the night. I requested to only play a few sets that weekend so I could party and enjoy the time with my family. Alex was trashed, I had never seen her that drunk before, and she and Lucas were practically making babies on the dance floor. Dylan and Aubrey spent the night on opposite ends of the room than us, and with the way Jeremy was acting I don't even know why they even bothered to come.

I wanted to have a minute to talk to Aubrey alone, and with Jeremy hovering over her the whole night I figured my best bet was the ladies room. She excused herself and Jeremy quickly followed her once again. I waited a few minutes for him to return then I made a run for it. I opened the bathroom door and gasped, locking it behind me, rushing to her immediately.

"Are you fucking kidding me, Aubrey? This shit is still going on?" I yelled, wetting paper towels under the faucet to bring them up to her bloody lip.

She hissed. "I fell. It's not what you think," she replied in a monotone voice.

"I'm sure you fell, right onto Jeremy's fist."

"Lily…" she pleaded.

"What, Aubrey? I've kept your secret, okay? Doesn't mean I have to fucking like it. I can't believe you're still letting him do this to you. He's a piece of shit."

"He's stressed out with work. He doesn't do it that often anymore. I swear." She was lying, I could see it all over her face.

"Why are you still with him? You know Dylan would have him behind bars in no time, all you would have to do is say the word."

She shook her head. "I'm not involving Dylan, Lily."

"He loves you. He fucking adores you, Aubrey. He wouldn't have kept this secret if he didn't. Don't you see this goes against everything he believes in for Christ sake? He puts people like him away where they belong."

She looked down at the ground. "Please don't say that," she whispered so low, the agony in her voice apparent.

"He can't keep doing this to you. You don't deserve it."

Tears fell down her face. "I deserve this and more, Lily. Don't talk about things you don't know."

"I don't understand. Help me understand. Let me help you. Let the boys help you."

She immediately stood. "No!"

"Aubrey, he's going to fucking kill you one day and you're letting him. This is nothing compared to the shit I walked in on that night, and something tells me when you went home it was—"

"It's none of your business. Not everyone gets their happily ever after, Lily." She tore the paper towel from my hand and looked back at the mirror, wiping off the blood from her lip.

"You're wrong."

She looked at me through the mirror.

"You couldn't be any more wrong. I hope by the time you realize that… it won't be too late."

Forbid Me

She looked at her lip.
And I left.

Chapter 25
Lily
then

It was my seventeenth birthday.

My mom wanted me to go out with my friends, but I refused. As far as I was concerned there was nothing to celebrate. I hadn't seen or spoken to Jacob since the day on the beach and that was three months ago. He moved to California to attend Stanford Law School a few weeks after. My mom was getting worse with each passing day, and Lucas was lost in his own drama. The only brightness brought to my day was my little dude, Mase.

"Leelee," Mason babbled, tugging on my dress.

"What's up, little dude?" He laid his head on my shoulder, grinning up at me. "Daddy said you can't have any more cake. You're going to get me in trouble."

He made that face. The face I couldn't say no to. He was a Ryder, it was in his blood to eat sweets, I could relate.

"Fine, we won't tell him." I grabbed a few spoonfuls, and he gobbled them down like a champ. I wiped his mouth, getting rid of all the evidence.

"Mase!" Lucas called out, walking into the kitchen. "There you are."

I smiled. "We were just hanging out. You taking off?"

He grabbed Mason from me. "Yeah, I gotta get him down. Even though he's definitely not going to sleep tonight with that extra piece of cake you just gave him."

I gasped. "I did no such thing."

He nodded toward the ends of my hair. "Did you forget that food goes in your mouth?"

"Mason, way to cover, dude." I kissed all over his face and he giggled, thrashing.

Lucas kissed the top of my head. "Happy birthday, baby sister. I love you."

"I love you, too. I'll see you later."

He left, and I started to help my mom clean up the kitchen.

"Lily, you don't have to do this. It's your birthday. I'm sure your friends would love to see you," Mom said, looking extremely tired.

"I'm fine."

"Baby, I'm worried about you. You're always home."

"I love being home."

She sighed deeply, cocking her head to the side. "What's going on?"

"Mom, I'm fine. I promise."

"Lily, does this have something to do with—"

"Honey, what are you doing? I thought we were having a date night in bed?" Dad interrupted.

"Eww…" I instinctively replied, wondering like hell whose name my mom was about to say.

"Why are your kids so stubborn?" she asked my father. "Happy birthday, sweetie. We will see you in the morning." She kissed my forehead and they left. I was in the middle of watching a girlie movie in the living room, I didn't like hanging out in my room anymore, too many memories.

I heard a soft knock at the front door.

Never expecting to see who was on the other side.

I couldn't miss her birthday.

I hadn't missed one since her birth. I didn't care that we hadn't spoken in months. I didn't care that we didn't end things on good terms. I didn't care that I was probably going to make things a lot fucking harder for the both of us.

Nothing else mattered but *her*.

I softly knocked on the door, making sure that it was late enough that everyone would be gone or sleeping. Lily was a night owl, always had been. She opened the door, stunned that I was standing in front of her.

"Happy birthday, Kid."

She immediately burst into tears, jumping into my arms and wrapping her legs around me.

"Shhh… shhh…" I coaxed, rubbing her back to soothe her. "Shhh…" I repeated until her breathing evened out, and all I heard was her sniffle.

"What are you doing here?" she wept, looking at me but still not letting me go.

"Where are your parents?"

"They're doing it in their room."

I laughed and she smiled.

God, I fucking missed that smile.

I carried her inside the house because I didn't want to let her go. I closed the door with my foot and carried her up the stairs to her bedroom, closing and locking that door as well. I placed her gift on the floor and set her on the bed.

"I can't believe you're here," she whispered, tears forming in her eyes again.

"No… come on now. I'm here. No more crying."

"What are you doing here?"

"Where else would I be, sweet girl?"

She smiled and it lit up her entire room.

"Did you have a good birthday?"

"Better now. I'm so happy you're here."

"Kid, I'm so sorry about—"

"No," she interrupted. "I don't want to talk about that. Not right now. We can talk about it tomorrow or the next day, or whenever, but I don't want to talk about it right now. Please."

I nodded. "I got you something." I reached for my gift and handed it to her.

"What is it?"

I laughed. "Open it and you'll find out."

"You didn't have to get me anything, you being here is enough."

"Lily, when someone hands you a gift all you have to do is say thank you."

Forbid Me

She tore it open and lifted the box. "Oh my God!" she exclaimed. "I've wanted these! How did you know?" She grabbed the cowboy boots and instantly put them on.

"I saw you looking at them when we were in Ohio. I ordered them online."

"You even got the right size!" She pranced around the room.

"Don't look so surprised. I know everything about you, Kid."

She beamed. "I love them. Thank you!" She hugged me and then placed them neatly in her closet. "I still can't believe you're here." She sat down next to me again and I grabbed her hand, setting it in my lap.

"How's school? Is it really hard? I bet California is beautiful. Alex says it's amazing."

I could tell she was nervous. "I'll take you there one day," I simply stated.

"Promise?"

I kissed her hand, nodding again.

We sat there for hours talking about everything and nothing. I loved being there with her. I didn't think about what was going to happen tomorrow. All that mattered was that we were together, after months of thinking of nothing but her. She was finally in front of me and I couldn't have been happier.

"When do you leave?"

"I should be leaving soon. It's near two am."

She frowned.

"Stay with me."

"Kid…"

"My parents sleep like the dead and with my mom… well, you know. They don't get up till late. As long as you leave by eight, we will be fine."

I took a deep breath.

"Please. It's my birthday, you have to do what I want."

"Your birthday is over."

"Not in California and that's where you're from so it's still my birthday there."

I laughed, shaking my head. "I'm sorry, Kid, I can't. It's one thing to stay when you're parents aren't home, but it feels wrong to do it right under their noses."

She sighed. "Let's go somewhere then."

"Where?"

"Anywhere. I'll go anywhere with you."

I couldn't say no to her so I grabbed her hand and drove us down to the beach, Lily grabbed a blanket and a pillow before we left. We walked around for a while, our feet in the water and the full moon above us.

"Come on."

I pulled her behind me as we walked up the beach into an abandoned house I had seen a few times in passing.

"Whose house is this?"

"It's abandoned. I've never seen anyone in this house. It's been sitting empty for years."

I shoved open the door and to our surprise there were already blankets, pillows, food, and water right in front of us. I lit the candles on the floor and grabbed one to use as a light.

"Hello," I called out. "Stay here."

She looked at me like I was crazy.

I chuckled. "It's not dark in here, Lily."

She looked around the room, the soft lighting only accenting the terrified glare in her eyes.

"Stay behind me. Do you understand?"

She fervently nodded. I grabbed the pocketknife I usually carried on me and checked the house to make sure we were really alone. The house had stuff in it for a reason, I figured they might be squatters, but nobody was there, at least not tonight. Lily was pretty much attached to my back and I couldn't help myself. I spun before she saw it coming.

"Boo!"

She screamed bloody murder and I laughed my ass off.

"You asshole! I almost peed my pants," she said, trying hard not to laugh.

"Come here. I'll make it better." I pulled her toward me and kissed her softly, then begrudgingly let her go.

"I wonder who's been using this place. It's beautiful," she said as she laid the blanket on the floor, placing the pillow on top of it. I took off my shirt to just sleep in my shorts, and she did the same thing she did the last time we slept together, she grabbed my shirt and used it as PJs. I blew out the candles and pulled her toward me as close as I could, wanting to mold us into one person. She laid on my chest in the crook of my arm, and I slept on the pillow.

"I miss this. I miss this more than anything. I have never felt as safe as I do when I'm in your arms, Jacob. It's like everything just goes away… how do you do that? How do you make everything go away?"

I kissed her head.

"I know you love me," she stated out of nowhere, catching me completely off guard. "You prove it time and time again with your actions. Words are cheap... you can tell anyone you love them, but proving it… that takes effort. You've loved me ever since I could remember."

"Lily…"

"I know you, too. I think you forget that." She was tracing hearts on my chest with her fingers. "I love you, and I don't care if you ever say it back to me because I know in my heart that it's real. That what we have is real. That the love you have for me is real. I can see it, I can feel it, and as much as I want to hear you say it. At the end of the day… I already know that the truth lies in your actions."

I held her tighter, taking in her words, and it didn't take long for her breathing to even out. I didn't sleep a minute that night, and I tried to tell myself it was because of where we were and how dangerous it was, but it wasn't.

It was the first night that I actually stopped seeing Lily as a child…

It was the first time I saw her as a woman.

A woman I was head over heels in love with.

Lily

He left the next morning.

The only thing that kept me from breaking down when I watched him leave was that I knew we would start talking again.

It gave me hope…

For the future.

Chapter 26
Lily

now

It had been a little over a month since my family had visited. We were eating breakfast when Jacob's phone rang.

"This is Jacob," he answered. "I'm good, just eating some breakfast. How are you?"

I couldn't hear the person on the other end, but Jacob's face quickly turned serious.

"Right… of course, I understand that. I have been going over some figures the last few weeks, and I think it's a good idea if we sat down and discussed it."

I frowned and mouthed, "Everything ok?"

He nodded, the expression on his face not changing. This was lawyer Jacob, the person I hadn't met yet.

"I'll have my secretary send over all that information, and as soon as I have things worked out here, I'll have her send my flight information as well. After that, we can figure out a date for the meeting."

Flight?

"I'll also have her cc the partners and we can come up with a date that works for everyone, but the sooner the better, Carl. Yes, you too. Bye." He hit end and placed his cell phone on the table.

I waited for a few minutes hoping he would share what that was all about, but he didn't. I even gave him the stare down, thinking he would get the hint to spill it. His silence tore into my insecurities of the past just a little bit. It's not like I knew what his plans were. I stood up from the table with my plate, more annoyed than anything and went to the kitchen. I didn't want to ask him what was going on, I just wanted him to tell me. To include me.

Simple as that.

Forbid Me

To finally include me in his life without me having to say something or constantly ask. Well, I'll show him, two can play at that game.

I started to wash the dishes when I felt him come up behind me and wrap his arms around my waist, turning me to face him. He grabbed my chin, making me look at him. Placing his arms on my shoulders, caging me in the only way he could.

"Say it," he demanded with a shit-eating grin on his face.

I shrugged, not wanting to give him an inch. I knew I was being a child, but I didn't care. After all we had been through he should just know. It was a given.

"You know, Kid, for someone who says they're an adult, you sure know how to act like a child sometimes." He half-laughed.

My eyes widened in shock, playing it up a little. I never wanted to punch him in the face more than I did at that moment for finding the situation funny.

"Do I need to provoke you to get the truth? Is it working?"

I narrowed my eyes at him and he laughed again, shaking his head and kissing my forehead. "It's been six months since I've been here."

I knew that. I had been counting down the days till he left me again.

"Before I found you, Lily. All I did was work. It was my whole life."

"What about your manwhore status?" I threw at him.

He pursed his lips, surprised that it had taken me that long to ask him about that.

"Nobody mattered but you. It's always been you, baby," he responded, not elaborating any further.

"You always seem to say the right things, Jacob," I replied, rolling my eyes.

"Are you trying to have an argument right now? Is that what's going on?"

I scoffed, ducking my head to slide out of his arms. He let me go without a fight.

"You're being an asshole!" I yelled, walking into the living room.

He followed, leaning against the wall in that Jacob sort of way. I call it his asshole stance. Probably one he uses in the courtroom to intimidate people.

"What?" I shouted, annoyed but also amused that he was treating me like I was on the stand.

"I just wanted to have front row seats to the temper tantrum of a lifetime, Kid, you may proceed."

"Temper tantrum? That's what you think this is?" I laughed.

"No. I *know* that's what this is."

"I'm sorry that you still haven't changed. I'm just supposed to accept it, right?"

He rubbed his fingers back and forth over his mouth, clearly amused with my banter.

"Just go, Jacob, go back home to your lawyer life, I'll stay here. We will see each other when we can. Maybe have some phone sex, some late night booty on Skype. Okay? I know you have to go back to work, I know you have a life over there, an apartment, a career, I get it alright! You're old and mature and got your shit together. It sure as hell doesn't mean I have to fucking like it."

"I see," he replied, trying so hard not to smile.

I put my hands up in the air in front of me. "That's all you have to say? I see?"

He pushed off the wall and headed to my bedroom. I watched him walk away and I was about to follow and give him hell, but he came back before I had the chance. He sat on the armchair, hunched over with his elbows on his knees, a piece of paper hanging in his hands.

"You know, Kid, if you want to start bringing up the past every time you overhear something you don't like, then the longevity of our lives together will most definitely be rough. You know I like it rough, baby, but I for one don't want to live like that. Do you?"

I didn't say anything. *What could I say to that?*

"Okay, that's how you want to play it? Giving me the silent treatment." He nodded, understanding. "Since you're so quick at throwing the past in my face every chance you get, I would like to discuss the past as well. As in the last six months," he stated.

"*I* came here to find you. *I* pursued you. *I* wouldn't take no for an answer. *I* bulldozed my way back into your life. *I* told you I love you… Do you see a pattern, Lillian? Because all the facts point to yes."

I still didn't say anything, mostly because he was right, and that irritated me as much as it made me happy.

He laid the sheet of paper he'd been holding on the coffee table. It was then that I noticed it was an airline ticket.

"You booked your flight back already? And you haven't even told me! This is exactly what I'm talking about! You don't include me in anything. Nothing has changed between us except NOW you tell me you love me!"

He cocked his head to the side. "Is that all I do now?" he arrogantly replied.

"No!" I shook my head. "You do not get to turn this conversation into a way to get laid! I'm closed up, buddy!"

He leaned back in the chair, laughing. "Check the ticket, Lillian."

"Why? Are you leaving this afternoon, big man?"

"With the way you're acting I just might. Stop being a little shit and check the fucking ticket, Lillian," he repeated.

I snatched the paper off the table, rolling my eyes at him. Looking at the name.

Lillian Ryder.

I almost died right then and there.

Wanting to eat my words.

"Do you like what you see, Kid?" I had to laugh at her.

She bit her lip with embarrassment radiating all around her.

"Lily, you already know how I feel about you. I've proved it to you then, in my own fucked up way, as much as I do now. Except now I use words to match my actions. You know that I'm committed to us, why question that? I finally have you. I don't want to lose you. Up until this point, this time around, it's been all me. I know you love me, but I need it to be your choice. We haven't spoken about the future. I want to keep it that way until you see how I've lived all these years. I think it will help clear up a lot of those goddamn insecurities you have. Come back with me. You need to see."

"To California?"

"I believe I made you a promise."

"Oh, so the first time I went there didn't count?"

He raised an eyebrow in a playful way.

"For how long?" I hesitated. "I mean this isn't me moving there, right?"

He grinned. "California couldn't handle you, Kid. It's for a few weeks while I take care of some business."

"Are you going to come back with me?"

"When I have more information for you, we will talk about it. For now, I want you to come with me. I won't take no for an answer."

"For only a second, I thought you were leaving me again. I never expected this," she expressed with glossy eyes.

I stood right in front of her, all joking aside, needing her to see how serious I was about the situation. "I'm giving you a choice, I can't force you to be with me. But, Lily, choose me again. Choose us," he pointed between us. "I promise I won't ever walk away from you, from us again. I promise to give you all of me, forever." I kissed all along her face, tears falling down her cheeks.

"I'm all in, sweet girl, damn the fucking consequences."

"I'm scared, Jacob. I know I've always been strong when it comes to us, but Lucas has been through the same shit I have. I don't want to lose my brother. I can't lose him."

"I would never let that happen, Kid."

"That doesn't mean it's not going to, you know my brother as well as I do."

"He's going to be pissed off at me. Not you. It will be my ass that he will want to lay out."

"Maybe… but I don't want you to lose him either. I don't want to come between anyone."

"I know, baby. The last thing I want is for you to have to go through any more shit."

"How are we going to tell them? How is this going to go down?"

I sighed not knowing the answer. "Let's worry about us for now. We can worry about everyone else later."

"Okay."

"Are you coming back with me?"

She grinned, nodding. "I need to tell my work."

"Not necessary."

She laughed. "I have to tell them I'm leaving, Jacob."

"It's already handled, sweet girl. I took care of everything."

She gasped, surprised. "I thought this was my choice."

I smiled. "Come on. Who are you talking to here? I gave you the option, doesn't mean I wasn't going to throw you over my shoulder and take you with me."

"That would have been quite a scene through security."

"Private planes exist for a reason." I grinned.

"You have all the answers, don't you?"

"It's part of my charm."

"Charm or annoyance?"

I slapped her ass making her yelp.

"Do I need to remind you who's in charge here?"

She backed away from me. "I know who's in charge."

"Good girl."

"Me," she giggled and took off running.

I spent the rest of the morning reminding her just how wrong she was.

JACOB

then

I was in town for a few weeks in between semesters. It had been six months since Lily's birthday. Even though we talked and texted almost every day, we had been spending every second we could together while I was in town, like every other time I was in town.

"Hey," I greeted my mom in the morning as I walked into the kitchen.

"Hey, honey." She looked like she had been crying.

"You okay?"

"Of course."

"Mom, you look like you've been crying."

She shook her head. "Don't be silly. Why would I be crying? Are you hungry? Can I make you something before I head to the store?"

"Did Dad leave?"

"Yeah. He had to go to town."

I frowned, I didn't remember seeing his car last night.

"I can fend for myself, Mom."

"Of course you can. Doesn't mean I don't want to take care of you. Your sisters should be flying in on Sunday. They can't wait to see you. I'll be back late tonight, and I'm not sure when your father..." she cut off, smiling. "Well, I'll see you later, honey. Love you." She kissed my cheek.

"Love you."

I watched her leave as I stood there concerned for what I just walked in on when I heard a soft knock coming from the back door. I found Lily standing there in a soft yellow spring dress, her hair loosely falling down the sides of her face and her back. She was wearing very subtle makeup, and I could faintly smell the coconut and vanilla on her skin. She was a sight for sore eyes.

"Did you dress up for me?" I asked, so goddamn turned on by the sight of her.

"I dress like this all the time for school."

"Is that right?" I arched an eyebrow.

She stepped inside. "I saw your mom leave. Are you hungry? I can make you something."

"So, tell me, Lily, do boys at school fuck with you?"

She bit her lip.

"Your silence is deafening, Kid."

"It's not like that."

"It's not like *what*?"

"Are you jealous?" She smiled big and wide.

"Jealous doesn't even begin to explain what I'm feeling. Jealousy is for boys, Lily, and we both know I'm not that."

"Oh yeah, big man?" she sassed. "It doesn't matter. I love you," she simply stated, slipping off her lips so easily and effortlessly. She said it all the time now, and, to be honest, it felt like a knife piercing my heart every time I heard it.

"What do you want to do today?" she questioned, walking toward me.

"You."

"I think I can arrange that." She stepped up on the tips of her toes, softly kissing my lips. Ever since Lily turned seventeen, she was getting ballsy. She didn't wait for me to make the first move anymore. She initiated several make out sessions, which would usually end with my face and fingers in between her legs. Nothing new had happened between us. I could tell she was getting frustrated that I wouldn't let her touch me.

Our kiss quickly turned into something else entirely. I gripped her ass, carrying her up my body. She wrapped her arms and legs around me, moaning her approval in my mouth. I carried her up to my old bedroom, kicking the door closed behind me. I laid her on the bed, falling on top of her, caging her in with my arms and body.

"I want you," she breathed out in between kissing, rubbing her pussy against my hard cock.

"Shhh…" I whispered against her lips, my hand already making its way down her gorgeous body.

"No, Jacob." She swatted my hand away. "You. I want you."

"It's not happening, Kid."

She sighed into my mouth. "Then let me touch you. Please, let me make you feel what you make me feel. I want to so badly."

I groaned, wanting her to do just that. I placed my forehead against hers, needing to gather my thoughts, trying not to let my overly eager cock take control.

"Jacob, I want to. You're always playing with me. Let me give you something for a change. I don't… I mean you know I don't…" she mumbled with the cutest fucking expression on her face. "Just tell me what to do. Teach me."

"Lily…" I whispered against her mouth.

"Please. Let me make friends with him. He probably already hates me. All I do is give him blue balls. That's not a very nice friend, Jacob. Don't make me beg for it."

I laughed so hard I fell onto my back to keep from crushing her. She quickly followed suit, sitting up on her knees, waiting for me to say the next word. My cock was already so damn hard from the sight of her let alone what she wanted to do to me.

"Kid, I never want you to feel like I'm pressuring you into anything."

"I'm offering. How is that pressuring me? You won the golden ticket, okay? Just let me suck your dick already."

My cock twitched from the filthy yet innocent way she spoke to me. I placed my arm behind my head, angling my body so I could watch her.

"Undo my belt and unbutton my jeans."

Her eyes dilated, shocked that I was granting her wish.

"Better hurry, Lily, before I change my mind."

Her hands immediately went for my buckle, anxiously undoing it. She went straight for my button next, vigorously working to free my cock. She pulled down my jeans and boxers, and I waited for the gasp when my cock jolted free, smacking against my stomach.

Her eyes widened and her lips parted. "Wow… your friend is beautiful, Jacob."

I chuckled. "Beautiful isn't quite the word he's looking for. In fact, beautiful will make him hide."

"Oh… right… I mean big and thick."

"Good girl."

"Your balls are nice, too."

I laughed, my head rolling back.

She blushed. "Sorry."

"Let's not talk about my cock anymore. Put him in your mouth the way I've been stroking myself to the image of you doing it for the last year."

She licked her lips and gently took me in her hand. I placed mine around hers. "Hard, baby, like that." I squeezed my hand around hers, showing her exactly the way I liked it.

"Use those take me lips and lick and suck around my head, slowly sliding me into your hot, wet mouth, inch by inch until all I can feel is the back of your throat."

She leaned forward, looking down.

"Don't take your eyes off me. Do you understand?"

I held in a breath when she licked along the tip. Her warm lips took me in, gliding down my shaft in a slow, torturous rhythm, taking me deep and then back out. Her eyes never left mine as I closely observed her making love to me with her mouth.

"Fuck… Lily." I groaned, the sight and feel of her being too much. "Good girl, just like that, baby, use your hand just like this." I showed her for a few seconds, watching as her tiny hand worked in sync with her mouth's movements.

"Mmm," she unintentionally hummed as she deep throated me again.

"Jesus Christ," I growled, pumping my hips against her movements, getting lost in the way she worked me over. I was about to grip the back of her neck.

When I heard, "Jacob!"

Lily

I didn't actually think he was going to let me do it so I didn't think twice about it when he said to undo his pants. I had wanted this for so long, he was finally giving in. For once he could feel something only I could deliver. I wanted to prove to him that I could give him pleasure, too. To feel that I loved him the same way he loves me every time his hands or mouth are on me. I listened carefully to every instruction he gave me, wanting to do it just right. By the sounds he was making and the intense, driven looks I had never seen before, I knew I was doing what he wanted. What felt good for him.

My heart soared…

His hips started moving against my hand and mouth, pushing his erection deeper down my throat. I wanted him to manhandle me. I wanted to feel his dominance over me as I had his dick in my mouth, and I think I was about to when we both heard…

"Jacob!" Lucas knocked on his bedroom door. "You ready? The waves are getting higher."

He tried to sit up and push my head away, but I wasn't going to have my brother's appearance take this away from me. I sucked harder and jerked him faster, his eyes widened in realization that I wasn't going to stop.

"Jacob, what the fuck, you in there?" The door handle turned.

"I'm here, Give me a few," he announced with an unsteady voice.

"What are you doing?"

He cleared his throat, breathing heavily. "Shower."

His face twisted in both pleasure and pain when he finally gripped the back of my neck, roughly moving against my mouth.

"I'll be in the kitchen. Why is my sister's truck parked outside?"

His dick throbbed and I swear it got bigger. He bit his lip and his eyes shuttered, as a thick substance spurted in the back of my throat. His chest heaved up and down as I sat back, wiping my lips not knowing what to do with his come in my mouth.

"Swallow it," he mouthed with a heated stare.

I did, not knowing I could even do that. I grinned, feeling all proud of myself as the thick, salty substance went down my throat.

He got up and went to the bathroom, turning on the shower and it didn't take long to hear Lucas's footsteps descend down the hall. He walked back in the room, buttoned up his pants and looked at me with a fiery glare.

"Jesus Christ, Kid, was that necessary?"

"Absolutely."

"Please enlighten me on how I'm going to explain your truck in my driveway?"

I looked around the room for an idea. "Tell him that I went to work with your mom for the day. I was doing a paper on tourism in Oak Island, and I needed to know how she buys all that tourist crap she does for their store."

"You're going to be the death of me." He changed into his board shorts.

"My brother will believe it. He would never think I would be in here with you. Relax. It's fine."

"I better go before he comes back up." He kissed my head and walked to the door.

"Wait."

He turned to face me.

"I did good, right? I mean... it was... it was good for you?" I nervously asked.

His body loosened from his tense composure, walking back over and sitting on the balls of his feet in front of me.

"Lillian, I have never had better. It was the best fucking blowjob of my entire life."

"You lie," I giggled.

He looked deep into my eyes and said,

"If there's one thing I need you to know, that I need you to remember, is that I have never lied to you nor will I ever lie to you. I can't."

He kissed me, left, and I believed every word he said.

We spent most of the day in the water.

Lucas believed me without a second thought, just as Lily suspected he would. We ate at Alex's parent's restaurant and it was weird to not have her serving us.

"How's law school?"

"It's law school. How's fatherhood?"

"Everything it's made out to be."

"That good, huh?"

"Never thought I could love someone like that. I think I got pretty lucky, though. He's a handful but a good kid."

"How's your construction business going?"

"I'm busy as shit. Stressed, overwhelmed, you know, all the bullshit that comes along with owning your own business. It's why I needed today, to work off some steam, it's good seeing you, bro."

"Likewise."

"It's been rough with my mom and Lily, I'm glad—"

"Lily?"

"Yeah… she's, damn, man, I don't even know anymore."

"What do you mean?"

"She's hurting, Jacob, and I know it has a lot to do with my mom and shit, but there's something else. Something she won't tell me, or anyone for that matter. For a while I thought it was a guy, but she never leaves the house. My mom says she has guys beating down the door, but she blows them off. I don't know, we're all worried about her. I mean she's going to be eighteen and she's never had a boyfriend? That can't be normal right? We're just worried that she's missing out on all the normal teenage shit because of my mom's cancer."

It was as if a stack of fucking bricks fell on top of me, and I tried to hide all the emotions that soared through my body at the speed of light. I couldn't pretend that I didn't know this was coming, but it was still like taking a swift kick in the fucking balls.

"The last thing I want is for Lily to look back on her childhood and only have shitty memories. My mom says she doesn't even hang out with her friends anymore, but she's constantly talking or texting on her phone so it doesn't add up. I don't fucking understand it."

I gazed down at my food, completely losing my appetite, and wondering how much more of the conversation I could take without wanting to beat my head on the goddamn table.

"But I'll tell you one thing, Jacob, if this is a guy. I'll beat the living shit out of him for doing this to my baby sister, and I know you and Dylan will be right there behind me."

I peered up at him and nodded, wishing like hell that I could beat the living shit out of myself, but something told me that it didn't matter because what I had to do next would kill me anyway.

Forbid Me

Chapter 28
JACOB
now

"Is now a bad time to tell you that I hate flying?" Lily said as I took my seat next to her in business class. I nodded to the flight attendant.

"Yes, Sir?"

"Can I get a coffee, extra cream with three sugars, and a whiskey on the rocks for her?"

"Of course. I'll be right back."

"Liquor will calm your nerves," I stated, looking at her.

"Or you could have just held my hand."

"Sweet girl, I'll hold your hand for the entire five-hour flight if that's what it takes."

"We can try your booze idea. If that fails maybe we can go in the bathroom and join the mile high club."

"As appealing as that sounds. I can barely fit my ass in the bathroom."

"I'm a tiny person."

"But I'm not."

The flight attendant handed us our drinks. The captain came over the intercom telling us to prepare for take-off. Lily reached for my hand as the plane started to move, squeezing the shit out of it until we were in the air.

"Drink."

She downed the entire thing in one swig. "When does the calming of the nerves kick in?"

"Clear skies the entire flight, Kid. You have nothing to worry about."

Forbid Me

I opened my laptop, planning on working while on the flight, but Lily wouldn't let go of my hand. I tried to keep her busy by distracting her. Talking for most of the flight worked.

We finally landed at one pm.

"Hello, Charles," I greeted the company chauffeur.

"Good afternoon, Mr. Foster, good to have you back."

"Charles, how many times do I have to tell you to call me Jacob, Mr. Foster is my father and I don't like him."

He laughed. "And who is this?"

I glanced over at Lily, who looked overwhelmed. "This, Charles, this is Lily."

"Ah… Lillian."

Her eyes widened, shocked that he knew who she was.

"I feel like I already know you, Miss Ryder."

"What?" she responded with a big smile on her face.

"Mr. Foster and I spend a lot of time together, all he does is work. I've chauffeured him around more than anyone else in the company. He's a very nice guy, also, head over heels in love with you. I'm glad to finally put a name with a face."

He extended his hand and she shook it, looking at both of us skeptically. "Did you pay him to say that? It's nice to meet you, too."

"The car is out front. I'll get your bags."

"I can get my bags," she stated.

"It's quite alright. I can handle it."

"Okay, mine are the bright pink ones."

"And you're familiar with mine, Charles."

"Of course, Sir."

I grabbed Lily's hand and walked her out.

"This isn't a car. This is a limo. Your firm owns a limo?"

"Among other cars." I opened her door.

"I've never been in a limo!" she happily exclaimed, jumping in.

I sat in front of her as she looked around everywhere, excitement written all over her face. I had to make a few phone calls.

"Good afternoon, Debra. How are you?" I asked. Lily pretending like she wasn't listening to every word.

"Were all the files emailed? Right. Have you talked to Robert? I'll be by the office in about an hour. You know how traffic is. Okay… Bye."

"Who's Debra?" she immediately asked.

"Do you always eavesdrop on private conversations?" I asked with a smirk.

"Just yours and only when they're in front of me."

"Debra is my secretary. You will meet her in a bit."

"Is she pretty?"

"I don't know, Kid. I don't see her that way, but I'm sure her husband does."

The response seemed to appease her. Once Charles started driving it didn't take long for traffic to hit.

"Why so far away? Come here, sweet girl." I guided her toward my lap and she came effortlessly. "I'm done playing twenty questions. Do you understand?"

She didn't falter. "Maybe… what do I get for it?"

I closed the partition.

"Isn't it rude to close that?" She smiled. "Or is he used to it being closed?"

I smacked her ass. Hard.

"Ouch!" She grabbed her ass. "I don't like this game."

"I don't like your sass. Now, be a good girl and I'll reward you. Be a little shit and you know what happens."

"I think I need to be reminded what my rewards are, Mr. Foster."

I traced her pouty pink lips with my thumb, pushing it into her mouth, getting it nice and wet. I slid her panties to the side, using my thumb to rub her clit.

She stirred.

"Need more reminding? Only good girls get to come… are you going to be a good girl from now on?" I eased my fingers into her warm, welcoming heat, never letting up on my circular motions around her nub.

She shuddered.

"Say it."

"Jacob…" she panted, her hips rotating against my fingers.

I smiled. "Tell me you'll be a good girl. Tell me you'll stop with the questions. Tell me you love me. Lastly, tell me to make you come."

I worked her harder, aiming my fingers to where she wanted me the most.

"I'll be a good girl. I'll stop… Oh God…" Her breathing hitched.

"And?"

"I love you, please… please… please make me come."

And I did.

Lily

We went to his office and Jacob introduced me to everyone. I swear by the way they looked at me, they had heard my name before. I made a mental note to ask him about it later. We stayed at his firm for a little over an hour, he was held up in a couple of meetings while I waited for him in his office.

His office had a killer view of downtown, but it was stale, so cold and empty. No pictures on the wall, no decorations anywhere. For someone who spent most of their time in their office, there wasn't very much appeal. His penthouse was the exact same way. The view was breathtaking, his furniture looked very expensive and probably not comfortable at all. The decorations on the wall matched perfectly, but it didn't feel homey. There wasn't a sense of warmth or love anywhere. The penthouse was immaculate, not one thing out of place, not even a speck of dust. It was cold and empty.

I felt like I was walking through a model home. There was no sign of the Jacob I grew up with, the man I had known all my life, anywhere.

I grabbed my suitcase when he went downstairs to grab his mail from the concierge, feeling sad for him. I walked into the bedroom ready to start unpacking my things. Even his closet screamed someone else to me. Expensive dress shirts, slacks, vests, and suit jackets, ties and fedoras in every color. It was like I had walked into someone else's wardrobe. Only the few pairs of flip-flops on the floor told me it was his.

When I walked back into his bedroom, a picture caught my eye on the nightstand. It was the only picture in the entire penthouse. I grabbed it, sitting on the edge of his bed. It was a photo of me when I held the lion cub at the zoo. I heard his footsteps coming toward the bedroom, but they stopped when he was at the door.

"Jesus... Jacob," I softly whispered. "I was sixteen here. That was seven years ago." I kept my gaze focused on the photo. "You really did love me, didn't you?"

"Was there ever a doubt in your mind," he stated as a question.

"There was so much shit that happened between us. After I left Oak Island, I was..." I took a deep breath, trying to gather my thoughts. "It was bad. Sometimes I felt like I imagined it. Our relationship."

"Our love, Lillian," he corrected. "Our love."

"I don't know when I stopped believing you loved me. It just sort of happened. I left Oak Island because I couldn't breathe there." I swallowed back the tears, the emotions running wild. "There wasn't anything left for me there. Did Alex ever tell you—"

"Yes."

I nodded. I figured she would.

"There's a lot of stuff you don't know," he said out of nowhere, making me raise my glossy eyes to him.

"Like what?"

"What happened between us that night. Fuck, Kid, I think about it all the time. I think I've thought about it every day for the last three years. Having you..." He rubbed his forehead like he had a sudden splitting headache. "It's a memory that I'll take to the grave. You have to know that? Please tell me you know that."

"I do now. I didn't know back then. I can't blame you for what happened that night. It takes two to tango, Jacob. I was just as responsible as you were. I hated you for what happened after. I didn't understand how you could do that to me." I shook my head. "After everything."

"I swear to you on all that is holy that if I could go back, I would have never done that. I would have never hurt you like that. It was a fucked up situation and I have every intention of telling you about it, but I don't want to ruin our time here. I promise you that I will tell you. I will tell you everything."

"Okay," I murmured, wanting to grant him his request. But just knowing that he's keeping something from me keeps me not at ease.

He walked over to me, sitting on the balls of his feet, swiping my hair away to hold my face in between his hands.

"I love you. I love you like I've never loved anyone before. I love you in a way I didn't even think was fucking possible. I loved you before I even knew what it meant. I'm sorry, sweet girl. I'm sorry for not seeing what was right in front of me. For all those years we lost. For every time I walked away from you. For every single time I felt your heart break because of me. I'm sorry for everything. All you ever did was bring light into my life, and all I did was take away yours. I will spend the rest of my life making it up to you," he paused to let his words sink in and looked deep into my eyes to say,

"Hurting you is my biggest regret, loving you is my only redemption."

I walked out of the meeting with a huge weight lifted off my shoulders. Finally after two weeks of negotiating, everything was done and taken care of. I tried to spend as much time as I could with Lily, showing her all around San Francisco. Her favorite was The Harbor where all the seals gathered. I found her there several times playing her guitar and singing. She swore the seals loved it.

"How was your meeting?" she asked as I came up behind her in the kitchen, tickling her. "I'm making dinner," she giggled, trying to wiggle her way out.

"Where you going?"

"It's going to burn."

"Fuck dinner. I'd rather fuck you," I groaned in her ear.

"Jacob!"

"Saying my name isn't going to help your disposition."

"Are you ever not horny? I thought testosterone was supposed to go down when you get old."

I bit her shoulder. "Watch it."

I let her finish dinner while I jumped in the shower. When I came out, she was setting the plates on the table. I grabbed a bottle of wine and poured us both a glass, leaving it to breathe on the table.

"You know what wine does to me." She took her last sip and I poured her another glass, knowing damn well what wine did to her.

"So, can you tell me what was going on now? Because I'm dying over here."

"I resigned."

She choked on her wine. "You what?" She wiped off her lips. "But you were trying to make partner, you had been working so hard for that. What do you mean you resigned?"

"I want to be with you," I simply stated, the realization slapping her in the face.

"You quit for me?"

"For us."

"You're moving to Nashville?"

I nodded. "Do you remember my friend Mark?"

"Yes."

"I wanted to make partner to be the boss, Lily. I don't have to do that in San Francisco. I could do it anywhere. I have been helping Mark with his firm for the last six months for a reason."

"Wait? What?"

"We're officially founding partners. You are looking at Foster and Daniels Associates. I had to handle some business here. Make sure all my loose ends were tied up before I could tell you about it. Just in case."

"Oh…"

"Oh?"

"I'm in shock, I don't know what to say."

I leaned back into the chair, rubbing my fingers over my lips, glaring at her.

"No! I'm thrilled. I'm so happy! I just wasn't expecting this, but I love it. Oh my God, Jacob! I'm shaking."

I cocked my head to the side. "What were you expecting?"

"I guess, I don't really know. I mean I was hoping for this. I was afraid you would ask me to move here and I'd say yes, a million times yes, but, to be honest, your office and your apartment scare me. They're so cold, Jacob, it's like you never wanted to be here, like you were just surviving instead of living."

"My home is where you are."

"Are you trying to make me cry? I'm going to cry in my spaghetti."

I laughed, taking in her adorable face, grabbing her wrist to pull her on my lap. I kissed the tip of her nose and looked deep into her loving eyes and spoke with conviction,

"You're mine."

JACOB

then

Three hundred and sixty-five days.
Fifty-two weeks.
Twelve months.
One year…
That's how long it had been since I last talked to Lily.
Since I stopped fucking living.

I said goodbye to her the only way I could. I told her I had met someone new. I was happy and in love.

She didn't talk to me again.

I was the only one to blame.

It was a lie. It was all one big fucking lie. A façade I conjured up. I never met anyone. There was no girlfriend. No committed relationship. I wasn't happy and madly in love.

It was all complete and utter bullshit.

I always knew what we were doing was wrong, not because I didn't love her but because of our circumstances. My conversation with Lucas just put everything in perspective. I was holding Lily back. It wasn't fair to her, she deserved to be loved without hiding, and she deserved so much more than I could offer her. People would say I was being a coward, a pussy. That I took the easy way out and they would be right, but when it came to Lily, I would lay myself down any day if it meant she got to be happy.

I told Lily what I had to, lying to those big brown eyes that I always saw myself in. Then planted the seed with Lucas and my mom, knowing damn well they would unintentionally tell her. She would believe it because I never lied to her before this time. This was the first and last time I ever did. I couldn't even look at myself

211

in the goddamn mirror anymore. I promised her, swore to her that I would never lie to her. That she could trust me wholeheartedly.

I'm a fucking bastard.

Their mom was getting worse. My mom said she barely recognized her anymore. She wanted to host Christmas Eve at her house. As much as I tried to come up with an excuse on why I shouldn't be there, I couldn't. She had been like a second mom to me, to all of us. I owed it to her to be there.

It may be her last.

"Hello," I answered my cell phone.

"Hey, honey," Lily's mom greeted. "How are you?"

"Good. How are you?"

"I'm great. Can't wait to see everyone. It will be nice to have all of you together again. It's a shame no one can get a hold of Austin, I would have loved to have all of you kids together one last…" she hesitated like she hadn't meant to say that. "Anyway," she laughed. "I was calling because I hear you're getting serious with someone."

"Mmm hmm…" was all I could say.

"Your mom said she didn't know if she was coming home with you. I wanted to make sure I prepare enough food and everything. Plus I'd love to meet her, Jacob," she requested in an unfamiliar tone. "I mean if you're serious and all, it would be normal for her to come, right?"

I didn't say anything. Not. One. Word. I was too disoriented by the way she spoke to me, almost as if she was testing me.

Did she know? No… Wait? Did she?

"Umm," I shook off the confusion. "I don't—"

"Jacob, I think it would be a really good idea if you brought her. For *everyone*."

"Do you… I mean…" I mumbled, not being able to form the words. "Do you know—"

She cut me off. "Honey, I have to go. Lucas just got here with the turkey. I'll see you tomorrow, okay? I can't wait to meet her! Have a safe flight. Love you." She hung up, and I sat there perplexed for the next hour.

She knew.

M. Robinson

Lily

I knew Jacob was coming to my house for Christmas Eve.

I just never thought he would have the balls to come with her. I watched him walk in, his hand firmly placed in hers with his gaze tightly locked on me. I didn't look at her at all... not for one fucking second. I hadn't seen him in over a year, a goddamn year. Not so much as a text. Nothing. He didn't even text me on my eighteenth birthday. He never missed a birthday, not one. I think that hurt most of all.

I was an adult.

A woman.

But I never felt more like a child than I did at that moment, the reality of his lies staring me right in the face. I was the first to break our connection, if I didn't, I would have called him a liar right there in front of our families and friends.

I watched him flaunt her in front of me, standing a little too close to her, touching her face a little too often, whispering things in her ear a little too much. It was like he was trying to make a point, I couldn't fathom his actions. After Cole had made his big announcement, which in my eyes was more of a pissing contest and a big fuck you to my brother, I witnessed Lucas physically break down in front of me. I just couldn't take it anymore. I needed to get the fuck out of there.

So I ran.

I ran out into our backyard, needing air, space, and a fucking sledgehammer.

"Fuck! I can't get a break," I shouted, running into Jacob, who was sitting on the patio steps. I immediately turned to go back inside, but the door locked behind me. "Of course, why wouldn't the door lock? Am I going to get struck by lightning now, God?" I peered up at the sky, shaking my head and staring back into Jacob's amused face.

"Where's your whore, I mean your girlfriend?" I spewed not being able to hold back.

His expression quickly turned desolate and I lashed out.

213

"I thought you said you would never lie to me."

He grimaced, it was quick, but I saw it. "I haven't."

"Liar!"

He stood and came toward me. "Kid, I—"

I pushed him. I shoved him with all the strength I could muster. He didn't even falter. I might as well have shoved a brick wall. I screamed out my frustration.

"FUCK YOU! I hate you! I hate you!" I repeated, hitting him all over his chest.

I took out a years worth of frustration on him. Beating his chest over and over again.

All my sadness.

My despair.

My love for him that wouldn't go away.

My hate for him because he lied to me.

I saw my mom's diminishing life. My brother's fucking misery over his star-crossed love. My dad being alone after she was gone.

I saw it all.

With each push and every blow that hit his body, I felt a little more of myself die. The carefree, happy girl was gone. All that was left was someone I didn't recognize anymore, someone I never wanted to be. I hit him harder and he let me. Not once did he try to block me or hold me. Not once did he try to comfort me.

And I didn't know which one was worse, which one hurt more. Tearing into my anguish of a future that didn't include my mother or him.

"Why? Why do you do this to me? Why do you hurt me all the time? Why do you keep breaking my fucking heart?" I shouted, moving away from him and not being able to look into his lying eyes any longer.

"Kid... I'm hanging on by a thread here."

"You think I'm so stupid. I'm one big fucking child! You think I don't know. That's what hurts the most, Jacob." Tears slid down my face. "Why would you lie to me?"

"Lily, I don't—"

"Stop fucking lying!" I yelled, raising my eyes to his. "I know! I know she's not your girlfriend. I know you lied! You made me think for this entire year that you had found someone and it's a lie. It's all one big fucking lie."

He jerked back for the first time like I had hit him, this time it wasn't by my actions but by the truth of my words.

"I knew it the second you walked inside with her. You can pretend all you want, flaunt her in my fucking face, but the truth is in your eyes, Jacob. It's always been in your goddamn eyes."

I bowed my head, shutting my eyes.

"Exactly. Go ahead and hide them."

It all made sense now. That's why her mom wanted her to come, but why? Did she want Lily to hate me even more? Nothing made sense. Not one fucking thing.

"Why did you lie to me? You owe me at least that."

"Lily, when was the last time you went out with your friends?" I looked at her with the sincerest expression spread across my face. "When was the last time you did something normal? Went on a date? Had a boyfriend? The last time you did anything but wait for me? You're still waiting for me."

"That was not your choice to make. It was mine."

"Not when your brother is telling me your family is worried about you. Not when he's telling me that they're terrified you're going to look back on all these years and regret missing out on everything. Not when he's telling me that you've become withdrawn, you never do anything, or leave your fucking house." I stepped toward her until we were a few inches apart.

"Not when he's telling me that all you do is sit on your phone, texting and talking to someone. To me." I hit my chest. "To fucking me, Lily. I'm taking you away from everything. That's not healthy. I'm hurting you when I'm with you, and I'm hurting you when I'm not. I can't fucking win either way."

"So you lie?" She wiped away her tears before I did it for her.

Forbid Me

"What other choice did I have? Tell me? What can I do? I can't be with you and it's fucking killing me that I can't be without you."

"You promised me! You swore to me that you would never lie to me. I believed you! I trusted you!"

"It was the only way."

"To make me hate you," she added the words I couldn't say, and I faintly nodded with bile rising up my throat.

"Where's your *girlfriend*?"

"Do you think if she mattered I would be out here?"

"Who is she?"

"Does it matter? Jesus Christ, Lily, I can't even look at you. Do you know how much that kills me? You're my favorite fucking thing to look at."

She slowly backed away from me and it took everything inside me not to throw myself on my knees and beg her to forgive me.

"That makes two of us." And with that she turned and left.

Leaving me with nothing but regret for the things I couldn't take back and the same things I desperately wished I could change.

Lily

I left him standing there.

I couldn't stand the sight of him. Not for one more second. He didn't deserve one more second. I barely had time to register everything that had just happened or what I was feeling when I heard soft whimpering coming from my garage. I walked toward the noise, the silence around me almost deafening. The bass from the music playing inside my house coincided with the crying as I got closer to the side door.

I ran.

I ran as fast as I could, barging inside the garage, halting as soon as I saw the sight in front of me.

Aubrey…

On the cement ground, clutching her stomach, and rolling around in pain.

Jeremy…

Looming, hovering above her like a monster, a villain in a horror movie.

I immediately hurled into action, sliding on my knees to Aubrey. "Get the fuck away from her! Dad! Lucas!" I screamed, fearing the music inside would be too loud for them to hear. Aubrey started to move her head back and forth in my lap. I didn't understand if she was telling me to stop or keep going.

"Dad! Lucas!" I yelled even louder.

"Shut your goddamn mouth, little girl," he gritted out.

"Fuck you!" He came at me just as the garage door opened, stopping him mid-action. We both looked behind me. There was Dylan standing in front of us, looking from him to us and back to him again. Putting together the pieces of the puzzle within seconds. Rage was written all over his face.

He closed the door and charged him, knocking him over with his entire body. They both fell to the ground and Aubrey shuddered, moving to the side to try to get up. I helped her as Dylan and Jeremy wrestled around on the floor.

"Please... please... stop," she begged for I don't know who, walking toward them. I grabbed her arm holding her back.

"You piece of fucking shit!" Dylan roared, hitting him. "You like to beat women, motherfucker!" He hit him again, slamming his head on the concrete.

"Lily, he's going to kill him."

I looked at her like she was crazy. "Who cares, he was hurting you."

"I'm fine. Please, Dylan, please stop!"

"You sack of fucking shit." He ignored her.

"Please, Dylan, if you ever loved me... please stop."

He instantly stopped, stood up and spit on his face. What happened next shocked the shit out of both of us.

Aubrey went to him.

She went to Jeremy.

The man who was fucking kicking her ass when I walked in.

"What are you doing?" Dylan asked, gripping her arm.

She roughly snatched it out of his grip. "Mind your own goddamn business. Leave!" she ordered, her demeanor quickly turning callous.

Forbid Me

"Have you lost your fucking mind? Get the fuck up, Aubrey! I'm taking this piece of shit in." He grabbed his phone and she knocked it out of his hand, the screen cracking on the floor.

"What the fuck is wrong with you? Why are you defending him?" he argued.

I stood there not being able to move or say one damn thing. Their problems making mine look childish in comparison.

"You know why. Leave. Leave now."

"You can't be serious? You think I'm really going to leave you with him? Give me some goddamn credit, Aubrey."

"If you don't leave, Dylan, I swear I'll never let you…" she hesitated, but she didn't have to continue because he understood her warning.

"Un-fucking-believable. I loved you. I still fucking love you and you stand there and defend this piece of shit."

She swallowed hard her resolve breaking.

"I guess I really never knew you at all."

She shut her eyes. I could physically feel her pain from the distance between us. Dylan took one last look at her before kicking Jeremy in the stomach, peering down at him with disgust.

"Mark my words, motherfucker, one day I'm going to fucking kill you."

He grabbed my hand and led me out through the side door, and I halted as soon as we were a few feet away.

"What are you doing? We can't leave her in there. We have to tell someone. You have to arrest him. Go back in there, Dylan!"

His teeth clenched. "I don't have a choice."

"Why?"

"Lily, just pretend you didn't see that tonight. Do you understand? For me. Do it for me."

"You can't ask me to do that."

"I'm not asking."

"Dylan, I—"

"Lily, you know I love you. Don't make me say it. We both know what I'm talking about. I've kept my mouth quiet, now it's time for you to return the favor."

I stepped back, the impact of his words being too much. He nodded in realization that I understood his simple yet powerful request. He kissed my head and left me standing there.

All I could think was…
What. The. Fuck?

Chapter 30
Lily

now

"Okay, hold on," I said to Alex on the phone, calling her on Skype from my laptop.

"Hello, it's you!"

"Hello, it's me!" I replied our standard greeting, hitting end on my cell.

"So, what is so important that we had to Skype," I asked, already knowing even though she hadn't told me yet.

I just knew.

Call it intuition.

They found out they made a little person on my birthday weekend. I like to say that I am the reason that child is in there. My awesome energy and vibes, but Jacob likes to remind me that it was actually Lucas's boys that got one passed the goalie.

She was glowing with her baby bump proudly showing, wearing a shirt that said, "If you didn't put it in there, then don't touch it." That right there was definitely my brother's handiwork.

"So we're having a…"

Lucas then showed a shirt on the screen that said, "I'm my dad's son in here so don't fuck with the belly."

I busted out laughing. "Oh my God! You're having a boy! Where does he keep finding these shirts?"

"He swears he's buying them, but I think he's having them made," Alex replied, Lucas looking at her lovingly with a shit-eating grin on his face.

"How far along are you now?"

"Eighteen weeks today."

"Wow! They fit you in fast then."

Her face frowned as she scratched the back of her head. "Yeah... well... they weren't going to see me till next week, but your brother called them back. Let's just say he's lucky they let him in the doctor's office at all."

I shook my head, typical behavior from my brother.

"Alright, baby sister, I have to go out for an estimate. We will talk soon. Love you."

"Love you!"

Lucas kissed the top of her head. "I love you." Leaned over and kissed Alex's stomach. "And I love you. Be good for your mom."

She beamed. "He's like the size of a potato, Bo."

"So are you."

We laughed.

"I'm so screwed."

"Yeah, have fun with that."

"Lily, he's already planning my entire day. What I should be eating, how much I should be exercising, telling me I can't carry anything heavy. He knows more than I do. He called the restaurant this morning telling them I won't be coming in as often. It's like I can't leave the house or something."

Alex owned her parents restaurant now. Her parents retired a few years back and pretty much handed it to her on a silver platter. She loved it, though, and I couldn't imagine her doing anything else.

"Yeah... like I said. Have fun with that."

"I may kill him before this pregnancy is over."

"I'm surprised you haven't killed him yet to be honest."

"Congratulations, Half-Pint," Jacob announced, leaning into the screen.

I slapped his chest. "You weren't supposed to say anything."

"She knows."

"You do?" I looked back at the screen.

"I do."

"Why haven't you said anything!?"

"Why haven't you?"

"Yeah, Kid, why haven't you?"

"Alright, so I recognize that tone. I'm going to go... have fun." Alex nodded toward Jacob. "With that." The call ended.

221

Shit.

"Did you say you wanted a blowjob?" I grinned, reaching for his pants.

He grabbed my hands. "As much as I would love to fuck your face right now, it wouldn't be for the right reasons."

"I'm in trouble, aren't I?"

"On so many levels. I should take you over my shoulder, Kid."

"Jacob, I thought we agreed we weren't going to tell anybody."

"Alex isn't anybody."

"Well, next time you can hand me a list of people who count. That way I know."

He arched an eyebrow, rubbing his fingers back and forth over his lips, his expression quickly fading.

"For someone who doesn't like my *game*, you sure do provoke me enough to spank that little fucking ass of yours. Don't you?"

I slid farther away from him, guarding my ass. He tried to hide his smile.

"I think you just like finding reasons to do it, you masochist."

"That's up for debate."

"I'm sorry I didn't tell her."

"That's not what you should be sorry for."

"Jacob…"

He narrowed his eyes at me.

"I need to know. I need to know now. Please. What happened?"

I didn't have to elaborate.

He knew exactly what I meant.

JACOB

"I want all that with you, Lily. The house, the white picket fence, the baby. I want the whole fucking nine yards. A complete life."

"I want that, too. More than anything. I've always wanted it. Except, I can't move forward without knowing everything. I know why you brought that girl to our Christmas Eve party. I get what you were trying to do."

"Do you?"

"I do now. I hated you for doing that. For flaunting another woman in front of me and thinking you needed to. It was the first time I hated you, Jacob. At least I thought I did. It wasn't until after you left me, that I felt true hatred towards you. I carried that hatred up until the moment I saw you at my bar. It was only then did I realize that I still loved you. That it never went away. I get it. I know you were hurting too. I've seen how you lived. I mean your pizza delivery boy addressed you by your first name, that can't be normal," she chuckled, but I couldn't bring myself to laugh.

The severity of what she wanted to know was too consuming.

"You were trying to be selfless by letting me go, allowing me to live my life or a life. I understand. That doesn't explain what happened after, though. Why did you do that to me?"

I stood, I had to. The memory of everything flooding back into my mind and it was just as painful now as it was back then. I felt like I was reliving it all over again, except this time I knew the outcome. She came up behind me as I looked out her back porch, wrapping her arms around my waist.

"I'm not going anywhere. I can promise you that. I just need to know the truth, but it's not going to change anything between us. You know it, Jacob. You know in your heart I'm not going to be able to move forward the way you want me to without you telling me what happened."

She kissed along my back, comforting me in a way that was unexpected. The memories of that day and the weeks that led up to it, like an old movie playing on a reel right in front of me. I couldn't stop it, not for one fucking second. Which is why I had been running away from it for the last three years.

"I love you. I'll always love you. No matter what, you're my lobster," she coaxed, assuming I needed to hear it.

"I don't even know where to start," I murmured, my voice seeming so far away.

"The beginning…"

Chapter 31

Lily

then

"I'm sorry. We've done everything we can. All that's left is to make sure she's comfortable," the doctor stated as if it were nothing, as if it was just another ordinary day, his voice lacked any sympathy, and I hated him as much as the cancer itself at that moment.

"How much time?" Mom asked not looking one bit surprised with the prognosis.

"A few weeks, give or take."

She smiled, nodding. Her face becoming hazy as tears formed in my eyes. My dad went to her. He held her face in his hands, resting his forehead on hers. Neither one of them spoke as he placed kisses all over her face. It was such an intimate moment shared between them that me and Lucas felt like we were intruders.

We wouldn't get to see any more moments like that. This was probably one of their last and the realization killed me.

The sounds of despair that came out of my father's mouth, a man I had never seen cry before, made me almost fall to my knees right then and there. Wanting to curse God for what he was doing to us. She soothed him by rubbing his hair and softly humming. The way she did when I was a child, and that's when I lost my shit. I felt so selfish for doing that. I didn't want to break their intimate moment. Lucas put his arms around me and hugged me so tight to the point of pain.

"It's okay, Lily. I'm here," he whispered into my ear, his tone composed and collected, which only made me cry harder. He was trying to be strong for me, for all of us.

"I can't do this, Lucas. I swear I can't do this," I bawled so low I didn't think he could hear me.

"Shhh… you're the strongest person I know."

I don't know how long we stayed like that. Time just sort of seemed to stand still. Next thing I knew we were home and all of it was one big blur of emptiness and sorrow. My dad took my mom up to their bedroom after talking to Lucas privately. His eyes were red and glossy when he left his office and walked into the kitchen.

"What's going on?" I immediately asked.

"Nothing you need to worry about."

"Please, please don't do this, Lucas, please don't treat me like I'm a child. I'm nineteen years old. I haven't been a kid for a long time."

He nodded with a downhearted expression.

"I can help. It shouldn't all fall on you. That's not fair."

He took a deep breath and let it out through his mouth. "Dad's going to call in a few favors to some of his alumni to see if they can take over his patients at the office, he's going to close it for the time being."

My eyes widened with the realization of why he was doing it. This was really happening. She was really dying.

"He wants to," he cleared his throat with an uneasy expression, trying to hold back his tears. "He wants to look over mom's will, make sure everything is in order and start checking out places," he cleared his throat again, shaking his head. "Places for the fu—" he hesitated for a few seconds. "The services." He couldn't even say it.

Fuck… I couldn't even say it. How were we going to live through this?

"Okay," was all I could say.

"He wants me to call everyone, you know, the boys, Alex, their parents. Immediate family only, so they can say their goodbyes."

"Yeah, that's probably a good idea."

"Can you call Alex and the boys? I'll tell everyone else."

"Yes."

I hadn't spoken to Jacob since Christmas Eve, but it didn't matter.

Nothing did…

Anymore.

Forbid Me

JACOB

Ten months.

That's how long it took for the phone call to come. I wish I could tell you I wasn't expecting it. As soon as I saw her name and beautiful smile pop up on my screen, I knew.

"Baby…" I drawled out, and she burst into tears.

"Shhh… sweet girl… shhh… calm down. Breathe, shhh… listen to my voice, breathe in and then out. Good girl… shhh… let's try again… in and then out. Good girl, baby."

"How do you know?" she wept, sniffling, barely getting the words out.

"You're a part of me. Always have been, Kid, always will be. How long?"

"A few weeks."

"I'm going to email my professors to let them know that I'm taking a leave of absence. I'll be on the next flight out."

"Okay," was all she could say.

I never wanted to tell her that I loved her more than I did at that moment.

"Lily, just remember to breathe alright? I'll be there soon, baby. Please just breathe."

She hung up first. Something told me it was because she didn't want to say, "I love you."

It took ten fucking days for my leave of absence to be approved by the Dean's office. That was after I raised fucking hell in student services for them to approve it immediately. I had to get home to Lily and fast. I talked or texted her every day, but with each passing day she became more reclusive, barely replying with more than a few words. My plane landed at eleven am two days later. My mom picked me up from the airport, taking me home first to drop off my things, before heading back to Lily's together.

The house had an eerie calm about it, the silence almost deafening around me. My mom led me to Lily's mom's room and the sight alone nearly brought me to my knees. Lily was passed out sleeping in her mom's bed, her head on her stomach with her arm wrapped around her like she didn't want to let her go. Her mom was rubbing her head and signaling with her other hand for me to come in. I closed the door and sat in the chair that was already placed by the side of the bed.

"It's okay, we can talk. She's passed out. She's not going to wake up for a while."

"Are you sure? I don't want to wake her," I replied, taking in her swollen eyes and pale skin, her already tiny frame looking skinnier. Even in her current state she still looked beautiful.

"She hasn't been sleeping lately. She's been walking around here like a zombie, barely any life in her. She's been my shadow. I know she's just trying to get as much time with me as she can. I made Lucas crush up a sleeping pill in her tea, and she fell asleep maybe an hour ago," she said, continuing to stroke Lily's hair.

I nodded not knowing what to say but wanting to say so much.

"Remember how much she hated to sleep when she was little? When she has trouble sleeping she loves her hair to be played with, it's the only way to get her to pass out."

My eyebrows lowered as I took in her words. Confused where this conversation was going.

"She's still so afraid of the dark, so I make sure to buy the scented plug-ins with the light on them. I scatter them through the halls, in the bedrooms. Anywhere I know she could get scared."

I narrowed my eyes at her, but she never took her eyes off her daughter.

"I have a notebook to give you that I started when she was nine. It has all her made-up words in it. I wrote down what they meant so when she talked to me I could get just as excited as she was when she was telling me something. It's much easier when you know what she means."

My eyes watered as I realized what she was doing.

"Music always makes her feel better. Her favorites are the classics, like Jimmy Hendrix, Santana," she said smiling down at her as tears started to fall down my face.

"I think you know why," she knowingly added. "She hogs the bed, it doesn't matter if it's a king size or a twin. You need to make sure that you start in the middle, that you fall asleep there first

227

because by morning you'll be on the end. It will give you a few more hours to be comfortable."

I wiped away my tears as her lip started to quiver. "She loves to be touched," her voice broke, and I swear my heart was too.

"It doesn't matter where. She just loves affection. You have to tell her that you love her often and all the time. It will always make her smile. She will tell you that she hates to be tickled on her inner thigh, but she absolutely loves it. You have to squeeze right in the middle, you always get the best laughs when you do that." Tears slid down her face as did mine, both of us getting choked up.

She breathed in and out, trying to gather her composure, and I reached for her hand, trying to give her any strength that I could.

"The last thing, Jacob, and it's the most important." She finally looked at me with an expression I would never forget.

"I spent too many years coming in between Lucas and Alex. I won't do that to Lily. To you. I know you love my girl. I've known you loved her since before you even knew. Your age gap was so big, I didn't think anything would ever come of it until she was older, but love is unexpected. It's beautiful that way. It's something that needs to be cherished. I need you to promise me that you will always look out for my little girl. That you will always love her, protect her, you will never hurt her again, even if you think it's the right thing to do. Can you promise me that?"

I nodded. "Yes, ma'am," I murmured high enough to where she could hear me.

"Okay." The instant relief on her face was like looking at a completely different woman. "I love you, Jacob."

I swallowed back the tears. "I love you, too." I kissed her hand, feeling like a weight had been lifted off my shoulders.

Lily

My mom passed away one week after Jacob arrived.

I spent every waking moment by her side, getting in as much time with her as possible. Silently praying that when she did die, it would be a little less painful, that the hurt I felt in my heart would ease just a little bit. Something, anything that would take away the empty feeling I felt every time I thought about her not seeing me get married, not meeting my kids and teaching them all the things she taught me. That was the hardest pill to swallow. I had been thinking about my wedding since I was a kid, what my dress would look like, how I would style my hair, the decorations on the tables, my color schemes, the list was endless. My mom was there in each and every scenario. I never imagined she wouldn't be there.

She was gone.

Forever.

She wasn't coming back.

I stared at the black dress on my bed that I bought for the funeral today. I wanted something I could throw away after wearing it. Something I would never have to look at again. I had been staring at it for the last hour, dreading putting it on. I knew once I did, all of this would be really happening. I was actually getting ready to attend my mom's funeral.

"You don't have to wear that, Kid," Jacob announced, leaning against my doorframe with his hands in his slacks.

"You look handsome. You clean up nice."

"You can wear whatever you want. Your mom would want it that way."

"I don't think I can put anything on. It doesn't matter what it is. I know what's it's for, so it doesn't change anything," I whispered so low I didn't think he could hear me.

He looked at me with an expression I had never seen before then he moved from the door frame to close it. He walked toward me, reaching his hands out for me to take.

I did.

"I'll help you get through this day, Lily," he coaxed, kissing the top of my head.

He slowly took off my dress, leaving me in nothing but my bra and panties. There wasn't anything sexual about the way he looked at me or handled me. He grabbed the black dress off the hanger and told me to lift my arms, gently easing it down my body, helping me with my shoes next and then combed my hair for me. The gesture brought me to tears.

He stood in front of me when he was done, swiping my hair from my face, placing it behind my ears.

"You look beautiful."

Forbid Me

"I don't feel beautiful."

I heard Alex's mom yell for us and he grabbed my hand, whispering all sorts of reassuring things to me before we left my bedroom. I barely remember any of it as I blankly stared at the hearse in front of us the entire drive to the church. I sat in between my dad and Lucas, Alex by Lucas's side and Jacob on the other side of her. I sat in a trancelike state the entire service. Everyone paid their condolences to us and all I did was nod when they were done.

If I heard, "I'm sorry for your loss," one more fucking time I was going to scream at whoever said it to me.

Lucas handed me my guitar at the funeral. I almost forgot I was singing This Little Light of Mine, a song my mom used to sing to us as kids as they lowered her coffin into the ground. There was no getting lost in the symmetry of the lyrics or the strings vibrating against my fingers that time.

Nothing but an empty feeling.

I was empty now.

After the funeral was over, I stayed seated in my chair, watching as they shoveled dirt onto my mom's new home.

"Let's go," Jacob said, standing beside my chair.

I raised my eyes to him and that's when someone caught my attention.

Austin.

He was standing in front of Lucas and Alex with some girl, dressed in a black pencil skirt and a matching colored shirt. Her sleeves were rolled up and I could see tattoos on her forearms. She was in sky-high heels and her hair was a dark shade of purple. She was beautiful in a hard and edgy kind of way.

"Who is that?"

Jacob followed my gaze. "That's Briggs, I'm assuming she's Austin's girlfriend."

That's when I took a good look at Austin. He was covered in tattoos now too, he appeared older, taller, and much broader than I remembered. I hadn't seen him in three years. No one had. We made our way over to him and when he hugged me, I swear I felt all of his remorse for not saying goodbye to my mom. They talked for a few minutes and then my brother said we had to go.

My mom was adamant that she didn't want anyone to mourn her death. She wanted us to celebrate her life. There was a get together at Alex parent's restaurant after the funeral. I don't remember much about it. All the faces seemed to blend together, my emotions becoming numb. I watched the good ol' boys, all four of them together for the first time in three years, their Half-Pint right beside them as they all stood on the beach.

For the first time, I didn't feel like I belonged anymore. I was like an outsider looking in. That's when I took one last look at them…

And left.

"Good to see you, man," Austin said, taking me away from my thoughts as I looked around for Lily.

"Likewise, bro. Where you been?"

"Everywhere."

"With the girl?" I nodded towards Briggs.

"For the most part."

"She looks like trouble."

"In more ways than one. You have no idea, man. I guess there's something about us good ol' boys and our women," he implied.

I stared at him not saying anything, because honestly what could I say to that? I scanned the area again looking for any sign of Lily while still giving my attention to Austin.

"Listen, man, I know." He nervously scratched the back of his head. "I know we… fuck… this was a lot easier in my head," he chuckled. "It wasn't my goddamn business. Lily… well, she's Lily. To know her is to love her."

I nodded understanding what he meant all too well. It was.

"She would be lucky to have you, Jacob. You both would," he said with sincerity in his voice.

"I wish it were that easy."

I was starting to get worried about Lily. I couldn't find her anywhere and now was not the time for her to be alone.

"Then it wouldn't be worth it," he simply stated, once again taking me away from my thoughts of her.

My eyes widened, surprised with how grown up Austin seemed. Maybe it was a good thing that he left. He definitely wasn't the same guy he was before he disappeared.

"Anyway, I gotta get back to Briggs." He motioned towards her.

"You sticking around for a while?"

He shrugged. "We'll see."

He smacked my chest a few times and left, and I looked back at the party with still no sign of Lily…

I knew where she would be.

Chapter 32
JACOB

then

It didn't take long for me to find her down the beach by the pier. Her hair blowing in the wind as the sun was setting, she looked fucking beautiful on the outside, but on the inside I knew she was dying.

I sat down beside her, placing my ball cap on her head.

"When is it going to go away?" she faintly asked, not taking her gaze off the waves in front of us.

"I wish I could tell you, Kid."

"There's so many things that I didn't get to say to her." Her voice laced with nothing but pain.

"She knows them already, Lily. She even knew about us, baby. It doesn't make everything that's happened between us right, but it makes me feel better knowing I had her blessing."

"I know, we talked about it. She told me to live my life, whatever that may be. Follow my heart, that it would lead the way. All that mattered was that I was happy."

"I agree."

"Liar. If you actually thought that, you wouldn't be doing this to us," she wept. "Everything hurts right now. I don't know what it feels like to not hurt anymore. It's a part of me now. I feel like I'm dying all the time, like a little bit of my air is being taken from my lungs each day, just enough to where I know it's missing. It's leaving me. And there's nothing I can do about it, knowing it's happening and I can't stop it. All I'm doing is waiting for the day where I can't breathe anymore," she cried, tears flowing down her cheeks, landing in the sand beneath her.

"Look at me, Kid. You have me. I am here," I reminded her, trying desperately to make her see she was not alone in this.

Forbid Me

"How do I forget about her? How do I forget about you? How do I go back to being that carefree girl that I was, when the two people I love the most are gone?"

"Please, Lily, don't say that."

She peered down at the sand and that's when it all became too much for her. She lost it. She bawled hysterically, her body shaking so bad with each sob. I don't think she even noticed when I shifted her onto my lap, hugging her tight against my body. Rocking with her, wanting to comfort her the only way I could. Expressing all sorts of soothing comforts, over and over again. It didn't help, her sobbing only became worse, her body nearly convulsing. I didn't know what to do.

"Baby... please... you're scaring the hell out of me right now." I hugged her tighter, her face hiding from me in the nook of my neck.

"I feel like I'm dying, Jacob. I feel like I'm fucking dying," she said, on the verge of hyperventilating.

"I know, sweet girl, I know. I wish I could take away your pain."

I could feel her physically crumbling, breaking apart in my very own arms, every part of her collapsing into a pile of nothing through sobs that will forever haunt me. I grabbed her face, needing to look into her eyes, trying to have her find her way back to me. She tried to push my hands away, moving her face around.

"Look at me. Stop fucking fighting me," I ordered.

"I can't," her tone flat and desolate.

"Look at me, Lillian."

Our eyes locked, except for the first time there was no light in hers. My Lily was gone and all that was left was her soulless body.

"I need you. Do you understand me? You can't leave me. I won't make it without you. I love you, Lily. I love you so fucking much it physically kills me," I whispered into her mouth.

She closed her eyes as if what I was saying was causing her even more pain.

"No!" I shouted. "You don't get to hide from me. Do you hear me?"

She shook her head not opening her eyes. I gripped her body, tighter like I was trying to mold us together.

Into one person.

"Open your eyes. Open your eyes and look at me. Look at my truths, look into my eyes, everything you want, everything you've known for years is there. Just fucking look at me."

She bit her lip and reluctantly opened her eyes.

"I. Love. You," I repeated and she sucked in air, her breath shuddering.

"Do you hear me? You. Have. Me."

I kissed her forehead, her cheeks, her neck, I wanted to kiss her everywhere all at once. I wanted to keep her there with me. When I kissed her lips, she let me, her mouth opened for me. I felt the silkiness of her tongue and the salty taste of her tears. I didn't feel her, my Lily. She was just giving me her body. I placed my forehead on hers and looked deep into her eyes. I didn't see it anymore, the light, the love, the happiness, that was for me, and it was fucking gone. Her eyes were just as beautiful as every time I looked into them, they were just no longer alive and full of life.

They were no longer for me.

I had ruined it.

I ruined everything.

"Please, don't do this," I whimpered in a voice I didn't even recognize, I was on the verge of tears. "My sweet girl…" I pleaded, grabbing her cheek.

Nothing.

Not. One. Fucking. Thing.

"I want to go home now."

I nodded with tears in my eyes.

"Okay, baby, I'll take you home."

I kissed her head one last time and took her home.

Lily

It had been ten days since my mom died, I know because I had been counting. My brother wouldn't let me out of his sight, barely leaving me alone for more than five minutes. My dad threw himself back into work, and all I tried to do was keep breathing. Jacob left to go back to school a few days after the funeral, saying

235

that the last thing he wanted to do was leave, but his leave of absence from school was up and if he didn't go back they would fail him out of his classes. I didn't care. I barely paid him any mind while he was here after the funeral anyway. He was as bad as my brother and at least now I only had one of them on my ass. I withdrew from my college classes the second the doctor told us about my mom's prognosis, and I had no intention of going back anytime soon. My mom's life insurance policy paid out in the next few weeks and my dad didn't want any of the money.

Not one dime.

She had a million dollar policy that was being split between Lucas and I. To be honest, I didn't want the damn money either, and I knew my brother felt the same. At the end of the day, it's what my mom wanted. She was adamant that we take the money and do what we wanted with it. All I knew was that I was donating fifty thousand of it to breast cancer awareness and so was my brother. My dad was setting up an appointment with a financial advisor for us, and I would just let them handle it. He was upset I wasn't going back to school, but I was an adult now and there wasn't much he could do about it. Being in my house was becoming suffocating, I had even crashed at Lucas's a few times with the hope that it would take away some of the ache.

It didn't.

I didn't know anything anymore. For the first time in my life...

I felt lost.

"Lily, you have to get off this couch today," Lucas announced, walking into the room with Mason.

"Lee Lee." He ran to me.

"Hey, little dude." I picked him up and sat him on my lap, hugging him tight. He scooted off my lap to go to his toys on the floor.

"Lily, you know you can crash here as long as you want, but you have to move from the couch every day. Your ass is leaving a permanent indent in it," he laughed, I didn't. "You have to do something, anything."

I shrugged, changing the channel to Elmo, and Mason crawled back up on my lap. We watched Elmo for the rest of the day together.

Much to my brother's disapproval.

"Hello," I answered my cell phone.

"Hey, man," Lucas replied.

"How are you?"

"Been better."

"I know, bro, it's going to take some—"

"It's not me," he interrupted. "I can throw myself into work, into Mason, I have stuff that can keep my head occupied. I can keep going. It's my baby sister, man. My dad's kind of lost in his head, and I guess he's doing what I am. Lily is… fuck I don't even know."

"I know. I've been texting with her on and off, but she doesn't answer or return any of my calls. Alex says she's getting the same non-response from her."

"Yeah, Dylan too. But it's actually why I'm calling. I need your help. Do you think maybe she can come to San Francisco, stay with you for a few days? Maybe it will help take her mind off things."

"Have you told her about this?"

"Not yet. I'm sure she would love it. She needs to get her ass off my couch. You know she loves to be around family. You're like another brother to her, Jacob. It's not going to be a problem, I know it."

Yeah… some brother I am.

"Alex and I… we're umm… do you think you could tell her? That way she can spend some time with Alex too while she's there."

I wanted to ask Lucas what happened between him and Alex. They seemed to be attached at the hip during the days leading to the funeral.

I didn't. Hell, it was none of my damn business, and I was going through my own shit.

I already felt guilty enough for ruining both Ryder's lives.

"You know Lily is welcome here anytime. You don't have to ask."

"Thanks, man," he sighed, relieved. "I'm just going to book her flight, pack her a bag, tell her we're going to dinner and drop her off at the airport instead. I'll carry her on the fucking plane if I have to."

I nervously chuckled. "I thought you said she would love to come."

"Under normal circumstances yes, right now? I don't fucking know anymore."

"Text me her flight information, and I'll be there."

"Sounds good. Thanks again, brother."

I hung up.

Excited to see Lily but never expecting the girl that got off the plane.

Lily

I sat on the plane fucking livid.

I had never been so pissed before.

Lucas stole my wallet, only giving me my license so I couldn't take a taxi back home. There was no one I could call. I had to take the damn flight. He said Jacob would be picking me up from the airport, he said this would be good for me. He said a whole bunch of bullshit that I didn't listen to because I tuned him out after he said Jacob's name. The plane landed at four pm, I purposely took forever to get down to baggage claim.

Jacob was already standing there looking fucking handsome as ever with my bag already sitting by him.

"Hey, Kid," he greeted as I walked up to him.

"Hi."

He pulled me into a hug, but I kept my arms down by my sides, I didn't want to be there. I didn't care if I was acting like a child. I was mad at both of them for doing this to me. Especially without my damn consent.

"How was your flight?"

I shrugged, walking beside him out of the airport.

He glanced over at me. "Are you hungry?"

I shrugged again and he grabbed my arm, turning me to face him.

"Is this how it's going to be for the next week?"

"I don't know, Jacob, you tell me. Since you and my brother are so great at planning my life, you can tell me how I'm supposed to act."

His eyes widened like he wasn't expecting me to lash out, but it was quickly replaced with a small grin. "Dinner it is then."

"I'm not hungry," I immediately replied.

"Kid, stop being a little shit. Just let me fucking feed you."

"Fine." I smiled. "It's your money, Lucas took all of mine." I opened the door and got in his car.

She didn't say one word at dinner.

I tried to initiate several conversations with nothing more than a shrug in response. She played around with her food, rolling it around her plate with her fork. She looked thinner than the last time I saw her, her eyes still vacant of life but full of sorrow. She looked empty and all I craved was that little piece of light that I loved so much about her. I rented movies for us to watch, thinking maybe she would let me hold her, try to comfort her, but she sat on the furthest couch from me. She passed out pretty early into the movie, and that's when I remembered Lucas said she hadn't been sleeping. I carried her to my bedroom and she had never felt so light before. She didn't stir when I laid her on the bed, placing the blankets on top of her. I sat on the edge of the bed, staring at her for I don't know how long.

The next thing I knew it was light out, and I'm brushing the sleep out of my eyes to find Lily looking at me with an unrecognizable stare.

I looked around the room, realizing I had fallen asleep at the bottom of the bed. She was still tucked in the same place I laid her in last night. At least now she looked somewhat rested, but the glow she always had about her was still gone. I was beginning to wonder if I would ever see it again.

"I must have passed out. I had every intention to sleep on the couch," I let her know.

"It's your bed."

I ignored her snarky comment, looking at the clock on the nightstand. "Damn, it's noon. You slept for fourteen hours, Kid."

"So."

"I just meant that's great. Lucas says you haven't been sleeping."

"You have a comfortable bed. It has nothing to do with you."

I sat up, shocked as shit by her reply. "Excuse me? Want to try that again?"

"Why? You heard me the first time."

I scoffed. "Who are you talking to, Lily?"

"You. You're the only person in the room."

I opened my mouth but quickly shut it, keeping my temper at bay. I had to remember she was still in mourning. She had been through a lot. I needed to cut her some slack when I wanted nothing more than to throw her over my knee and remind her who she was speaking to.

I stood. "I'm going to take a shower and make some breakfast. You're free to join me if you want." I walked away.

"To the shower or the breakfast? Because neither sounds very appealing."

I froze. Now she was just fucking provoking me.

Take a breather, Jacob, she's hurting. Her mom just died. Breathe… it's not you. It's her pain.

I spun to face her. "Kid, you need to eat. You're rail thin. After you eat, you can come back and lay in bed, I don't fucking care. But I will feed you while you're here. Do you understand me?"

She narrowed her eyes at me in a destructive kind of way. "What about the other thing? Or does my rail thin body not do it for you anymore? At least I'm not a kid anymore. Or do you just find excuses not to be with me? What, Jacob, do I need to gain weight for your feelings to come back?"

"Come back? What the fu—"

"If you're not going to take a shower then I am." She jumped out of bed and went right into the bathroom, ending our argument as abruptly as it started.

The rest of the day she barely spoke to me. She carried on like that for the next three days. It didn't matter what I did or what I said, her behavior didn't change. I had to keep reminding myself that she was hurting. That it was her pain spewing out hurtful things and that it had nothing to do with me. I was allowing her to take out her frustrations on me and as much as she fucking provoked me to reply, I played nice.

For now.

Alex came to hang out with her while I was at school. She said Lily hadn't really been talking to her much either. No one seemed to be able to get through to her so I decided to try something different. I ordered her favorite kind of pizza, pineapple and pepperoni. I couldn't stand that shit, but I would try anything at that point. I rented an obscene amount of chick flicks and even picked up some of her favorite ice cream, mango apricot sorbet. It took three different stores to find the damn thing, but I was hoping it would all be worth it. I wanted to see her smile. Once. That would be enough for me.

I was sitting on the couch with everything laid out on the coffee table when she came out from my room after she took a shower. She froze as soon as she saw the spread on the table, but her expression didn't give away anything she was feeling. She just sort of stood there.

"I thought we could hang out tonight like we used to," I said, breaking the silence between us.

"Why?"

"I miss you. I'm worried about you."

"Of course. That's always your motive."

"Kid, if you're finally going to talk to me, I'm going to need you to not speak in fucking code."

"Fine, then I won't talk to you at all." She spun and I was over to her and turning her to face me before she even took her first step.

"Enough of this bullshit. I have been giving you space, time, letting you be. But there's only so much I can take. I have reached my goddamn breaking point with you. I get it, okay? You're hurting, Lily. Everyone is. But you don't see all of us shutting people out and saying shitty things. I don't know what more I can do for you."

"I didn't ask to come here. I don't need you to babysit me. I don't even want to be here."

"Then what do you want, Lily? Because no one fucking knows, not even me."

"Especially not you! You never know anything about me! So that's nothing new."

"Is that right?" I gritted out.

"Yes." She tried to pull her arm away, but I wouldn't let her, only holding her tighter.

"Let go of me!"

"Not until you tell me why you're acting like a little shit."

She didn't falter. "Fuck you."

I immediately yanked her toward me and she lost her footing. I grabbed both of her arms and sat her up on the counter, placing my body in between her legs. She tried to move away, but I held her firmly down with my hands around her waist, she wasn't going anywhere unless I wanted her to.

"Let's try this again. Stop testing me, little girl, because I promise you it won't end well for you. Now, what the hell is your problem? I know this can't all be about your mom."

Silence.

"For fucks sake, Kid, just tell me," I urged.

"You can't do this!" she yelled. "You can't—"

"Try and stop me, Lily."

She tried to shove me away, tried my hands, my body, anything for her to be able to break free and run away. "You always do this. You always manhandle me, it's not fair!"

I gripped her hands, locking them by her sides and she screamed out in frustration, whipping her body around.

"What's not fair, Kid? That you love it? Is that what's not fair?"

"No!"

"We can do this your way or we can do it mine? But either way, you'll fucking tell me."

She thrashed a little bit more until she realized she wasn't going anywhere. "You're being a dick!"

"Unlucky for you... I don't give a fuck." I gripped her inner thighs, right in the middle for the first time, exactly how her mom told me to do, and she immediately stopped. We locked eyes, the realization of what I was about to do was clearly written across her face.

I grinned.

Squeezed, and she lost her shit.

Lily

I kicked, my legs flaying everywhere, my body shaking uncontrollably. I bit my lip so damn hard I thought it was going to bleed.

I would not laugh. I could not laugh.

Which only made him squeeze harder, twitching his fingers right on the muscle to the point of pain. It was like when you hit your damn funny bone, it hurt like a son of a bitch, but it made you laugh from the sting. I couldn't take it anymore and I squealed, laughing hysterically and screaming all at the same time. His body firmly locked on mine, the counter giving him the advantage to torture me mercifully and with no remorse.

"Spill it and I'll stop." The enjoyment in his tone was evident.

He pressed harder, my throat burned and my voice sounded hoarse.

"You have five seconds to stop being a stubborn little shit before I really have no mercy on you at all. Five... four..."

I fought harder and laughed louder.

"Three... two..."

"I waited so long," I screamed out, trying to catch my breath, and he finally fucking stopped.

"For what?" he impatiently added.

I breathed heavily, in and out, my chest rising and falling with my heart pounding out of my chest. My body hot all over with sweat forming at my temples. I swallowed the saliva that had pooled in my mouth.

"For. What?" he repeated, gripping my sore thighs just a little. The expression on his face quickly turned heated.

"God, Jacob, for someone who is going to be a lawyer, you sure can't catch a clue." I took a deep breath, my lip quivering from what I was about to say. "I waited so damn long to hear you say those three words to me, and when you finally do it... when you finally say it to me... I'm at my lowest. I don't need your pity. I was hurting enough. You didn't have to add to it."

His face frowned with confusion. "What the fuck are you talking about?"

"Oh my God, do I have to spell it out for you? You told me you loved me because my mom died. I was falling apart in front of you and you told me you loved me to only make me feel better. I never wanted it to be that way. I wanted you to mean it the first time you said it to me, not because you felt bad for me."

He shook his head, and I couldn't get a good look at his face before he lifted me off the counter, carrying me as if I weighed nothing to the couch. He sat us down together, making me straddle his lap and grabbing my chin so that I would look at him.

"That's what you think?" he asked, looking staggered that I could even think that.

"How do you expect me not to think that? You looked at me with pity, not with love," I countered.

"You know me, Kid. You know me better than that."

"I thought I did. I hoped I did. It was just too much, Jacob. You lied to me for a whole year, making me think that you fell in love with someone else. Do you have any idea what that did to me? How that made me feel? Then you bring her and flaunt her in my face? That's just cruel, even if I knew the truth. What if I didn't?"

"I wanted you to hate me." He sighed his expression fill with nothing but remorse.

"I did," I paused to let my words sink in. "But I also loved you. I never stopped loving you, and I hated you more for that. Then my mom took a turn for the worse and then her funeral... it was one thing after another. I never expected you to say it to me that day. Not like that. Not ever like that. That's not the way I wanted it, I never wanted to look back and remember that you told me you loved me for the first time the day of my mom's funeral because you pitied—"

"I love you."

My lips parted and my eyebrows rose. I wasn't expecting that.

"I. Love. You," he repeated with so much conviction.

I didn't know what to say. I barely knew what to feel.

"That day was one of the worst days of my life, Lily. I had never seen you so lost, so empty. It scared the living shit out of me. I didn't pity you, sweet girl. I had wanted to say it for years. Having you break down, crumbling to pieces in my arms, feeling your pain. I had to say it to you at that moment. I love you. I've always loved you."

Looking deep into his green eyes, I could see his truths. I took in his words, each and every one of them since my mom's prognosis.

"I love you, too. Of course, you already know that, though," I half-laughed and so did he.

I bit my lip suddenly nervous. Jacob reached over and eased it out of my mouth, tracing it back and forth with his thumb. I don't know what came over me, but I started to trace his thumb with the tip of my tongue. His eyes dilated, watching me with a predatory gleam in his eyes. I sucked it into my mouth, gently biting down on it. He let his thumb linger for a few seconds, not breaking our eye contact as I twirled my tongue around it, loving the effect I had on him.

He suddenly pulled it out of my mouth, reaching around and roughly gripping the back of my neck. My breath hitched as his mouth collided with mine.

Kissing Lily after all that time was like coming home.
She was my home.
So pure, so innocent, so angelic.
So *mine*.
She possessed my thoughts.
She owned my heart.
She fueled my wants and desires.

"You're so fucking beautiful," I groaned, wanting to claim every inch of her body.

I touched her face, her lips, her neck, stopping once I reached her heart. It was pounding profusely, beating rapidly against my fingers.

"It's yours." She reached for the hem of her shirt and lifted it over her head, throwing it on the floor beside us. "I'm yours. Always."

"Lil—"

"Please, Jacob, don't make me beg."

I growled, kissing her fervently and lifting her off the couch. I kicked open my bedroom door and laid her body down on the bed, never breaking our connection. I took off her bra, tossed it aside and her panties quickly followed, leaving her completely naked for me. I leaned back to take in her beautiful body, touching her soft silky skin. She had the softest fucking skin I had ever felt.

"I love you. I love you so damn much," I expressed again, wanting to brand it in her heart and soul.

"Prove it to me," she panted. Ready for whatever I had planned to do to her. I peered up at her face and all I could see was yearning in a way that had never been there before.

"Make love to me," she pleaded in a raspy tone. "I belong to you. I've always belonged to you. Please, Jacob—"

"Shhh…" I leaned in, whispering against her lips. "Let me take care of you. I don't want to hurt you." I kissed her one last time before I made my way down her body, kissing and softly licking every inch of her skin.

"Jacob," she murmured, her body shuddering as I brought her pussy to the edge of the bed. I gently kissed around her thighs, blowing air the closer I got to where she wanted me the most. My hands gripped her thighs as I lightly pecked her clit, spreading soft kisses all around her mound. Her hands instantly went into my hair. I opened her wider, lightly kissing and licking all around her heat. I could already taste her on my tongue. Her breathing escalated as I took her clit into my mouth, moving my head in a side-to-side motion.

I never took my eyes off her as I watched her grasp the sheets so fucking hard from her climax building higher and higher. That's when I eased my finger inside, she was so fucking wet. I tried to push a second finger in, wanting to stretch her as much as I could. Knowing it didn't matter what I did, it was still going to be painful for her. I could feel her getting close when her hips started moving on their own against my fingers and tongue.

"That's it, baby, fuck my face like you love." Not a minute later I tasted her climax, and I didn't stop until she was shattering above me, holding her legs down and begging me to stop. I stood, and with hooded eyes she watched me undress. I opened my nightstand and grabbed a condom.

"You don't need that. I'm on the pill. It regulates my period. Have you been tested?"

I crawled my way up her body, positioning myself at her entrance.

"I'm clean, I've always used a condom."

She beamed.

"Tell me if I'm hurting you."

She nodded, biting her bottom lip as I gently pushed in, the feel of her wrapped around me, inch by inch, was immediate and almost too much to bear. I could tell I was hurting her by the look on her face. I reached down and rubbed her already sensitive nub, her breathing hitched and her lips parted. Making her pussy much fucking tighter.

"Are you okay?" I thrust in a little more.

"Mmm…" was all she could reply.

"I'm almost there. Fuck, baby, you're so fucking tight."

"I'm sorry," she breathed out.

I laughed against her lips. "You're mine. Forever mine."

I had never been with a virgin before, never gone unprotected either. The fact that I was experiencing it with Lily was the best thing that had ever happened to me.

She was the best thing that had ever happened to me.

I took a moment when I was fully inside of her, leaning back to take a good look at her, wanting to remember her just this way, always. Her long silky brown hair spread all over my sheets, the way her cheeks were slightly flushed and how the blush crept down to her neck, how her lips were swollen from my touch and her serene eyes glazed over.

So beautiful.

So fucking beautiful.

So fucking mine.

Forbid Me

I placed a soft kiss on the pulse on her neck, loving the feel of it beating against my lips. Her dark brown eyes watched me adoringly as I took what I needed.

What she gave.

I peered up at her and she shyly smiled while I kissed my way down to her breasts, taking her perfect round nipple into my mouth, making her moan.

I fucking loved it when she moaned. It made my cock twitch inside her.

"Jacob, come up here. I want to feel all your weight on me."

I placed my body completely on hers, like I knew she loved, caging her in with my arms around her head so that my hands could caress her face. My torso touching her chest and my legs firmly locked beside hers. Every time I thrust in she could feel the mass of my body movement, inclining her a little higher each time. I softly kissed her, taking my time with each stroke of my tongue as it weaved with hers. Savoring the velvety feel of my mouth claiming hers, thrusting in and out of her tight wet core a few times before I pulled away needing to look into her eyes again. I loved seeing every emotion I felt through her gaze. It mirrored every feeling that was displayed inside of me, to a degree I never quite understood, but I didn't care because it was there.

It was for me.

Just. For. Me.

My thumb brushed against her cheek, and she smiled as I kissed the tip of her nose, thrusting a little faster. I positioned my knee a little higher and her leg inclined with mine. Her breathing elevated, and I knew I was hitting her sweet spot better from that angle.

"Does that feel good?"

"Yes... it still stings, but it feels good."

I reached down and played with her clit again.

"Yes... that's... that's so much better... ah..."

I gently grabbed the back of her neck to keep our eyes locked. My forehead hovered above hers as we caught our breaths, trying to find our perfect rhythm.

"Don't close your eyes."

She nodded, panting profusely, her heart pounding against mine. Her body started to tremble, and I brought her lips to meet mine, pushing my tongue into her eager, awaiting mouth.

"Say it," I growled in between kissing her.

"Jacob," she breathed out, and I swear my cock got harder.

Our mouths parted and now we were both panting uncontrollably, desperately trying to cling onto every sensation of our skin on skin contact. I felt myself start to come apart and she was right there with me.

"I love you." I found myself saying before I even gave it any thought.

"Jacob, Jacob, Jacob," she repeated over and over, climaxing all down my shaft and taking me right over with her. I shook with my release and passionately claimed her mouth once again.

Mine.

Chapter 33

Lily

then

"Wow, so that's what the big fuss is about, huh?" I asked as he hovered above me, looking down at me with so much love in his eyes that it made me weak in the knees.

"No, baby, that's just with me."

I smiled.

"Did I hurt you?"

I shook my head, loving the weight of him on top of me. "It hurt a little bit at first, but I knew that was going to happen. That was the best thing that's ever happened to me."

"To us, baby. To us."

"There's an us?"

"There's always been an us."

"Does this mean… I mean are we… do you—"

"I'm never leaving you again. I love you."

My heart soared. It's everything I ever wanted to hear coming from his lips.

"Do you mean that?" I needed to hear him say it.

"You're mine, Lily."

We stayed like that for I don't know long, but the next thing I knew it was morning and I was wrapped in his arms, both of us still naked. I felt like I had run a fucking marathon. My body sore all over. I moved my leg a little higher, my eyes widening, but Jacob was already awake and staring down at me.

"How is my friend up already? I played with him last night."

"He's addicted to you like I am."

I grinned.

"Are you sore?"

I nodded. "I am, but it's the good kind of sore."

He smiled, rubbing the back of my head.

"What time is it?"

He looked over at the clock. "Shit. Almost noon. What is it with you and me sleeping in all morning?"

"That's what lobsters do," I simply stated.

"I love you."

I beamed, I couldn't help it. My heart soared every time I heard it.

"I don't want to leave," I expressed, remembering that I'd leave in three days.

"I'm coming back with you."

"You are?" I asked, sitting up, taking the sheet with me.

"Lily, I've stayed away all these years for a reason. I made both our lives miserable for a reason. I was not supposed to be with you like this, but now that I've had you… there's no going back. I meant what I said last night. You're fucking mine," he stated, possession laced in his tone.

"So where do we go from here?"

"I have less than a year and I will be finished with law school. We will make it work. I'm coming back with you to talk to Lucas, talk to your dad. Let them know what's going on. What's been going on for years, Kid."

"Really? You promise?"

"I won't lie to you again. I can't."

I jumped on him so fast that if he weren't sitting up against the headboard we would have fallen back. I straddled his lap, my entire body laying on him, hugging him so tight.

"You make me so happy!" I sat up, looking at him. "We're really going to do this? For real this time? All of it?"

He nodded, gazing at me with adoration and love in his eyes.

"My dad probably already knows. My mom knew, there's no way she didn't tell my dad."

"It doesn't matter. I'll take care of it. I'll take care of you, baby."

I licked my lips, my mouth suddenly dry. "My brother… Lucas is…"

Forbid Me

"I'll handle everything. Don't worry about Lucas, don't worry about anything. I promise, Lily, everything will be okay from now on. I'll make this right."

"I really want to kiss you." I grinned. "But I have to brush my teeth."

He laughed, grabbed the back of my neck and kissed me anyway. We showered together for the first time. He did all sorts of incredible things with his tongue as he backed me up against the tile wall and then again in his bed. We spent the entire day in there, exploring our bodies in ways we never had before. I loved every second of it. Never wanting this moment to end.

The next three days went by entirely too fast. He showed me around a few places in San Francisco. He was adamant that we couldn't stay in bed the entire time, even though that's all I wanted to do. I had turned into a minx, as Jacob called me, but he definitely made up for lost time, spending most of his time inside me. We christened his entire apartment and then some, with him always making sure that I was okay after. It was the sweetest side I had ever seen of him, and it made me wonder how many things I still would learn about him.

The possibilities were endless.

I blinked and it was Sunday, but it didn't matter because Jacob was coming back with me. He was going to drop me off at home first so I could spend some time with my dad and Lucas. He already texted Lucas telling him he wanted to meet up at Alex's parents restaurant for breakfast the following morning. He wanted to talk to Lucas by himself first. He didn't want me there. Same thing with my dad, he was going to stop by his office around lunchtime. Talk to both of them, let them know what was going on, and then hopefully by Monday night we would have their blessing.

We could move forward…

Together.

I would be lying if I said I wasn't nervous. Not so much about my dad, but definitely about Lucas. This would probably be the hardest news to swallow. Jacob said he wanted to be completely honest with both of them, tell them what we had been doing on and off for the last several years. He was over all the lying, and I prayed the truth would set us free. I was prepared for the worst, though, I didn't want to lose my brother, not after everything we just went through. Him and my dad were all I had left. I couldn't lose them.

But for Jacob...

For Jacob I would.

I loved him that much.

I loved him more than anything.

He rented a car when we got to the airport, saying it would be easier for him to get around. He held my hand the whole ride back to my house, the anxiety and nervousness radiating off of me though Jacob was calm and collected. He didn't seem to have a care in the world. If anything he looked happier than I had seen him in a long time. The burden of all of our lies about to disappear. It was like he had found peace.

By the time Jacob pulled into my driveway it was three pm.

"Everything will be okay, Kid. I promise. Relax. The next time I see you there will be no more secrets. Do you understand me?"

I nodded because I couldn't find the words to express how I really felt and it didn't matter, he already knew.

He kissed me deeply, grabbing the sides of my face the way I loved.

"I love you, Lillian. Don't ever forget that. I'll call you later, and I'll see you tomorrow night.

"Okay." I bit my lip and got out of the car. Jacob helped me with my bag, kissed me one more time and stepped back into the car.

"Jacob!" I enthusiastically shouted before he took off.

He stopped, cocking his head to the side.

"I love you, too."

He smiled. "Bye, sweet girl."

I watched him leave and went inside, counting down the hours till tomorrow night.

I wasn't nervous.

For years I thought I would be. It was different now. I had her mom's blessing and as cheesy as that sounded it made me feel better. I knew her dad had to know something, maybe not to the extent her mom did, but enough to where he wouldn't be surprised to see me standing in his office. Lucas on the other hand would be a fucking time bomb. There was no question about that, and I didn't even want to guess how he would react. It didn't matter. I would take every blow, verbal or physical. I would be coming back for her, with or without his consent.

I was praying he would understand.

My parents' cars weren't in the driveway. It was still fairly early, so I assumed they were at the farm in town like they were every Sunday since I was a kid. I wanted to surprise them, I hadn't seen them since the funeral and I knew they were taking it just as hard as everyone else. They were all best friends. I unlocked the door and walked inside my house, leaving my luggage by the door and going into the kitchen. I grabbed a glass of water and made my way up to my parents' bedroom, needing to grab my social security card and my birth certificate from the safe for some internship applications.

I opened the door and stopped dead in my tracks. Instantly, the glass fell from my hand, shattering on the floor with glass shards and water spilling by my feet. Everything suddenly happened in slow motion.

"Fuck!" Dad shouted, pulling out of her and yanking up his pants. She shrieked, jumping off the bed, running around to grab her scattered clothes.

The fucking bastard doing the same.

I. Stopped. Breathing.

All I could see was my father as he fucked her from behind, her tits bouncing, gripping her hips as he slammed into her, both of them covered in sweat.

A woman...

A woman who wasn't my mother.

I recognized her as she ran past me and out of the room. She'd been working at the store for years. My mom…

Fuck, my mom.

That's when I lunged for him, shoving him up against the wall. "How could you do this to my mom? You piece of shit!"

"Jacob," he roughly gritted out, gripping my hands that were on his collared shirt.

"Answer me, goddamn it," I demanded through clenched teeth.

"Let. Go. Now," he ordered in a tone that I could never respect again.

I did, but not because I wanted to. I did it for my mom.

"I can't believe you're doing this." My hand gesturing to the bed. "In the house she made you a fucking home! In your goddamn bedroom! You're such a fucking bastard," I roared, ready to go at him again.

He put his hand out in front of him, knowing what I was thinking. "It's not what you think."

"It's not? I didn't just walk in on you fucking another woman?"

"Jacob… your mother and I. Jesus Christ." He rubbed his forehead. "It's been years. Years since we've been happy."

"So that excuses you having an affair? You can't be fucking serious?"

"She knows."

I jerked back like he had hit me with a goddamn sledgehammer.

"Your mother betrayed me."

"I don't understand. What the fuck are you talking about?"

"You wouldn't. I didn't want to tell you like this. I never wanted you to find out like this. I swear to you."

"What?"

He shook his head like he didn't want to say it.

"WHAT!" I yelled so fucking loud, pushing over the lamp and making him jump.

"A few years ago. Fuck… Jacob. Oh, God." He looked up at the ceiling.

"Just fucking say it!" I yelled at him, trying to keep my fists at my sides.

He looked deep into my eyes and spoke with conviction,

"I'm not your father."

"NO!" Mom screamed from behind me, making us both look back at her.

"How could you do this, Lee? How could you fucking do this to me? You said you would never tell him! You promised me he would never know! How could you betray me like that!" she shouted not moving from the door.

"Betrayal? Oh, come on, Ginger, you want to start talking about fucking betrayal?" Dad replied, both of them lost in their own conversation as my whole world came tumbling down.

"That's not what happened. I told you—"

"I don't fucking believe you! I've never fucking believed you! Why do you think I got a DNA test? How many times did I have to fucking hear from people that he looks nothing like me? From our friends, from our families, from goddamn strangers at the fucking park! Tell me! How many fucking times is it okay to hear that until you start to question it yourself?"

I sat down on the edge of the bed, I had to. Bile rising in my throat, my body giving out on me. I had heard that I didn't look anything like my father ever since I could remember, the boys, Alex, fuck... even Lily telling me we looked nothing alike.

Some kids don't look like their parents? Right? Isn't that normal?

"I never betrayed you, Lee. Never."

"What the fuck is going on? Someone needs to tell me before I lose it," I murmured loud enough for them to hear.

My mom watched me with an expression that will forever haunt me as if she was dying right in front of me.

Fuck... I couldn't go through this again.

"Tell him, Ginger, lie to your son like you have to me."

I looked at her with pleading eyes, and she bowed her head not being able to meet my gaze. "Jacob, you know your father and I had been friends for years before we got together. We all have... he had been pursuing me for months and I...I... I don't know. I was young. We both were. We were graduating from high school. Lily's mom and I... we went to a college party one night and we had been drinking. I met this guy, he was nice, God... I don't even remember his name. I barely remember what he looks like. It was all one big blur, it was over before it even started." Tears slid down her face, her body shaking.

"I'm so ashamed... I swear, Jacob, I wasn't like that... that's not who I was."

"Right, Ginger? Because you didn't spread your fucking legs for me three days later. You fucking trapped me, I was your ticket out of being a single mother."

I snapped.

I charged him. I rammed my body as hard as I could into the man who raised me like I was his own. To the man who I thought was my father for the last twenty-six years. To the man who I loved and respected. To the man who I know as nothing but my father.

"YOU DO NOT TALK TO HER LIKE THAT!" I yelled loud enough to break glass. His back hitting the wall with so much force that he broke through the drywall. I moved away from him, hunching over and dry heaving from the adrenaline on the floor. My mom immediately came toward me, rubbing my back, apologizing profusely.

"I swear, Jacob, I swear on your life that I didn't know. I never knew. I wouldn't do that to you or to your father. I swear on everything I didn't know. We used a condom. I didn't with your dad. Please, believe me…" she sobbed into my back.

My dad stumbled from the wall, shaking drywall off his body from the impact of my blow. I stood and we locked eyes.

"If you believe her, Jacob, you're a very stupid man."

I didn't falter, the emotion taking over. "It still doesn't excuse you fucking someone in our house. In the home you built a family. In the bed you have shared with my mother, your wife, for the past twenty-six years. This is your kid's home. This is the only house I've ever known. Now when I think of this place all it's going to make me feel is fucking sick. So no, Dad, it doesn't fucking excuse that. You tainted everything."

"Jacob, I—"

"Leave."

"Jacob—"

"Leave. I won't ask you again." I stepped toward him in a menacing way.

He shook his head, looking at me with disappointment in his eyes before he turned around and left. I walked to the bed, needing to sit down. My legs giving out on me, I didn't know anything anymore. I was in a daze where I couldn't feel, I couldn't see, I couldn't even fucking think.

Forbid Me

My mom sat in front of me on the balls of her feet. "Baby, please tell me you believe me."

I shook my head. *Was I crying? How long had I been crying?*

"Mom, I can't. I can't right now. Please don't ask me anything. Please...not now."

She nodded in understanding. I fell into her lap and cried like a fucking baby. I bawled for hours while she held onto me so tightly. Whispering soothing words of comfort and rocking me back and forth.

I didn't think about Mr. Ryder.

I didn't think about Lucas.

I didn't think about Lily.

All I thought about...

That I had no clue who I was.

They ripped me of my identity...

And they didn't even know it.

Lily

Jacob didn't call me last night and I figured it was because he was spending time with his parents. I left him alone the next day because I knew he was going to be with Lucas in the morning and then my dad after that. I didn't need to burden him with my worries, he was confident that everything was going to be okay and I didn't want to burst his bubble.

I trusted him.

I woke up early that morning, feeling like I hadn't slept the entire night. I watched the clock, counting down the hours until my dad got home, or till Lucas walked through the door. I watched for Jacob's car to pull up into my driveway. I waited for it all. When I heard my dad parking his car in the garage, I sat on the couch patiently waiting for him to walk inside and tell me everything was okay.

He walked inside like it was any other day. He kissed my head, asked how my day was, not mentioning Jacob at all. Not a word about his afternoon, or their talk, nothing. I immediately called my brother, mentally preparing myself for the wrath of Lucas. It never came. It was the same with him as my dad. I didn't mention the breakfast because I didn't know about it as far as Lucas was concerned. It didn't matter anyways, he didn't say a word about it either. He talked to me like he always did, nothing had changed. When I got off the phone with him, it was near eight o'clock.

What the fuck was going on?

I hadn't heard from Jacob, which was really unlike him. I told myself I was just being paranoid, but panic was creeping up on me. I couldn't shake this awful feeling. Maybe I was reading too much into it. He would never hurt me again. He wouldn't lie to me again.

He promised.

He loved me. He told me he loved me.

I waited…

I waited all night. Finally, my phone pinged with a text message and Jacob's name appeared on my screen. I smiled, for the first time that day, finally able to breathe again. My anxiety easing. I swiped over the screen and all it said was…

I'm sorry. I can't.

Chapter 34

Lily

now

"Oh my God, Jacob," I wept with tears falling down my face. "That's why you left?"

He nodded. There were no more words left for him to say.

"I can't... holy shit. Does anyone know?"

"Alex."

My eyes widened. "You told Alex and not me?"

"Not because I wanted to. Fuck, after I left, I knew I broke your heart. I knew there was no coming back from that. I couldn't lie to you again. If there was one promise I was going to keep it was that one. I wasn't ready to be honest with you either. So I shut you out. It took me almost two years to admit it to myself, Lily. Two fucking years of my life I spent trying to figure shit out. Trying to figure out who I was. I didn't know who to fucking believe. My parents were both in the wrong. Both of them fucked up. I couldn't talk about it with my sisters because they didn't even know. Do you have any idea what it felt like finding out that the man you thought was your father... isn't? And not even being able to contact the man who is, because your mother doesn't even remember his name?" he asked, trying to keep his composure calm as he sat in front of me in the living room.

"I was so mentally fucked up. You didn't deserve that. After everything I put you through, and with your mom's passing being so recent, I just couldn't put more on your shoulders. I didn't want you to have to deal with this too. I couldn't. I couldn't even admit it, Lily. I pretended my parents were getting a divorce because my dad had an affair, that's the only way I could look my mom in the face. I hated both of them. That's what killed me the most. I was in therapy up until a year ago. I threw myself into work. When Lucas and Alex got married, I was so fucking happy for them. Me, Kid." He placed his hand on his chest. "The same guy who kept them apart for years. I thought… no, I hoped that if they could find their way back to each other then so could we. After every obstacle they conquered, their love so consuming, it was that fucking powerful."

I took in everything he was saying, my heart breaking for him.

"I knew I was going to see you at their wedding, and it had only been less than a year since I found out the truth. I still couldn't face you. I waited, Kid. I waited on the curb until I saw you leave. You looked so fucking beautiful dressed in that soft pink dress, it was the first time I ever saw your hair curled. I almost got out of the damn car, but I couldn't get my legs to move. I was paralyzed. When I watched your car leave, I sat there for probably another hour just thinking about how fucked up everything was. I made up some excuse that my plane was delayed and that's why I was late, but when Alex told me that you had to leave early… I knew it was because of me. I knew you left because you didn't want to see me. Which helped me."

My face frowned, confused.

"It made me feel better that you didn't want to see me. Made me feel like maybe you weren't hurting as bad anymore. That maybe you found some peace. I hated my goddamn self for making you hate me. I wasn't the man you needed at that point. You leaving proved that to me." He took a deep breath, grabbing my hand to place gentle kisses on it.

"Alex showed up at my apartment a few weeks after I left you, I was drunk as shit. I think I spent the first six months in a haze, just moving on autopilot, trying my best to finish school. Alex called me every name in the book, told me that you were devastated. She tried to make me see that what I was doing was killing you inside. That you told her everything that had happened, that you bawled your eyes out until you passed out from the exhaustion. She asked how I could do that to you… I had never seen her so fucking livid before." He shook his head, ashamed. "I broke down, she caught me in a moment of weakness. I told her everything. She told me I needed to tell you. That you were moving away, going to Nashville. I couldn't. I wasn't ready. Alex knew it, too. She didn't pressure me or anything. She just listened. Stayed with me all night. We never talked about it again, not until recently. She's been telling me to tell you the truth since the third time you kicked me out, and I actually listened this time."

I smiled. "You kept count?"

He faintly grinned. "I never told the boys. They all had perfect families. The last thing I wanted was for them to feel sorry for me, when I already felt sorry for myself. I wanted to win you back first. On my own. Not because you felt bad for me. I didn't want you to take pity on me. I wanted you with me because you loved me. That we were finally together for the right reasons, I know it's wrong what we've been doing behind everyone's backs, but I just needed you to be mine again before we told anyone."

"So your mom really knew that your dad was having an affair? Why did they stay together all those years? I remember some of their fights, you used to talk to the boys about it."

"Yes and no. She suspected it, but I confirmed it. I think it was his way of punishing her."

I nodded not wanting to ask any more questions about it, sensing it might be opening old wounds.

"I stopped going to therapy a year ago because I finally believed her. My mom would never hurt our family like that. It's not in her. I'm her son and I knew that. My dad has known her for most of his life. He knows the truth in his heart. They got married after they found out she was pregnant, they had only been together three months at that point. Which is why my grandfather gave them the store, he was getting old and they took over everything. My mom says my dad has always felt like he could have done something more with his life, he was never happy. He did the paternity test when I was eleven, and that's when they're marriage went to shit. I think he used it as an excuse to get what he wanted, and that's why I can't forgive him. He will always be my father, Lily. Blood's not going to change that for me, but as of right now... I don't want anything to do with that bastard. Who's to say that won't change down the road but for right now, I'm okay. I'm finally fucking okay."

He smiled lovingly at me, kissing my hand again.

"My colleagues were all starting to get married. All I did was work. I was exhausted, mentally, physically, and emotionally. One day I woke up calling your name. I rolled over searching for you. It was the weirdest fucking thing that's ever happened to me. I hadn't been with you in three years, and I woke up thinking you were there, beside me. I immediately sat up in bed disoriented, looking for you, and then I remembered you weren't there. You hadn't been there in a long time. I called my boss that same morning and told him I needed to go. I knew that I couldn't fucking fight it anymore. I explained I had some personal shit going on and that I would work from where I was. We were able to hit common ground, and I booked my flight out for the next day. As I was packing, Mark called me and told me that he was opening up a firm in Nashville and asked me if I was interested. Everything came together, you, Mark's call, Nashville. It was fate. It was the right time. I firmly believe that."

"Wow," I breathed out. "I don't know what to say. I'm so sorry all that happened, Jacob. If I would have known... you know what? I don't want to talk about that. It's in the past. We're together now. I'm so happy to finally know the truth."

"Do you understand why now? Can you forgive me?"

"I had already forgiven you before you told me."

"I want to tell Lucas. I want to tell everyone. I don't want to hide anymore. It's wrong and there's nothing wrong about us."

I was taken aback, never expecting him to say that.

"I want to handle it all. The way I was supposed to. I swear, Lily, I had every intention of doing this three years ago. I want to make it right. I don't want you involved."

"When?" I simply stated.

"As soon as possible. We could take a flight out tomorrow."

I hesitantly nodded.

"What? You don't—"

"No," I interrupted. "Of course I want him to know. It's just that Alex is pregnant. Don't get me wrong us being together is amazing, but it's not going to be for Lucas. I don't want to take away from Alex's pregnancy. They've waited so long for this. It took them three years to get pregnant."

"Kid, we've waited a long time, too."

I nervously bit my nail on my thumb. "I know that, trust me. More than you... but that's my nephew in there and this is going to cause stress on Alex, she will have to deal with Lucas. She could... I just wouldn't forgive myself if something happened to him. You know?"

He nodded, but I could tell he wasn't happy.

"You can tell them as soon as he's born. I promise."

"Lily, you know you're not going to want to do it then either. You're not going to want to take away from his birth. I know you. You're going to be excited, so is everyone else, and you're not going to want to take away from their happiness."

I bit my lip. He was right.

He sighed. "I love you. We can wait. We will wait a bit until after he's born, let things calm down. As much as I hate this idea, I will do what you want."

I smiled, reaching for his pants to show him just how appreciative I was.

JACOB

It had been a little over five months. We flew in for the birth of Bo. He was six pounds, seven ounces and looked exactly like Lucas. Which made Alex very happy, all she wanted was a baby Bo.

Time just seemed to fly by…

I had moved in with Lily within those months. Our shit was everywhere. The house was not big enough for the both of us, but we made it work. We opened up the law firm, hired some amazing employees, and the office sort of ran itself. I worked fewer hours, wanting to be home before Lily left for work. It was hard to adjust. Our schedules were completely opposite. We spent as much time together as we could on the weekends. I even went to work with her just to be able to have more time together. I didn't mind it, though. I loved seeing her perform. That being said, I was over her fucking working there, she didn't need to. I made more than enough money to support us both. She could do whatever she wanted. The world was her oyster, but I knew all she wanted to do was perform, and any place she would work would be those types of hours. It was pointless to tell her how I felt when I didn't have any solutions.

She would Skype with Alex nonstop, wanting to see Bo, fearing that if he didn't see her then he wouldn't know who she was. If that kid cried when Lily picked him up it was going to break her heart. I could tell she missed home, she had been running from it for so long, I guess we both were. Our lives were complete. We were together. I think she was waiting for the rest to fall into place.

When I walked in from work, she was cooking in the kitchen. It smelled amazing, but not nearly as good as her. I came up behind her, wrapping my arms around her waist and kissing all over her neck.

"Mmm," I groaned and she sniffled, immediately making me turn her. She had been crying.

"Baby, what's wrong?"

"Bo rolled over today and I missed it. Then Alex tried to make him do it on Skype and he wouldn't," she wept.

I laughed at her. I couldn't help it.

"It's not funny. I never missed anything with Mason, and now I'm missing everything with Bo."

"Kid, you've been here for the last four and a half years," I stated, trying to keep the smile off my face.

"Yes. But I didn't leave until Mason was three, so at least he knew me. He knows who I am when I come home."

"I understand."

"No you don't..." She playfully tried to push me away, and I spanked her ass.

"Come here." I grabbed her hand.

"Jacob, dinner is going to burn."

I turned off the stove. "I'll order your disgusting pizza," I said, trying to make her smile.

It worked.

I sat her next to me on the couch, both of us sitting sideways with my arm placed on the backrest. "What do you want, sweet girl? What are you not asking for?" I asked, rubbing my fingers across my lips.

She shrugged. "I don't know."

"Yes, you do."

"You're not going to like it."

"Try me."

"I miss home. I miss my family. I have you now. We're together and... I guess I don't want to run away anymore."

I narrowed my eyes at her, grinning.

"What?"

"I knew that's what you were going to say."

She mischievously smirked. "Then why are you asking, old man?"

"Watch it."

She giggled, leaning into my arm. I caressed the side of her cheek and said, "Then it's a good thing we're going home."

She instantly pulled away, sitting back up. "What?"

"This isn't working, baby. This house is too fucking small, I hate lying in bed without you at night, I worry about you constantly when you're at the bar, do you need me to keep going?"

She shook her head no, completely confused.

"Good. I talked to Mark and the firm is doing amazing, he can run it on his own. I'm going to open a new branch in Oak Island. You can do whatever the fuck you want, but I do know this Half-Pint girl that owns a restaurant there. I'm pretty sure I could put in a good word for you, but it's going to cost you."

She beamed. "You're being serious?"

"I don't lie to you."

"Jacob, you are seriously moving twice for me?"

I grabbed the nook of her neck, bringing her to my mouth.

"I told you, baby, my home is where you are."

Chapter 35

JACOB

now

It had been a month.

We were getting everything in order to make it official and the timing worked out perfectly with Alex's party. We weren't just coming back to town for their party, we were moving back. Lily was beyond ecstatic. I had told Lucas that I was moving home and asked him to help me find a house. With his connections in construction it didn't take long for him to find me a place. It had four bedrooms, three baths, and a study. It also had a pool and a huge backyard. It was perfect. When he asked why I needed a house so big, I told him I wanted something I could grow into. He was completely unaware that I was planning on living in it with his baby sister.

When I told Lily I wanted to buy the house for us, she was adamant that we were buying it together. At that point, I didn't give a fuck as long as we were together. Her house in Nashville sold within a week of being listed. It may have been small as shit, but it was in a prime location. There wasn't much packing we needed to do besides our clothes and some odds and ends. The aquarium was a pain in the ass to transport to Oak Island. So was the damn cat. We had to drug Maverick for the plane ride. Lily made me do it, claiming that he was going to hate whoever did it to him. Since he already loved me more than her, this would even the scale. He was staying at her dad's house until we closed on ours. We sold all of our furniture, wanting to start fresh with everything.

We arrived at Lucas and Alex's house, deciding to park the car a few doors down.

"Thank you for looking so beautiful for me today," I whispered into her ear as we walked beside each other down the street.

Forbid Me

She was staying here tonight, wanting to catch up with Alex. Mind you they talked on the phone multiple times a day, but she swore it wasn't the same. I knew she wanted to spend time with Bo, it was written all over her face. She was only twenty-four but I think she was starting to get baby fever. If it was up to me I would knock her up tomorrow. I couldn't wait to see her belly grow with my child. The future and having her as my wife was the only thing I was thinking about recently. The only thing I looked forward to.

"You're not going to tell, Lucas, tonight right?" she asked for the millionth time.

"I think you need to get your hearing checked, Kid. I've told you no over and over again."

"But you're the one that's old," she tried to say with a straight face.

I spanked her, hard.

"Ouch!" She jumped. "How many times do I have to tell you that I don't like this game?"

I pulled her toward me, kissing her head. "Then stop being a little shit."

"That's like asking me to not breathe," she sassed, making me want to spank her again. Before I could get the chance, she grabbed my ball cap off my head and took off running.

We were the first to arrive, but it didn't take long for the house to be packed with people.

"Jesus Christ, man. If you want her so fucking bad then just tell her," I argued with Dylan.

He glanced at me. "What the fuck are you talking about?"

"You're staring at Jeremy like you're ready to kill him. They've been together for years, bro, I don't know if you have a chance anymore, but you're never going to know unless you try."

He cocked his head to the side with a shit-eating grin. "Oh, so now that you're permanently attached to Lily's pussy you're an expert on relationships, are you?"

I jerked back and he arrogantly shook his head. "I'm a Special Ops Agent, Jacob, I read people for a living. You do remember that right?"

"How long have you known?"

"Since she was ten?" he laughed. "Always knew you liked little girls, I should arrest your sorry ass."

"You're such a fucking dick."

He laughed harder. "Being in a relationship is making you soft, Jacob. Do I need to worry about your feelings now, too? Do you guys sit around and braid each other's hair and shit?"

"This coming from the man whose hair has been down to his shoulders since he could walk? Who's the one that grew a fucking pussy?"

"You are what you eat."

"But it tastes so damn good," I rasped, and he clinked his beer with mine.

"Touché, motherfucker, touché. When are you telling Lucas?"

"Soon."

"Good thing you're a lawyer, Jacob, because he's going to need it after he tries to kill your ass."

I took a deep breath.

"And you?"

"And me what?"

"You're okay with it?"

"What other choice do I have? I love that girl. Even when she was a kid and annoying the shit out of me with her guitar early in the morning."

I nodded, chuckling.

"Don't hurt her again. It's good to see her smiling."

Lily and I locked eyes from across the room.

"I love her, Dylan. I love her more than anything. I always have."

"No shit. If Lucas wasn't so far up Half-Pint's ass since she could walk, he would have noticed it, too. But, I'll tell you something."

I looked at him.

"You hurt her again and I'll be standing right there with Lucas while he buries your body. We clear?"

"Crystal."

He patted my back. "Good talk."

The rest of the night went by pretty fast. I could tell Alex was ecstatic about having Austin and I both moving back home. She had been waiting for this since her and Lucas got married. Lily had

Forbid Me

conned me into spending the night, knowing that I hated to sleep without her. I followed her to the guest bedroom, which thankfully was on the other end of the house.

"See, I told you no one would notice," she rasped into my ear, hovering above me on the bed. Wearing only her tank top and panties. She sat on my cock and I instantly got hard. I rubbed my hands up her soft silky thighs, her nipples hardening through her white top.

"When do we go sign the paperwork for the house again?" she asked, grabbing my hands and moving them up to her waist.

"Thursday."

"That's five days away. Where are we going to stay till then?"

"I'm talking to Lucas tomorrow…" I reminded.

"I know."

"Baby, you've wanted this for so long and now I feel like—"

"No! I do. I swear I want this more than anything. It's just everyone is so happy and in a good place. I don't want to ruin that." She whined, sticking out her bottom lip. I wanted to bite it.

"I know, sweet girl. But Dylan knows."

She didn't seem surprised by that.

"Does Austin?"

"I think so."

"Wow, the boys noticed and my brother didn't? Maybe I should thank Alex more often." She leaned over. "I don't want to talk about this anymore."

"Is that right?" I asked, rubbing my lips against hers.

"Yes."

She moved my hands up to her breasts and I cupped them, kneading her nipples. She moaned into my mouth and then Bo started crying.

"Remind me again why that's in here?" I joked.

"I told them they could have a date night in their bedroom. I would get up with him tonight."

"Well, he's up, too, baby." I gestured towards my cock.

She pouted. "Sorry, I'll make it up to you." She jumped off my lap to attend to the baby's needs. I turned on the TV. I just got cock blocked by a baby.

I must have fallen asleep. I felt Lily flipping me over to lie in the crook of my arm and put her head on my chest, sighing contently before sleep once again took over.

Lily

"Hey, you leaving me?" I groggily asked as Jacob stirred.

He kissed my closed eyes and tried to scoot away. "Hell, yeah. I should have left last night."

"Where would the fun be in that?" I grabbed the edge of his boxers and pulled him on top of me. "Give me a curl, it's cold." I grinned not opening my eyes. "Mmm... so much better," I happily moaned. "My friend is up." I kissed his neck and along his jawline, his beard prickling my skin.

"I have to go, Lily."

"No, you have to stay, Jacob."

"Kid—" I gyrated my pussy against his hard dick and he stopped talking. I took the advantage to flip him over.

"The sun's not even up yet. I've never seen Lucas get up before noon." I pulled down his boxers, freeing his cock. I never took my stare off his as I kissed my way down his chest and slid his dick into my mouth. His hand immediately went to the back of my neck, making me deep throat him further down his shaft.

"Fuck," he groaned, his body shuddering. I worked him harder and then all of a sudden my heart sank.

"I'M GOING TO FUCKING KILL YOU!" Lucas screamed, lunging toward him. I shrieked, jumping off the bed with Jacob shielding my sheet covered body.

"You need to calm down, Lucas," he coaxed his hands out in front of him, grabbing his boxers from the edge of the bed and throwing them on.

I couldn't take it anymore. The years of waiting for this to happen and it was finally here. I needed to make my brother understand that Jacob was everything to me.

"Lucas, stop it! I love him!" I shouted from behind Jacob.

Forbid Me

His face went from rage to shock. All the color drained from his face. All that was left was the truth standing in front of him. He worked his fists at his side.

I didn't falter. It was now or never.

"Lucas, I've loved him since I was a kid. You of all people should understand. Get over it!" I desperately yelled. Pleading with him to calm the fuck down.

Jacob turned around and glared at me. "You aren't helping," he informed with clenched teeth.

I shook my head. "I don't care. I love you and it's time he knows! It's none of his business anyway."

Jacob turned back around. "Luc—" My brother's fist connected with Jacob's jaw so fast I didn't see it coming. Jacob's body whooshed back almost taking me with him. He stumbled, trying to catch his balance, and I stared with wide eyes back and forth between them.

Lucas shook out his hand and Jacob massaged his jaw, both of them waiting for I don't know what. Alex walked in with Bo in her arms, her expression matching mine.

"Lucas, come on, this isn't the right way. He's your best friend and that's your sister. Okay, stand down," she reasoned with him.

His intense stare immediately directed at her. Alex didn't even seem fazed.

"You know?" Lucas simply stated.

Jacob and I locked eyes, both of us feeling awful for involving her.

"I do. I've known since the beginning. Now come on."

"Are you fucking kidding me, Half-Pint? Did you not think that I needed to know?"

She shook her head. "No. I didn't."

"Alex, don't—"

"Don't what?" she cut Jacob off. "I can't stand by and have him do this to you. It's not fair. Especially after everything you two have been through."

"What the fuck is going on?" Lucas argued, looking at all of us.

"Bo, she's always loved him. He's always loved her."

M. Robinson

"He's seven years older than her? When could this have possibly started?"

I stepped toward him and he stepped back. "Lily," he warned.

"Lucas, you of all people should understand this. After everything you and Alex went through?"

"That was different."

"How? Please, all mighty one, tell me."

"Because it… I… she wasn't… I… fuck…" he mumbled, uncontrollably.

Jacob put his arm out, pushing me aside to stand in front of me.

"Lucas, I have loved your baby sister ever since I can remember. I wasted too many years in denial and sabotaging us when I could have been with her. I let her age, our parents, the boys and you, especially you, make my decisions for me. It's over I can't live without her and I won't," he confessed, shaking his head.

His eyes widened in realization of what Jacob was saying.

"I did everything I could to keep you and Alex apart because I didn't think you were good enough for her. You have no idea how much I regret that. If I could go back and change things, I would. It's obvious that you were meant to be together. I wanted to protect her, the same way you want to protect Lily. I understand. I understand more than anyone. I can't tell you how sorry I am for coming in between you and Alex, but I won't ever tell you that I'm sorry for loving Lily. I'm not sorry for wanting to be with her. She's fucking everything to me. She always has been."

Lucas lowered his eyebrows with an unreadable expression. "How long, Jacob?"

He sighed. "The first time I kissed her she was fifteen."

Lucas scoffed, stepping toward him, but Jacob didn't move a muscle, ready to take whatever blow my brother was going to throw at him.

"You're telling me you put the moves on my fifteen-year-old baby sister when you were twenty fucking two years old?" Lucas gritted out, his fist clenching at his side with a deadly stare.

"It wasn't like that. Your mom had just been diagnosed. I found her on the beach—"

Forbid Me

"You fucking took advantage of her? You piece—"

"Stop!" I screamed, coming in between them. "Please stop this. You're ruining it," I said with tears forming in my eyes. "He didn't take advantage of me. He was there for me... he's always been there for me. I'm not going to let you or anyone make that into something that it's not. Do you fucking understand me? I love you more than anything, Lucas. But I won't let you make our already fucked up situation into something seedy and ugly. I won't let you take away some of the best memories of my life. Not after everything we've been through," I stated, my voice shaking.

"Lily, I just found out that this has been going on since you were fifteen years old, behind my back and you expect me to stand here and be okay with that?"

"I stayed away from her after that. I shut her out because she was a kid and I was a grown ass man. I had the same thoughts as you do right now. It's always been my number one concern, Lucas. Up until a year and a half ago, I hadn't seen her in three years. Three fucking years, I stayed away from her. I won't do that again. I didn't want you to find out this way. I never wanted you to find out this way. I want a life with her. I want what you have with Alex. I want that more than anything in this world. I promise you that I will never hurt her again. She's mine. She's mine forever. This isn't us dating or getting to know each other, I want to marry her."

Lucas jerked back, stunned. "What?"

"You heard me."

"Bo."

His gaze went to Alex.

"I told you. They love each other. He loves her as much as you love me and vice versa. They're meant to be together like we are. Please, let them be. They want your blessing. That's all they've ever wanted." She gritted out.

"Half-Pint... I... I'm sorry... I just..." He shook his head and my heart pounded in my chest with the words I knew were coming.

"I can't... I'm sorry I can't..."

"Lucas," Jacob called out after him as he left the room.

I bowed my head, tears falling down my face.

My brother's words breaking my heart.

JACOB

I took her into my arms, hugging her as tight as I could.

"I'm sorry, I'm so fucking sorry," I whispered into her ear. I had promised her she wouldn't lose him.

"I'll talk to him. He'll come around. You know how Lucas is, he's stubborn and he needs time to reflect. I promise he will come around," Alex sympathized, rubbing Lily's back.

I held her the entire time she broke down, and all that I feared was that she was thinking about her mom, sad that she had lost another person. If this would have been before she died, I know Lily would have been stronger, but she didn't want to lose another member of her family, especially not like this. The longer she cried, the more pissed off I got, my temper looming and I could feel it fucking pumping through my veins. After she had calmed down, Alex told her she needed to take a hot bath, that it would make her feel better. I had never been more grateful to have Half-Pint there. She knew me and what I wanted to do. Lucas and I needed to work this out without having Lily present.

Man to man.

I knew where I would find him. He would be taking out his frustrations on the waves. I walked down the patio stairs and onto the beach as he was getting out of the water.

"Don't fucking try me, Jacob, not right now," he spit out with a menacing tone.

"Or what? You're going to hit me again? Fucking do it! Hit me. Come on hit me, as many goddamn times as you want, if it's going to make you realize that this isn't going away. I'm not leaving her. I'm right fucking here, waiting!"

He threw down his board into the sand and shoved me. "I thought you were my friend!" He pushed me again. "I thought you were my brother!"

"I am! Don't you fucking see that! Jesus Christ, Lucas, it's been almost ten years, ten fucking years for us to get to this point!"

"You think that matters to me? I don't give a shit if you would have waited twenty! She's my fucking baby sister, you piece

275

of shit!" He charged me, ramming his one shoulder into my ribs. His momentum propelled my body into the sand where he landed on top of me, having the advantage. "I can't even fucking look at her! All I see is your hands all over her!" He threw the first punch, his fist connecting with my cheek. I laid there taking it.

"Do you feel better? Hit me again!"

He did, he hit me four more times after that. Twice in the jaw and twice in the ribs, before getting off of me, stumbling back a little. He regained his balance and hovered above me. If looks could kill, I'd be dead.

I rolled over getting on my hands and knees, spitting blood in the sand.

"I loved you. I fucking trusted you, man! I sent her to you! What, Jacob, did you fuck her the entire week? Huh? I guess you made a fool out of me didn't you?"

I stood, wiping my mouth, never taking my gaze off his. "That's not what happened, you have to fucking know me better than that."

"I don't fucking know anything anymore. I can't think about how many times I left you alone with her. I was supposed to protect her, yet I handed her right fucking to you. Do you know how sick that makes me?"

"You know that's not true." I touched my ribs, hissing upon contact.

"I don't know shit. I don't know you at all."

"Fuck, Lucas! What do you want from me, man? I'm telling you the truth," I roared, spitting more blood into the sand.

"Its too late for that, Jacob! I already saw my baby sister sucking your fucking cock!" He shoved me hard. I stumbled but remained upright.

I winced, that was a low blow.

"Yeah... so you tell me. What am I supposed to do now? Since you have all the answers, asshole?"

"You can hate me. You hate me all you want. I can take it. But Lily? Lily is upstairs bawling because she thinks she lost another family member. She doesn't deserve that. She's done nothing wrong."

He jerked back.

"She loves you. She loves you so damn much. I hate that this is happening. I hate that I can't do anything about it. But please, do not take it out on her."

"What the fuck, man? How could you do this? How am I supposed to get passed this?" He started to pace back and forth, hands pulling at his hair.

"I didn't do it to you, Lucas. I love her. I've tried not loving her. I've tried for years… I can't. I'm sorry, bro. I never wanted to do this to your family, especially after everything you guys have been through. You know that."

He shook his head, disappointed. "You know what really fucking kills me is that I didn't know. How did I not know? I love Lily more than anything in this world. How did I not see it? Am I that fucking blind?"

"I… don't…" I sighed not knowing what to say.

"I can't look at you right now. I can't even stand to fucking look at myself either. After all the years and everything you did to keep Alex and I apart… you were fucking around with my baby sister? You're such a goddamn hypocrite."

"I love her," I simply stated not knowing what else to say. "I'm so fucking sorry, Lucas. I don't know what else I could say other than you're right and I'm fucking sorry."

"Everyone knows, don't they?" he asked out of nowhere.

I faintly nodded.

"Since the beginning?"

"For the most part."

"My mom and dad too?"

"Your mom knew. She gave us her blessing on her final days. I'm sure your dad knows something, but I was going to talk to him next about it. I want to ask for Lily's hand in marriage."

"Shit…" was all he could manage to say.

"I told you. I'm not fucking around. She's mine."

He took a deep breath, looking all around the beach and then back at me. "You hurt her, Jacob, you so much as make her cry one fucking time and I will bury you alive. You hear me? You will fucking die."

"I'll bring the shovel."

"I don't fucking like this. I'm not going to pretend like I do. I'm not saying that's not going to change, but for right now I'll accept it because what other choice do I have. We're not okay." He shoved his finger into my chest.

I nodded again.

He grabbed his surfboard and I followed him back up to his house. Lily was sitting on the couch with Bo in her arms, Alex standing in the kitchen making some breakfast. She took one look at me and then at Lucas.

"I'll get you some Ibuprofen, Jacob." She kissed Lucas on the neck. "Feel better?"

He shrugged and grabbed a beer from the fridge, throwing me one. I took it down in three swigs, walking into the living room. Lucas never took his eyes off me, burning a hole in my back. I knew he was watching Lily and I like a fucking hawk.

"You okay?" she asked as I sat on the coffee table in front of her. I could tell she wanted to comment on my appearance but didn't want to add any more fuel to the fire.

"You hit harder." Cracking a smile for her, trying to lighten the situation.

She smiled, biting her lip.

"Everything will be alright, sweet girl. I promise," I murmured. "I'm going to meet with your dad. I'll be back later."

She nodded. "I love you."

"I love you, too." I kissed her forehead.

And left.

Jacob left and we all ate breakfast in silence. Lucas didn't say a word to me, not that I expected him to. After breakfast, I put Bo down in his crib for a nap. I turned around to find Lucas standing in the doorway, watching me with a look in his eyes I had never seen before.

"Lucas, you scared the shit out of me," I said, grabbing my chest.

"Are you happy?" he questioned. His arms were crossed over his chest with his back leaned against the wall.

"I've never been this happy in my entire life," I paused to let my words sink in. "I pursued him, Lucas. For years it was all me. He never wanted to disrespect you, our families, or me. For the longest time I didn't understand his reasoning. A little part of me resented it. I felt bad that I didn't feel that way and he did. When mom died everything changed for me. Even up until now I was terrified of you finding out. I can't lose another family member, please don't make me choose." Tears formed in my eyes and he immediately came over, putting his arms around me.

"Shhh… you're not going to lose me. I promise."

I nodded into his shirt and he pulled away. "Lily, all I've ever wanted is for you to be happy. You're always going to be my baby sister. I may not understand you and Jacob, but as much as I hate it right now… I'll respect it for you."

It wasn't what I wanted to hear but I said, "Okay."

"Do you love him?" he questioned.

"More than anything in this world."

"If he hurts you, I may have to kill him. You've been warned."

I laughed. "He won't hurt me again."

"So he's hurt you before?"

"Lucas, I don't want to talk about that. It's in the past. He won't hurt me again. I trust him. But I will say this, every time he walked away from me it was because of you. I won't let him push me away again."

"I promised mom that I would take care of you, but you've always been able to take care of yourself. I need to remember that. I need to let you grow up."

"That's probably a good idea."

He smiled. "I'll always be here, Lily. I'm your big brother, you're stuck with me."

"Good. I wouldn't want it any other way."

He kissed my forehead and left. I knew he was going to talk to Alex, and I hoped it would go as smoothly as it had with me. Even though I knew he was hurt that she lied to him. Alex would find some way to make it up to him though.

"You may get a sibling before you know it, Bo," I giggled, shaking my head.

Forbid Me

It was late by the time Jacob came back from talking with my dad. At least this time he didn't have more bruises. His lip was swollen with a cut down the side, his left eye had light bruising starting to form around it, and he had bruised ribs.

I felt awful.

"It looks worse than it is," he stated as we lay together in the guest bedroom.

"So, you were being honest about the whole letting him kick your ass thing, huh?"

"Look what it's done for his perspective."

"Hmm… not much." I laughed, kissing the cut on his lip. "But at least he knows now. How was my dad?"

"Your dad was not surprised in the least. Which makes me think your mom told him more than what we thought."

JACOB

I wasn't going to tell Lily that her dad wasn't pleased with the fact that everything started when she was only fifteen. He yelled, a lot. I think he debated on hitting me himself. The only reason he didn't was because he took one look at me and knew Lucas had already handled it for him. As soon as I took the ring from my pocket, he shut up fairly quickly. After he threatened me a few more times, he gave me his approval before I left. I didn't tell Lily I went to see her mom's grave to thank her for everything. I sat there for a bit also telling her how Lucas reacted and what my face looks like from it. Before I left, I told her that I would always take care of her little girl.

No matter what.

Lily laid down on my chest, and I hissed from the pain.

"Shit!" She instantly sat up. I pulled her back down wanting to feel her.

"I'm fine."

"I just hurt you. You're not fine."

I thought about it for a second. "You know what… I'm really not fine. I'm actually really hurt. I've never hurt this bad in my life. I think I may be dying." I grinned.

"Oh yeah, big man? What can I do to save you?" She smirked right back.

"I don't know. I think this is serious. I may not make it through the night."

"Maybe I should check on my friend? You know, make sure he's okay after all this. It's important that he still loves me."

I nodded, placing my hands behind my head. "Whatever you think is right, baby."

She kissed every one of my bruises, working her way down to "her friend" as she called him. She placed me into her wet, hot mouth, sucking my cock like she had something to prove. I couldn't take it anymore. I flipped her over and fucked her until she begged me to stop.

I didn't.

JACOB

It was Lily's twenty-fifth birthday. She loved to take every opportunity possible to remind me that I would always be seven years older than her. We were having a party for her at Alex's restaurant where she was currently their entertainment. Word got around fast about Lily's talent. People from all over the world come in just to watch her perform. She's been in the papers and on the news. She was called a hometown celebrity. It never fazed her though. All she wanted to do was play and sing. I opened my law firm a month after we moved and so far things were running smoothly. Our house was finally furnished. It took fucking forever. Lily was constantly changing things left and right... Alex wasn't helping the situation either. Lucas's company remodeled a few things for us.

We were not as close as we used to be, but slowly we were getting back there. Lily didn't pay him any mind and neither did Alex, who was now four months pregnant with a girl. Lily laughed her ass off for like ten minutes when we found out the sex. She said one word, "Karma."

Dylan was working crazy hours doing God knows what. We barely saw him anymore. Every time I tried bringing it up to Lily, she blew me off. Changing the subject to something else, which I found odd. Austin moved back a few weeks after we did. No one knew what the fuck was going on with him and Briggs. I could tell some shit went down with them. Who knows when it would stop, if it ever would.

"Phew... I need to sit down," Alex breathed out, putting her hand on her belly.

"Don't let Lucas hear you. You'll never leave the house again," Lily responded. "You know what? I'm actually surprised he let you out tonight, Half-Pint."

"You think he could make me miss your birthday party? Hell no." She continued to rub her baby bump.

Lily laughed. I lugged her toward me, hugging her tiny frame into my chest to look down at her. "Have I told you how beautiful you look?"

"Once or twice, but you're thirty-two now so…" She winced. "Your memory must be going, old man," she giggled.

"You little shit." I spanked her.

"Hey, hey, hey what are your hands on?" Lucas chimed in, rubbing Alex's bump.

"What's mine," I replied not taking my eyes off Lily.

"You're lucky I don't kick your ass, *again*."

"You would be lucky if I *let* you do it, again."

"Alright, boys, let's remember it's my birthday. This pissing contest ends now. We're nice to each other today!" Lily sang out loud.

"Bo, I need help with the cake. Come help me." Alex pulled him with her.

"Is this code for kitchen fu—"

She put her hand over his mouth. "Oh my God!" She shook her head with wide eyes while Lily and I tried not to laugh.

Dylan walked in as they were about to leave, making his way to the bar.

"Fuck, man, what the hell happened to you?" I asked, taking in his bloody lip, bruised eye, and his knuckles all cut up. He looked like he had been in a fight.

"Bad day at work," he simply stated, grabbing a beer from the bar.

"No shit," was all I could reply.

"Happy birthday." He pulled Lily into a hug.

"Thanks, are you okay? Do you need me to get you something?" She looked him over.

"Don't fuss over me. I'm fine. Comes with the job."

"Okay." Lily gave him a knowing look.

Forbid Me

There was something about the way she looked at him that I couldn't quite place or even understand.

The night continued with its usual festivities, everyone together exactly how I wanted. Just like the old days.

"You want your birthday present, Kid?"

"What is it?"

I laughed. "It doesn't matter how many damn times I tell you to just say thank you, it's never going to happen is it?"

"Highly unlikely, let me see it, big man! Where are we going?" I took her to the middle of the room, nodding to the DJ to turn down the music. Everyone looked at us. Lily only stared at me with a questioning expression.

"The first time I realized I was in love with you, I knew I was in trouble. Not because of your age, or our families, or your brother, or even the boys.

She lowered her eyebrows, confused.

"I knew that I would never be able to let you go, no matter how many times I tried. I soon discovered there was no going back for me. Only moving forward. I could stand here and tell you all the things that I love about you, Kid, each and every one of them, but you know them already. You know them because you know me. You've always known me."

She smiled and it lit up her entire face as she took in the meaning of my words. "What's this all about?" she nervously asked.

I got down on one knee and her breathing hitched.

"I have had this ring." I placed it out in front of me. "Since I left San Francisco."

Her lips parted and her eyes widened. I would never forget the look on her gorgeous face at that moment.

"The morning I realized I was finally coming home to you, I went and bought a ring. It's taken everything inside me not to ask you to marry me about a hundred times at this point. I have missed so many birthdays. I wanted you to remember this day as one of the happiest of our lives…" I opened the box.

"Oh my God. It's huge!" she blurted out.

"Lillian Michelle Ryder, my sweet girl, will you put me out of my goddamn misery and be my wife. Will you marry me, Kid?"

She tackled me to the ground. "Of course! Yes! Yes! Yes! I will marry you, Jacob!" she screamed as everyone started clapping.

She kissed all over my face as I picked us back up.

"I love you."

"I love you, baby."

Her dad was the first one to come congratulate us, followed by Alex and the boys. Lucas stood back watching me warily, and then he finally approached.

"Congratulations, baby sister." She smiled as he kissed the top of her head.

He stuck out his hand for me to shake. "I guess this officially makes you my brother," he stated with a neutral expression.

"Guess so." I shook it.

He nodded, pulling me toward him into a hug, slapping my back.

"Take care of her, Jacob."

"Always."

Lily beamed, I didn't remember ever seeing her so happy. To know that I was finally the cause of it warmed my heart in ways I never thought possible.

"What the fuck?" Austin chimed in, making us all turn in the direction of his gaze.

Three police officers walked in going right for Dylan. He was sitting down at the table beside us, sipping his beer like nothing was going on.

"Agent McGraw, we hate to have to—"

"Just fucking do it," he interrupted the officer, standing to look at all of them.

And the rest played in fucking slow motion…

"Dylan McGraw, you have the right to remain silent. Anything you say can and will be used against you in a court of law. You have the right to an attorney. If you cannot afford an attorney, one will be provided for you. Do you understand the rights I have just read to you? With these rights in mind, do you wish to speak to me?"

THE END.

Forbid Me

For Jacob and Lily.
It's only the beginning or is it *the end* for...
Dylan and Aubrey.
(Next in The Good Ol'Boys Standalone Series)
Coming Early Spring 2016

Website:
www.authormrobinson.com

Like my Facebook page:
https://www.facebook.com/AuthorMRobinson?ref=hl

Join my VIP Group on Facebook:
nf
https://www.facebook.com/groups/572806719533220/?fref=nf

I share EXCLUSIVES & hang out with my readers

Follow me on Instagram:
http://instagram.com/authormrobinson

Follow me on Twitter:
https://twitter.com/AuthorMRobinson

Amazon author page:
http://www.amazon.com/M.-Robinson/e/B00H4HJYDQ/ref=sr_ntt_srch_lnk_5?qid=1425429982&sr=1-5

Sign up for my newsletter:
http://eepurl.com/beltYj

Email:
m.robinson.author@gmail.com

CPSIA information can be obtained
at www.ICGtesting.com
Printed in the USA
LVOW10s1502141116

512902LV00047B/2065/P